CRIMES OF LOVE

ALSO BY DONALD LEVIN

The House of Grins

In Praise of Old Photographs

New Year's Tangerine

CRIMES OF LOVE

DONALD LEVIN

A POISON TOE PRESS BOOK

This is a work of fiction. All of the characters, establishments, events, locales, and organizations portrayed in this novel are either products of the author's imagination or are used fictitiously and are not construed as real.

ISBN-13: 978-1466431621

ISBN-10: 1466431628

First edition published November 2011

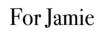

For Jamie

The child is mortal; but Poor Child
Creeps through centuries of bone
Untransient as the channelling worm
Or water making sand of stone.
Poor child, what have they done to you?
　　　　　 — *"Poor Child," Jay Macpherson*

Wednesday, November 5, 2008

1

She rushed out of the house so fast she forgot to take her coat.

She remembered it as soon as the cold night air hit her bare arms, but she was in too much of a hurry to get away.

So she kept going.

Short legs churning, she turned right at the end of her front walk and continued toward Livernois in the darkness of her street. She shuffled through the oak leaves that blanketed the sidewalk. The familiar dry rattle gave her the courage for what she was doing, as did Bea Bunny, her favorite stuffed toy that she hugged tightly to her chest.

At the corner she paused. Now, then. Where to go? She left the house without thinking this through. Who did she know who would take her in? Who would let her stay until she could call her mother to come get her?

Sirens passed on Woodward a block away. When they faded the sound of traffic on the busy main road started again, reminding her of the sighing of the ocean her parents had taken her to last year during their vacation on Cape Cod. Shivering, she remembered how good that had felt—the heat of the sun on her back, the sand between her toes, the salty tang of seawater on her lips . . .

At once she thought of Jamie Sparks, who was in her class at school. Jamie didn't have a father because he moved out when Jamie's parents got a divorce, but her mother was nice and her grandmother lived with them. And they had an in-ground pool in their backyard where all the girls went swimming in the summer.

The Sparks home. Perfect.

Jamie lived two blocks down, so she turned right. She was starting to feel better already.

She had not eaten yet even though it was late. Now with a place to go, she knew Jamie's mother would feed her. She whispered, "Gonna eat soon," into Bea Bunny's floppy ear.

Not as many tall trees grew on Livernois as on her own street, so she had a clear view of the stars in the cloudless November sky. She spotted Orion. Her father had started teaching the constellations to her, but Orion was the easiest to recognize. There were his wide shoulders and belt cutting across his body. There was the knife hanging at his waist.

She stopped and stood, lost in thoughts of stars, of heroes and warriors, of rescue and safety, of oceans and pools and summer.

She didn't see the shadow moving in the trees behind her.

Or the headlights sweeping toward her from down the street.

Or hear the crazy screaming.

Or notice anything else at all . . . not even how her beloved Bea had slipped from her grasp and dropped into the pile of leaves beside where she herself had fallen to the ground.

Thursday, November 6, 2008

2

"Seven-year-old girl," said Tony Tullio. "Madison Kaufman." His voice was low and hoarse, a life-long smoker's croak. "Left the house by herself around 8:30 last night. Not seen since."

It was just after two in the morning. Martin Preuss said, "Look like a runaway?"

"Parents say no way. Good girl, happy, well-adjusted, never any problems."

Standing with Tullio in the hard-edged kitchen, remodeled, high-end, everything granite and stainless steel and white light, Preuss shook his head. This could be a bad one.

"Mom's in the living room with Janey and a neighbor," Tullio said. "Dad's out driving around looking for her. Neither knew she was gone till Mom went in to give her a nightly dose of medicine. She takes medication for seizures. When they realized she wasn't there, they searched the house, then drove around the neighborhood and checked with her friends before they called it in."

Tullio slid a 5 x 7 out of his folder across the counter. "This is her."

Preuss tried to will the fog out of his brain so he could focus on the picture. The call from the line supervisor of the detective bureau woke him from a sound sleep. Missing child: we need you in. He rolled out of bed and raced to the house in his Explorer; he was still logy.

The photograph was a school shot of a little blonde girl smiling with dimples in front of the standard mottled blue school photo backdrop. She had sharp intelligent blue eyes and a sheepish grin, as though embarrassed by the camera's attention. Her face was round and her hair parted straight down the center.

"Pretty little girl," he said.

"Pretty enough for the wrong kind of attention, out by herself at night."

"What's she wearing?"

Tullio checked his notebook. He was a stout man a few inches shorter than Preuss, with pitted skin that looked grey under the fluorescent lights of the kitchen.

He breathed a raspy sigh sour with old coffee and cigarettes. It ended with a tremendous coughing fit. His face turned the rich color of eggplant.

Preuss took an empty coffee cup from the counter, rinsed it in the sink, and filled it with cold water.

Tullio bobbed his head in thanks and drained it. When he got his breath back, he cleared his throat and said, "So, pink short-sleeved top that says, 'Princess in Charge,' pink jogging pants. Top is like a tee shirt but with those little frills around the collar."

"No coat?"

"Still hanging on the hook in the back hall."

"So a little girl's out in the middle of the night without her meds in thirty degree weather in a tee shirt."

"About the size of it."

"All right," said Preuss. "I'm going to get out and look around the neighborhood. First I want to see her room."

"First door, top of the stairs."

Preuss leaned closer, lowered his voice. "Any chance of another Susan Smith situation here?"

"Doubt it very much," Tullio got out before another spell of coughing, loose as a bag of pebbles, made him double over. Preuss refilled his cup with water and Tullio took another drink.

"What happens when you wash down cigarettes with scotch for forty years," he gulped out when he caught his breath.

Preuss patted his shoulder and left the kitchen.

Upstairs Madison's room faced the street in the front of the house. The room was smaller than the one his son occupied in his group home, but while Preuss tried to furnish Toby's room like a young man's with rock posters and photos of his family, this was impossible to mistake for anything but a little girl's bedroom. She was deep into pink bunnies. Stuffed bunnies on the bunny spread on the bed, frolicking bunnies painted on the headboards, bunny pillowcases, doll bunnies on the chest of drawers, Beatrix Potter bunnies on posters, plush mother and child bunnies on the bunny throw rug beside the bed.

He glanced through the closet, saw a full wardrobe for a little girl who didn't lack for anything. Shoes for every occasion lined up neatly on the floor beneath her clothes, with the emphasis on pink. Nothing seemed missing.

He wondered who was so compulsive, the little girl or one of her parents.

Back downstairs, on the sofa in the living room the three women were still sitting together. The dark-haired woman, whom he assumed was Mrs. Kaufman, sat with her head in her hands. Two women sat on each side of her, one with her arm around her shoulders, the other writing in a notebook. She was small and sinewy, with dishwater blonde hair that stuck up in finger-thick ringlets around her head.

Janey Cahill looked up when she noticed him standing there. She shook her head.

Nothing new to report.

He continued outside. In the dark November night, a fine flurry of snow had begun. A trio of blue-and-whites bristling with antennae surrounded the house. It was a big Dutch colonial circled by lanky bare oaks arching over the street. Lights blazed in every window.

He walked slowly up one side of the block and down the other, shining his flashlight into the bushes of every house. Flurries winked in the beam of light like fireflies.

Most of the houses were dark. Preuss hoped for a neighbor to step onto the front porch of one of the homes and say, "You must be looking for Madison," then produce her from behind her robe.

No one did.

Lawn signs from the election on Tuesday still stood in some front yards, and he made sure he checked the shadows for the girl.

This was a solidly Obama neighborhood, and his supporters kept their signs up to gloat; the few McCain followers kept theirs up to protest the results.

One of the political signs was for the candidate who had just been elected as the city's first openly gay mayor. Ferndale was changing fast, Preuss reflected as he walked along. An aging inner-ring suburb across Eight Mile Road from Detroit, within the past ten years Ferndale had been reborn as affluent young people moved in, including a large gay population. The newcomers changed the cultural and social landscape with improved housing and new business. Every year brought more trendy bakeries and sushi bars and salons along Nine Mile and Woodward.

Ferndale was changing so fast some of the older residents couldn't deal with it. Why couldn't it stay the same as it always was, with the traditional values they had all grown up with, they wondered.

For Preuss there was no ideal Ferndale to pine for. Change was supposed to happen. The only things that didn't change were dead. And there were already too many of those.

With luck Madison wasn't going to be one of them.

His search turned up only patrol officers shining their own lights into the darkness and the glowing eyes of raccoon and possum. The bunny girl had to be out here somewhere, he thought. Maybe trapped and cowering in a dark place like her favorite animal.

Wherever she was, he sent her a mental message: We'll find you, sweetheart. Sit tight and we'll bring you in.

He trudged back to the house and told Tony Tullio he was going to expand the search in the Explorer.

3

Madison had been missing for eleven hours when the five detectives, grim with worry and fatigue, assembled at 7:35 a.m. in the conference room at the Eugene Shanahan Law Enforcement Complex on East Nine Mile in Ferndale.

Patrol officers had started their full canvas of the street shortly after seven, Tullio told them. He passed around copies of the photo of the girl's clear, bright features.

"What's your sense of the parents?" Tullio asked Janey Cahill, the Youth Bureau detective.

"They seem like good people. Dad's an accountant for Triple A. Mom's a sales clerk at Nordstrom's out at Somerset. Solid citizens, I'd say. Madison's their only child. They're beside themselves."

"So far we've been thinking she just got lost," Martin Preuss said. "We need to consider alternatives."

They fell silent. All five of them had children, in Tullio's case grandchildren. A missing child was never just another case.

"Reg," Tullio said, "check the Sex Offender Registry, see if anybody in the area has a history with kids and pay them a visit."

"Will do," Reg Trombley said. In his thirties, he was the youngest member of the detective squad, lean and model-handsome with close-cropped hair and perfect, taut caramel skin.

"Janey," Tullio said, "have you notified the state or the county?"

"Not yet. Been tied up at the house."

"I'll do it, soon as we're done here," Tullio said. "I'll get her name in the MMCIC, too." The Michigan Missing Child Information Clearinghouse. "Can't do an Amber Alert yet till we're certain she isn't a runaway or the parents aren't involved. I'm also requesting a tap on their phone. Any relatives nearby?"

"No," Cahill said. "They're not from around here, so there's no family in the immediate area."

"Where are they from?" Tullio asked.

"Buffalo. They moved here eight years ago. Loads of aunts, uncles, and cousins, but none local."

Tullio nodded, then said, "Hank, check hospitals and police agencies in Oakland and Wayne. Run a check on the parents, too, just to see what's what. Priors and so forth."

Hank Bellamy nodded. He was a placid and pear-shaped man with a mustache and buzzcut.

To Janey, Tullio said, "I'd like you back at the Kaufman home in case she shows up. She does, I want to be the second to know."

"Probably also worth a conversation with her school," Cahill said. "See if they've noticed anything unusual."

"And follow up with Madison's friends and their parents, see what they know."

"You got it."

"Marty, you coordinate activity on the street. I'll bring the chief up to speed. I'm sure he's going to want to make a statement to the press, she doesn't turn up soon."

"Right," Preuss said. He had sad eyes under bushy brows, with a narrow face and sandy hair going to gray. "I'll take another run around the neighborhood, too, maybe have another talk with the parents."

"Okay, then," Tullio said. "Anything else?"

Dead quiet around the table.

"Let's get busy. We'll meet again at eleven."

The meeting broke up and they went their separate ways. Unease radiated off them all like body odor.

4

Could someone really have snatched her off a street like this, Preuss wondered as he drove up and down the quiet blocks.

You didn't expect a child to disappear from one of the better neighborhoods in Ferndale. West Woodland was in what the local realtors called, with a straight face, the Gold Coast of Ferndale—a desirable, newly upscale section of three streets in the northwest corner of the city.

Though who really knew . . . anybody could have been driving down the street, seen a little girl walking along by herself in the dark of night, and there you have it. Girl gone.

After making another fruitless circuit, he checked in with each of the four officers ringing doorbells around the neighborhood, then called Cahill's cell.

"Any word?" he asked her.

"Nothing yet. I'm sitting here with Mom."

"Dad still out driving around?"

"No. He went into work."

"Seriously? His daughter disappears and he goes into the office?"

"Uh-huh," Cahill said in a flat voice.

Then she said, "Listen, were you going to swing by?"

"I can. What's up?"

"Mrs. Kaufman gave me something that might be important. I'm getting ready to head over to the school and talk with the teachers, but I'll wait till you get here."

"Detective Cahill said you had some thoughts about your brother?"

"Well, I wouldn't call them 'thoughts,'" Sharon Kaufman said. Dark smudges under her eyes gave her a blowzy, haunted look. She and Preuss sat together at the kitchen table. Her red plaid shirt hung open over a charcoal grey turtleneck. Her sadness and fear hung in the air like smoke.

The pain of missing children: nothing worse, as he knew.

"She asked me if anybody seemed overly attached to Maddie," she continued. "I told her Kenny always spends a lot of time with her whenever we see him."

"How often is that?"

"Not often. Holidays, mostly."

"What do they do together?"

"Mostly they play 'bunnies.' Maddie brings out all her bunny toys, and she and Kenny make up stories about them."

"You've never seen him roughhouse with her, or do anything that seems unusually physical?"

"It's all very innocent. Kenny's really a sweet guy. He's just lost his way."

"What do you mean, 'lost his way'?"

She paused, as though debating whether to say more.

"Mrs. Kaufman, the sad fact is, most missing children are taken by relatives. The family's always where we start looking."

"He's had a drug problem the past few years, and it's taken a toll on him," she admitted. "I don't know more than that. I try to stay out of my family's business and hope they stay out of mine. I just know he's been having a rough time of it."

Preuss looked over the list of relatives she had given Janey Cahill. They were all from Sharon's side of the family. Her husband seemed to be the only one left of his line. He ran a finger down the list of names until he got to her brother, Kenny Meredith.

"You say his address is the same as your sister Peggy's. In Hamburg. That near Buffalo?"

"Just south. Kenny lives with her."

"How old is he?"

"Thirty-two."

"When was the last time you heard from him?"

"I can't even remember. You really don't think it's Kenny?"

"We don't know anything yet for sure," Preuss cautioned. "But we have to keep every option open right now. It's a possibility we'll have to put to rest," he said gently.

And thought: It's always the uncle.

He filled in his notes sitting in the SUV.

Uncle Kenny.

When he was finishing his degree at Wayne State a woman from a criminology course cornered him in their classroom one day to tell him how her uncle abused her. Making her give him a blow job was part of an elaborate ritualized performance when she was eleven.

It had been the first time the woman had talked to him all semester. He guessed she was working through her anxiety at having to make a public speech in their class. She saw it in the context of performing for her uncle, and it caused her to freeze.

She dropped the class finally and he lost track of her in their program. Ever since, whenever he heard a story of child abuse, his first thought was, It's always the uncle.

Even though of course that wasn't always true. Sometimes it was other family members.

He tapped Kenny Meredith's number into his cell. The line rang three times and a woman's voice answered.

Preuss identified himself and said, "I'm calling for Kenneth Meredith."

"Kenny can't come to the phone at the moment."

"Who am I speaking with?"

"His sister. Is he in some kind of trouble?"

"His name came up in connection with an investigation and I just need to ask him some questions. Is he around?"

"He lives in an apartment above our garage. He comes and goes as he pleases, so I don't always know where he is."

"So you don't know if he's been home the past few days?"

"No," she admitted.

"Could you see if he's there now?"

He held on for ten minutes before her tense voice came back on the line. No sign of Kenny in his room. He didn't look like he'd been around recently, either.

Always the uncle.

Back to the Shanahan Complex he called the Police Department in the Town of Hamburg, New York, and asked them to look for Uncle Kenny.

5

"Oh Christ," the man moaned and leapt to his feet.

He was paunchy, pale, and unhappy looking with mousy hair thinning over the crown of his head and bags under his eyes. "Have you found my daughter?"

"No," Preuss said, "sorry. There's nothing new. I just need to go over some things with you."

Kaufman's shoulders slumped, then he recovered and held a hand toward one of the chairs across from his desk on the second floor of the Automobile Association of America branch office on Woodward in Royal Oak.

They sat on opposite sides of Kaufman's desk. "Don't you have to bring the FBI in or something?" Kaufman asked.

"We will if we need to. For now we're going over any possible way she might be with somebody you or your wife knows, for whatever reason."

"We've asked ourselves that. Nobody comes to mind."

"Your wife mentioned her brother, Kenny. Have you seen him lately?"

He shook his head. "I can't image Kenny could get it together enough to do anything to Madison."

"Have you ever seen them together?"

"He's mostly useless, detective. Trust me on this one."

His tone put Preuss on alert. "You don't like him?"

"Let's just say I never thought he was a good influence on Maddie. My wife thinks he's harmless but I'm not so sure."

"You didn't answer my question: Have you seen him around lately?"

"No, I haven't seen him in a while."

Preuss considered the information.

"Mr. Kaufman, something's bothering me here. Can you walk me through what happened last night before Madison left? I'm troubled by what made her leave the house without a coat."

Kaufman shifted uncomfortably but remained silent.

"Was there something going on last night she was trying to get away from?" Preuss probed.

"It's not what you think," Kaufman said finally.

"Maybe you better explain it to me."

"It was nothing to do with Madison. My wife and I were talking. Madison must have overheard. And over-reacted."

"What were you talking about?"

"Sharon was late for dinner. Again. It's a point of contention between us."

"Did she say where she was?"

Kaufman gave a huff of exasperation. "What does this have to do with finding my daughter?"

"I'm just trying to get a sense of Madison's home life."

"Our home life is fine. Whatever's going on between my wife and me has nothing to do with Madison."

"You'd be surprised how sensitive kids are, Mr. Kaufman. If you and your wife were fighting about something—"

"We weren't fighting. It was a discussion that may have gotten loud."

"It never turned physical? You didn't strike your wife and Madison saw it and left for fear of her own safety?"

"No! It wasn't anything like that. Sharon and I were talking. We may have gotten a little excited. You're getting the exact wrong idea about this."

Kaufman was getting heated so Preuss decided to take a step back. "Whatever happened, it seems to have upset Madison enough to drive her out of the house."

Kaufman looked pained. "I didn't realize she was listening." He murmured something else that Preuss didn't catch.

"Sorry, what's that?"

"I said I'll never forgive myself is something happens to her because of this. I don't know how I'd go on."

Preuss stayed silent. You'd go on, he knew. You'd put one foot in front of the other and you'd go on. You'd feel like your heart was ripped out of your chest, but you'd go on. You'd survive.

Even if the ones you loved didn't.

6

The eleven o'clock meeting was a quick one.

Janey Cahill, on speakerphone from the Kaufman home, talked about her meeting with Madison's teacher, who said she never saw any evidence of a problem with Madison or at home. Preuss talked about what he had learned from the parents. Trombley was still working through the Sex Offender Registry. Bellamy, whose specialty was fraud, had been temporarily detailed to investigate an assault on an elderly woman who was bilked out of $8,000 and then beaten by two scam artists.

Crime marches on, Preuss thought.

"I'm calling in the K-9 unit," Tullio said. "I put in a request for one of Oakland County's dog-handlers. He's going to meet us at the Kaufmans' this afternoon after the news conference. Reg, after the press thing today we're going to have tips up the wahzoo. Can you start sorting through them along with doing the Sex Registry?"

"No problem," Trombley said.

They agreed to meet again at six and the meeting ended.

"I'm feeling worse about this by the hour," Tullio said to Preuss when the others had left. His face was the color of a fish's belly.

"Yeah," Preuss said, "if she was just lost, she would have shown up by now."

"Unless she's hurt somewhere and can't get to anyone."

"She could have hurt herself walking around in the dark."

"Even so, where would she be? She would have turned up by now. We've looked everywhere in the neighborhood. Unless somebody took her in."

"And won't let her out. Or she got locked in a garage and can't get out."

The older detective pressed a hand to his sternum. He couldn't seem to speak.

"Tony?"

When he caught his breath Tullio said, "It's nothing."

"Doesn't look like nothing."

Preuss waited. Tullio had spoken longingly of retirement. In a few more years he would have his thirty in and move north, where he had property near Indian River at the top of the Michigan mitten.

With luck he'd live that long.

After a few moments, Tullio made a sour face and said, "Look, can you draft the news release? I have to liaze with the Sheriff's SIU."

"Sure. Getting calls from the media already?"

"Last hour or so, yeah. It's like they smell blood in the water."

"Little white girl gone missing, gift from the gods for that bunch."

For the next forty-five minutes, Preuss worked on the statement and sent a copy to Tullio to review before sending it on to the chief. It was short because there wasn't a lot to say.

Tullio made no changes, so Preuss emailed it to the chief's administrative assistant to duplicate for the reporters.

As soon as he sent it off, a scream from down the hall pierced the quiet of the detectives' section.

7

Preuss was down the hall in a flash. In Tullio's cubicle the older man was sprawled face down across his desk, a cup of coffee overturned and spreading black liquid over the papers on the desktop.

Tullio's face was pasty and sweating and twisted in agony but he was breathing. He tried to lift his head off the desk to say something but couldn't force anything out. One arm was trapped between the top desk drawer and his body, the other flopped uselessly out to the side.

Using his desk phone, the records clerk called for an ambulance.

Preuss undid Tullio's tie and the top buttons of his shirt.

"Hang on," Preuss said. "Help is on the way." The older man stared at him with full, imploring eyes.

It wasn't long before a pair of big EM techs burst into the office with their paraphernalia. In short order they got him loaded onto a gurney and rolled him out to their rig.

He was still breathing.

The news conference began a half hour late. It was held in the chief's conference room, a square room that was not large enough to accommodate the crowd that showed up.

Video news crews from the major stations, Channels 2, 4, and 7, crammed into the square meeting room, the tripods for their ENG equipment making a metal forest of angled legs and the lights from their video cameras raising the temperature of the room twenty degrees. Cable and radio reporters were also there, along with print reporters from the *Free Press* and *Oakland Tribune*, and a young woman who looked about twelve whom Preuss didn't recognize.

The chief of police, William Warnock, was a tall, spare man with pitted scars on his jaw from an ancient bout of acne. He began by explaining the lead investigator had just been rushed to the hospital with a medical emergency. At the front of the room with him were Lieutenant Russo, the chief of the detective unit, and Preuss. The other detectives were in the field.

The chief read his statement and Preuss distributed press packets to the assembled group. The press packet contained the text of the chief's statement, the photo of Madison Kaufman, and instructions for contacting the department.

Immediately after the chief finished, the TV reporters all shouted the same question: "Why do you say there's no foul play?"

The chief looked at Russo, who looked at Preuss and gave a barely perceptible nod toward the podium.

Stepping up to the cluster of microphones, Preuss said, "Right now there's no physical evidence at the scene or any communication to the Kaufman family that suggests foul play. But we're not ruling anything out and we're pursuing a number of lines of inquiry."

"Have you gotten any ransom demands?" the reporter from Channel 2 asked.

"No."

"Has there been any contact from anyone about her kidnapping?"

"At this point we have no reason to believe she was kidnapped."

"Are you saying for certain she wasn't kidnapped?"

"I'm saying we have no reason to believe it right now. That may change."

"Can you talk about what your lines of inquiry are?" the reporter from Channel 7 asked.

"I can't comment on those specifically. But we're giving all available resources to finding this girl."

"Have you checked on local sex offenders?" asked the young woman Preuss didn't know.

"Yes, that's happening as we speak."

"So that's one of your 'lines of inquiry'?"

"It is."

"Can you say anything about what you're finding?"

"I can't comment on that."

"Are all the men on that list accounted for?"

"I can't comment on that either."

"So it's possible other children in this community may be at risk?" the woman pressed.

Russo jumped in. "No," he said, "that's not the right conclusion at all." With his dark plum dress shirt stretched over aging bodybuilder's muscles gone to seed, he resettled his feet as though prepping for a physical confrontation with the slight young reporter. She seemed barely out of her teens, with matte black hair cropped close to her head and geeky black glasses.

Good-looking despite the square studs in her eyebrow and right nostril, Preuss noted.

"If you don't know what these men are up to, how do you know they're not involved?"

Russo glared at the reporter as thought trying to decide which Ninja move to use on her.

Preuss stepped back to the podium and said, "A detective is working with the Sex Registry to account for the whereabouts of the people on the list. There's no reason at this time to think any child in our community is at increased risk. Parents should maintain their usual level of caution."

The young woman adjusted her glasses and gazed at him as if taking his measure. Her fingernails were painted black. She seemed satisfied and looked down to make a note on her pad.

"In the meantime," Chief Warnock said, "we've put a picture of Madison Kaufman in your press packets, and we're asking all residents of the area to be on the lookout for her. At this point, our entire force is trying to find her."

The TV reporters began asking questions that repeated information from the news release so they could be seen on their news reports actively pursuing the truth. When they were finished the young woman who had given Russo a hard time raised her hand.

The chief nodded to her and she said, "Did you say the head of this investigation is now off the case?"

"He was taken to the hospital an hour ago. He'll return to duty as soon as he gets a clean bill of health."

"Any idea how long that might be?" she asked.

"I couldn't say when he'll be back. We all wish him well and as soon as there's any word, I'll make that known."

"So who's going to take over in the meantime?"

The chief looked at Russo, who stepped forward and said, "Detective Martin Preuss is now the lead investigator." He spoke as if it killed him to say Preuss's name.

The reporter from Channel 2 shot back up on her feet. "Detective, how do you intend to proceed?"

"In exactly the ways we've just outlined."

The reporters made another clamor about the spelling of Preuss's name, and once that was settled the chief said, "That's it for now. Thank you all."

The video camera operators turned their lights off and prepared to pack up their gear. With the lights out, the room cooled and it was as if anything of possible interest was over.

As the chief and his detectives were leaving the room, the young woman who had pressed Russo intercepted Preuss. Russo gave her a hard look and told Preuss, "See me when you're through."

"Detective Preuss," the young woman said. "Shelley Larkin from the *Metro Voice*."

Her hand was cool and boney as Preuss shook it. The *Voice* was the local alternative paper. Since a messy newspaper strike and the takeover by conglomerates had turned the two major dailies into fillers for advertising, the *Voice* did most of what passed for investigative journalism in town.

"What's the *Voice's* interest here?" he asked. "You're a weekly. You don't usually pursue breaking news."

"It's my own interest, actually."

Up close Preuss could see she was older than he thought, maybe by as much as ten years, which would put her past thirty.

"I'm doing a piece on media attention to minorities compared to whites."

She gestured to the empty room around them. "All this attention for a little white girl. Not that I begrudge it to her, but black children are proportionately the victims of vastly higher numbers of crimes. Yet when a cute little white girl is missing, that's what gets the media's attention."

"Just so you know," Preuss said, "we work every case equally hard. It's not Madison's fault she's white. So let's not get ahead of ourselves—we don't know if a crime has been committed here or not."

"I understand that. And don't worry," she said with a wry smile, "my knives aren't out for you." Despite the hardware on her face, she was an attractive woman, slender as a nail with fine, sharply etched features. "I'm interested in a larger issue that has to do with the priorities of the mainstream media."

She adjusted the glasses on her nose. "So where do you think this girl is? Off the record?"

"We really have told you all there is to know about it for now. We're not keeping anything back."

She dug in the messenger bag she used as a purse and came up with a business card. She extracted one and handed it to him. "Keep me in mind if you do hear anything?"

"You'll be the second to know."

She narrowed her sly, black, smiling eyes.

Russo said, "Twenty-four hours. She isn't back by tomorrow morning, we're calling in the cavalry."

Before Preuss could answer, Russo continued, "And stay away from the media. Anybody wants information, they come to me."

Preuss nodded, remembering Shelley Larkin's crafty smile.

8

"What's your problem?" Brian Mobius demanded.

Rebecca Johnson took a look at the joint they were passing around and screwed up her mouth.

"You lipped it," she said.

"So?"

"So it's gross!"

"You don't want it, give it back."

Mobius made to grab it and the two fell into a mock struggle with giggles and much grabbing at breasts.

In the corner of Blair Park, a mile down the road from Ferndale High School, where they all should have been in class, Stevie Matuzik said, "Knock it off."

The girl shrieked and danced away from Mobius.

Stevie said again, "Knock it off!"

Mobius said, "Who the fuck made you king?"

Rebecca said, "Shut up, you two. Just gimme the doobie,"

"At least let me wipe it off first," Mobius said. He took a deep toke and showily lipped it clean before passing it over.

She took her own long, satisfied drag.

"Yo," Mobius said to them, "check this out."

He pulled a brand new Ipod Touch from his pocket and stuck the buds in his ears. He turned it on and closed his eyes and did an exaggerated head-bang to unheard music.

"Where'd you get that?" Rebecca had to yell to get through.

"Fell into my hands a couple nights ago."

"You liar. You stole it, didn't you? You're such a thief!"

Stevie watched this with growing disgust.

Finally he said, "You both suck," and stomped away, moving with his gangly round-shouldered shuffle past the line of a half dozen trees that separated the swing set from the rest of the park.

He went deeper into the park, toward the baseball diamond at the far end.

Stevie ignored him and continued on his long legs past the picnic shelter. He needed to be alone.

Back at the swing set Mobius grabbed up the remaining Labatt's and set off after him. "Hey! Dude!" he called.

Stevie stopped abruptly when Mobius caught up with him.

"What's the matter?" Mobius asked.

Without replying, Stevie bent to pick up a rock from the cold dirt of the field and heaved it with all his might toward the backstop. It fell short.

Mobius said, "Oh, right, I know what it is. Dude, I told you about that girl."

Stevie didn't answer.

In his fury he could find no words to respond with, so he picked up another rock and hurled it with all his might into the wooden backstop. The rock shattered into a hundred tiny pieces and left a white dent in the weathered wood.

"How many times you gonna let her shit on you before you get the picture? You got to get over it, man."

Stevie turned on Mobius. "She loves me."

"Dude, are you ever stoopid. She may love somebody, but it ain't you."

"She loves me," Stevie insisted. "I know she does."

"Yeah, right. That's why she was with another guy."

At the thought, Stevie went apeshit. He went to shove Mobius but the other boy was too quick for him and did the rope-a-dope backwards.

Instead Stevie searched for another rock to brain him with, to beat his stupid fucking head to a pulp until nothing was left but a little puddle of shit in the snow.

Fortunately for Mobius, the ground was bare.

Stevie sought release from his rage in a long, piercing howl of anguish.

9

"Right here's the last trace we found of your girl," the dog handler said.

He was an earnest young Sheriff's deputy from Oakland County named Steele. Preuss bent over to give his dusky German shepherd a scratch behind the ears.

Steele pointed to a patch on the lawn, cleared of leaves. Preuss judged it to be about a hundred yards away from the girl's house, down the street and around the corner on Livernois.

"There's a strong scent coming directly from the house," Steele continued. "But then she disappears right here."

"What do you mean, disappears?"

"Her scent stops cold."

"And nobody heard anything?" Preuss wondered. "If a car stopped and snatched her, wouldn't you think she'd have put up some kind of fuss?"

Cahill said, "I'd like to think she'd scream bloody murder. That's what I tell my kids to do, anyway."

"Yet none of the canvasses turned up anything like that."

"Maybe somebody stopped and threw a bag over her head or disabled her somehow," Steele offered.

"Or," Cahill said, "it was somebody she knew. Somebody tried to throw her in a bag, she'd still make some noise."

"Unless she was disabled," Steele repeated.

"She has epilepsy," Preuss said. "A seizure could have disabled her enough so she wouldn't yell."

"The strongest scent comes from the house to here and stops," Steele pointed out.

"All right," Preuss said. "It's bad news, but it's helpful. It means our theory is now that somebody physically grabbed her right here and carried her off."

"That's what I'd say," Steele said. "Rickie's got a nose on him I'd trust with my life."

As though that gave him permission to move, the dog stood suddenly and strained at his leash toward the street.

"Rickie!" Steele said. "Calm down!"

"Wait, let him go," Preuss urged. "See what he's after."

Steele let Rickie off his lead and the dog bounded into a tremendous mound of leaves in the street by the curb. The pile had not been there the night before, Preuss was certain. The homeowner must have raked them into the street earlier in the day in preparation for the city's leaf collection.

Rickie rooted around in the leaves and trotted back to his master. In his mouth he gingerly carried a stuffed rabbit toy. He dropped it at Steele's feet and sat as though waiting for further orders.

The three police officers knelt around Rickie's find. Along with bits of brown oak leaves and debris from the leaves on the rabbit's shabby velveteen fur was a ragged dark red stain.

"Oh, shit," Cahill murmured.

"We need the tech squad down here," Preuss said. "Right now."

He snapped a photo of the stuffed animal with his phone, taking care not to show any blood.

Preuss left Cahill to wait for the crime scene investigation unit while he went to the Kaufman residence. When she looked at the photo on his phone, Sharon Kaufman collapsed with her head in her hands in the corner of the sofa in the living room.

The wail she let out sent an electric chill down his spine.

10

Even though he had been in the detective unit for almost four years, Reg Trombley was still amazed at how many Ferndale residents wound up on the Michigan Sex Offender Registry.

When he went to the State Police website he found sixty-three matches with Ferndale addresses, four full pages, all men. Even more disconcerting were the photos accompanying the entries, happy smiling faces from the driver's license photos of asshole perverts, indecent exposers, perpetrators of incest, rapists of thirteen-year-old girls, sodomists of children and incapacitated women, pornographers and consumers of pornography.

And last but not least my neighbors, he thought sourly as he printed out the list.

He had two girls, Jessica, nine, and Reva, eleven. Every time he thought about them walking home from school with the likes of this skeevy rogues' gallery on the loose, he wanted to follow the girls around with a shotgun locked and loaded and ready to blow away the first one who gave them a second look. Crimes against children were the worst, no doubt about that.

What a sad, sick world we live in, he thought.

At his desk in his cubicle he paged through the printout. Look at these smilin' shitheads, he reflected with disgust. Like they didn't have a care in the world after raping a child.

One face in particular jumped out at him. Wayne Joseph White, Criminal Sexual Conduct 2nd Degree, person under thirteen. Thirty years old and big, five-eleven and close to three hundred pounds, with blue eyes and brown van dyke that hung on his double chin as though pasted there.

Thinking about what a man that size could do to a seven-year-old brought a great rage boiling up inside him. Sometimes it was hard to remember he was supposed to be a force of social order, and not an agent of vengeance.

What had caught his eye was not White's appearance but his location. He lived on Roanoke in Oak Park, a few streets away from Madison Kaufman. Of all the scumbags on the Sex Registry, Wayne White lived closest.

Isn't that interesting?

He found the name of White's parole officer and had a brief phone conversation with him. He was keeping his nose clean, the p.o. said. Had a job at Buzz McMillan's Chevrolet Service Department on Main Street in Royal Oak.

Trombley found the number in the Yellow Pages and talked to the service manager, who told him Wayne White did work there but had called in sick that day.

Even more interesting.

Wayne, Trombley silently told him, I believe you and me'll be seeing each other real soon.

11

"I go back a long way with this guy," Cahill said. "His last bit was Criminal Sexual Conduct Four. Vic was a fourteen-year-old girl, I think." She and Preuss sat in Trombley's Taurus across the street from Wayne White's house.

"Maybe he's moved on to the littler ones," Trombley said.

"You know him," Preuss said to Cahill. "You want to take the lead?"

"Delighted."

"If he's not home or gives us trouble, we'll get a warrant."

"He won't give us trouble," Janey said. "Trust me on this one. He's just a big pussycat."

"Little pussyhound, more like it," Trombley said.

Cahill rang the doorbell and when she got no response tried the storm door, which was locked. Though the houses around it were neat and well-maintained, Wayne White's home was a frame structure with peeling white shingles and an enclosed porch stuffed with boxes and old lamps and chairs without seats, the windows gone and protected by torn cloudy plastic sheeting.

"Neighbors must love the way this guy keeps his property," Trombley said.

Cahill started banging on the door frame now, which made the whole front porch shake. "Wayne White!"

She stopped pounding to call his number on her cell phone, and then resumed hammering until the front door opened inside the enclosed porch and an enormous man hove into view.

"Hey, Wayne," she said through the glass of the storm door. He was blimp-like in a soiled Red Wings 2004 Stanley Cup Champions sweatshirt and a pair of multicolored red and blue sweatpants that looked like clown pants. He was completely bald, with quizzical eyebrows arched over sneaky suspicious blue eyes that looked from one to the other on his front porch.

"Open the door for us, Wayne," she said. "We need to talk to you."

Breathing hard, he unlocked the storm door and led the way inside.

"Got nothing to hide," he tossed back over his shoulder.

"That's what I like to hear," Cahill said.

Following White, she led Preuss and Trombley into a living room that smelled of old musty socks and stale beer. Preuss looked hard around the room, lighting up different parts of it: the old food and empty cans of Miller, the shabby furniture, the general disarray. Especially the lack of evidence of a child.

"Watching your step, Wayne?" Cahill asked.

"Trying."

He stood behind them like a guest in his own house. Then flopped his bulk onto the ratty purple sofa in the corner of the living room. The house shook.

"Trying, or doing?"

"Doing."

"How come you're home, Wayne? Why aren't you working?"

As she spoke, the other two detectives silently fanned out through the downstairs of the small home, opening doors, even looking inside cupboards.

He told her about his job at McMillan Chevrolet.

"You like it?"

He shrugged. "Pays the rent."

He turned around to check out Preuss and Trombley. "Hey," he said, "what are you all looking for?"

Ignoring him, Cahill said, "Wayne, you didn't answer my question. Why aren't you at work today?"

"Didn't feel so good when I woke up. Called in sick."

"Feeling better now, are we?"

"Little."

"We're just going to take a look around, okay?" It was not a request for permission as much as a statement. The big man sat on the sad filthy sofa without replying.

Cahill and Preuss climbed the staircase to the second floor while Trombley kept an eye on White. The master bedroom, where White laid his bulk at night, had a disheveled bed and a dresser with all the drawers open and leaking clothes. Preuss looked inside the closet, knocking on the walls to see if any were hollow. He heard the satisfying "thunk" of solid wood.

The other two bedrooms were empty.

Preuss looked inside the bathroom, which was filthy, with dank towels scattered across the sink and the back of the toilet. He whipped the shower curtain back, unconsciously holding his breath at what he might find there but seeing only a bathtub with a serious ring. Imagine trying to get clean in that, he thought.

Out in the hallway was an entry to the attic in the center of the ceiling with a rope tied to a hook. Preuss pulled it and down came a folding stairway into the attic. He pulled a penlight from his inside coat pocket and climbed the rickety stairway. He shone the light around the attic, which was completely empty.

Four by eight boards were set over pink insulation between the floor joists. He satisfied himself there were no hidden rooms, no crawl spaces, no doors leading into torture chambers. It was an attic much like his own, except his was filled with boxes of old stuff from his previous life.

Downstairs Cahill was in the living room again, sitting on the sofa talking with Wayne White. Trombley was standing by the fireplace. He and Preuss raised eyebrows at each other, and both shook their heads. Nothing here.

Preuss said, "Wayne, is your garage locked?"

"Yeah." His voice sullen and high, like a brooding boy's.

"Toss me the key, will you?"

With great and obvious resentment, White heaved his bulk off the sofa and padded into the kitchen.

"Can't say I like this," he told them, speaking on the way into the kitchen and without looking at them so it wouldn't seem as if he were directly confronting them. "Coming into my house like I got no rights."

"You know why we're here?" Cahill said.

"No fucking idea."

He came back into the living room and handed the key to Preuss and collapsed on the sofa. The house shook again.

"I ain't done nothing wrong and you're all in my face about some shit."

Cahill said, "A little girl's missing."

He got very still.

"She lives over there on West Woodland. Her name's Madison Kaufman. I don't suppose you know her?"

"Never heard of her."

"Little seven-year-old. Been missing since last night. Not spending any time with little girls, are you, Wayne?"

"No, ma'am."

"Telling me the truth?"

"God's truth, ma'am."

At that, Preuss and Trombley went out into the back yard and unlocked the garage door. More junk inside: an old push lawnmower, pieces of bent and discolored drywall, a couple of rusted metal rakes and shovels, old lawn chairs with impossibly twisted aluminum tubing and tattered plastic seats.

Cahill came out the back door to join them.

"I still don't like this guy," Trombley said.

"I don't either," Cahill said, "but I don't see anything here that gets us closer to Madison."

Preuss said, "There's just no place to hide a kid here, unless we're missing some secret compartment somewhere."

Trombley said, "Could have her stashed someplace else."

"That's a thought," Cahill considered.

Preuss said, "All right, I'll order a car on his house. We'll trace his movements. If he's got her in a hidey hole somewhere, we'll find it."

They went back inside the house. White was still on the sofa, staring into space and breathing hard through his mouth.

"Okay, Wayne," Cahill said. "We're going to keep an eye on you. I better not find out you did something to this little girl."

"I swear on my mother's grave I didn't. I've been keeping my nose clean."

"That was true," she said, "you wouldn't have the pleasure of our acquaintance today."

12

In his cubicle Preuss settled back with a cup of coffee and a cheese sandwich of uncertain age from the machine in the canteen. The sandwich had no taste and the coffee was bitter but he wasn't focused on the food.

With his lunch sitting like a brick in his belly, he blew a huff of air out and realized how tired he was.

By the clock on his desk, it was quarter to six already. The whole day was gone and they were no closer to finding her than they had been in the morning.

He brushed a layer of dust off the timepiece, a present from his older son Jason when Preuss was promoted to the detective squad and the only personal item on his desk. Jason had the department's motto, "Midwest's Finest," engraved on a plate at the base of a clock set into the wheel of a sailboat.

That was back before everything went bad in their lives and Jason disappeared. Thinking of Jason was always painful, and this case brought him right up against the lost child in his own life.

He forced himself back to the present. He called Cahill and Trombley to check in and told them not to worry about meeting that night. They agreed to meet in the morning after roll call.

He spent the next hour word processing a report for Russo. The chief of detectives was gone for the night, though he had left instructions to be called if anything developed. Not only were there no developments, but it was sounding like they couldn't avoid calling in help.

Before he left the station he called Cahill again.

"I'm home now," she said. "Sam Kovachs is at the house. Reggie's on duty, and the night patrol is heavier than usual. So we're covered."

"Still no word?"

"Nothing."

"What's going on at your place?"

"All present and accounted for."

"Mitch doing okay?"

She sighed. "He calls me and tells me about his job and it reminds me of something out of the pioneer days. But hey, we're lucky we still have the house. Kids miss him like crazy. Me not so much."

Her husband was a union carpenter who couldn't find work in the area so he was out in Las Vegas on a job for a contractor that was a step above a sweatshop. But it was the only work he could find. Things were terrible in Michigan, and not likely to get better any time soon. She often talked to Preuss about how hard it was to be a suddenly single mother of two boys at the same time as she was glad to get her husband out of her hair.

Preuss knew their marriage was rocky, though neither one would ever consider divorce. They believed you made your bed and then you had to lay in it, no matter what.

She said, "What have you been up to?"

He told her about his afternoon, and the increasingly bad feeling he had about how things were going.

"I've been thinking about Wayne White," she said. "It's just too coincidental he lives a couple blocks from the Kaufmans. Guys like that never change, except when they get worse."

"We should ask the Kaufmans if they've ever seen him."

"Want me to do that?"

"No, stay put. I'll swing by their house when I leave here."

"I'm sure RT isn't going to let him out of his sight," Cahill said. "Seems like he has the same feeling about him."

"He's a good guy, Reg. Going to be good police when he learns to keep a cool head."

"What's on your plate still, beside the Kaufmans?"

"I promised Toby I'd stop in and see him."

"How's the little guy?"

"Doing great."

"Give that sweetheart a kiss for me. And you get yourself some rest."

When he didn't say anything, she said, "We'll find that girl, Marty. I can feel it."

"I know we will. What worries me is the shape she'll be in when we do."

13

"Did that animal take my child?"

Sharon Kaufman stared with revulsion at the driver's license photo of Wayne White.

"We don't know that. We're just trying to find out if you know of any link between this guy and your daughter."

"What's his name?"

Preuss told her. "Never seen him before."

"Mr. Kaufman?"

Standing behind his wife, Stanley Kaufman shook his head, murmured something that Preuss took for a negative.

Before he took the picture back from them, he had a sudden thought. "What kind of cars do you both drive?"

"I drive a Tahoe," Sharon answered. "Stanley a Malibu."

Chevys. "Where do you get your cars serviced?"

"The Chevy dealer on Main Street in Royal Oak."

"McMillan?"

"That's it. Why?"

When was the last time you took your car in?"

Sharon thought for a few moments. "Last month. I went in for some brake work."

"Do you remember if you brought Madison with you?"

"Yes," she said, "I think I did. It was on a day when she was off from school. Is that important?"

"Might be."

Stanley Kaufman walked him to the door. He said goodbye glumly. He seemed to have given up all hope already.

41

By then it was 8:45. His son was probably in bed already. Even if he was asleep, Preuss would be able to satisfy himself the little guy was safe.

He drove west on Drayton to Scotia, crossed over the 696 expressway, cut through Huntington Woods into Berkley. Lucky the new group home was so close to where he lived and worked. Other homes further out, in Bloomfield Hills or Novi, may have been bigger but this was close and new and well-equipped. Toby seemed to enjoy it, and most importantly, the staff was stable and took good care of him.

They also appreciated him. They understood his subtle responsiveness, his humor, the range of nuanced communications in his expressions and tones of voice.

He pulled into the driveway of the one-story house off the corner of Eleven Mile and Scotia and parked in the rear. It was a long building angled on its plot of land with room for vans to pick up the residents for their day programs without having to back up or turn around, newly built within the past six years.

He entered to the sound of a TV in the living room. To the right was the kitchen and dining room. As he walked in he threw a wave to Charlie, the young man who was Toby's friend in the home. He had been in a car accident that killed both his parents and left him with a traumatic brain injury. Charlie raised his palsied hand to greet Preuss from the dining room table where he seemed to spend most of his time, either being fed or waiting to be fed by the staff.

Preuss peeked in to the living room but no one was watching the dance contest on the TV, so he continued on toward the back of the house, where the residents' bedrooms were. The night nurse, Kim, was in the med room and he said hello to her as he passed.

Except for Charlie, all the other residents were in their beds already. The rooms were pink and frilly, girls' rooms. Like Madison's, he thought. Besides Charlie and Toby, all the other residents were young women. Music or the television played in all the rooms. One of the girls, Kathy, was still awake and laughing to herself with a rowdy infectious whoop.

Toby's wheelchair was in the hall outside the open door to his room. The light was off. Preuss stood at the doorway and looked in, trying to see if his son was already asleep under the covers. He was small for his age, seventeen, but at almost ninety pounds he was a real handful to lift and transport. Preuss still remembered the time when he could hold the boy in one hand and hoist him over his head while Toby chortled madly.

Now Toby lay curled like a comma on his right side, his sleeping side, and his eyes were closed and his breathing deep and even. Sound asleep. Judy Collins played softly on the CD player Preuss gave him for his birthday two years ago.

He tiptoed up to the bed and leaned over his sleeping son's form and kissed him softly on his temple and his cheek, inhaled the clean smell of soap and shampoo. He would never get used to feeling stubble on the boy. He had a heavy beard already, from the medicine he once took for his seizures.

Dilantin, he remembered. The same thing Madison took.

Preuss lightly laid a hand on Toby's shoulder, overwhelmed, as always, by the complex feelings the boy engendered . . . love and tenderness at the child's eternal innocence and vulnerability, but also sadness, guilt, and loss, emotions associated not so much with Toby himself as with what Toby reminded him of as the last remaining member of the family.

And tonight, with a missing girl out in the world somewhere, his feelings were also charged with gratitude the young man was here, safe and still present in his life. Unlike his brother Jason, who was also out there, though at twenty-one better able to fend for himself.

He bent over and kissed his son again, bade him a silent goodnight, then stole quietly out of the room.

14

He couldn't remember the last time he was this glad to get back to the big empty house.

He just wanted to shut the door on everything for the night. The case would be waiting for him in the morning. Others were moving it forward.

In the kitchen he peered into the refrigerator. On the top shelf was a white container of leftovers of take-out from the Thai place on Nine Mile. He dumped it in a bowl and put it in the microwave. Even this minor task drained the last ounce of energy from him. He sat slumped at the table while the food heated.

When the microwave stopped, he found a pair of chopsticks and ate right from the bowl sitting at the table. The food was not hot all the way through, but he was too tired to care. After a few lukewarm bites he felt refreshed enough to get up and pour a glass of water, which he drained in one gulp.

He took his food and another glass of water into the living room and flicked on the CD player. Dylan's *Highway 66 Revisited* came up. He had been listening to it on Wednesday night, which seemed like a month ago.

"Like a Rolling Stone" started, Bobby Gregg's snare drum and Al Kooper's plaintive organ instantly sending him back to when he had first heard this song.

It reminded him how long past his shelf life he felt.

He flopped down on the reclining chair and put his feet up and let the music flow over him as he ate.

For the past few years the house had been feeling too big for the narrowness of his life. Periodically he thought of selling it. He imagined himself as a ghost drifting through the vacant remains of his former existence.

All the central people in his life had left him . . . his wife, Jason, even Toby, now cared for by strangers. Toby was the only one in the car the night of the accident who was not seriously injured. Toby, born with cerebral palsy and a list of disabilities that filled a whole page of his yearly IEP . . . mental retardation, seizures, visual impairment, scoliosis, paraplegia . . .

It was Preuss himself who had pushed most of them away. No illusions about that. With more control over himself, he would have been a better husband, better father. Their life together wouldn't have been one long screaming match.

Screaming at each other constantly. Like the Kaufmans.

Jeanette wouldn't have piled the kids in the car and tried to escape their life. Wouldn't have been on the road to her mother's in Traverse City when a drunk driver in the dead black of a Michigan country night t-boned the Windstar, killing her instantly and putting Jason in the hospital with a closed-head injury. Piled around with pillows to keep him propped upright in the back seat bench, Toby sustained only a broken leg.

Jason blamed him for all of it, and once out of his year-long rehab he took off. For a few months he kept in touch with Preuss by phone, mostly when he needed money, but then the intervals between those calls lengthened and finally Jason stopped calling altogether. Preuss had not heard from him at all for four years now, though he had tracked him down using the boy's social security number and his contacts with police agencies throughout the country. The boy was currently in jail in Needles, California.

A member of the ranks of lost children.

Preuss kept track of him long distance, but let his son have the space he seemed to need away from his father.

Preuss was left with only his sweet, loving Toby, who was the happiest person he knew, who enjoyed everything and everybody, whose crooked smile, tender brown eyes, and buoyant laugh brought the only joy his father knew.

After Jeannette died, Preuss hired nurses to care for Toby. Finally it didn't work. At first it broke his battered heart even more, because he knew Toby was also dealing with his mother's loss; being nonverbal, he couldn't talk about it but expressed his sadness through his cries and whimpers and distress for the first year after the accident. But he had to get Toby someplace where he would get the care he needed.

Now Preuss visited and took him out as often as he could. Jeannette's mother Agnes came down for a weekend each month to see him. She avoided Preuss, and had been happy when Toby went into his group home because she no longer had to deal with him for her visits because she blamed him for her daughter's death.

So did Jeanette's father, his boss Nick Russo. Russo was why Preuss became a policeman. When Jeanette became pregnant with Jason and they got married, they settled in Ferndale and Russo convinced him to join the department. Now Russo could barely look at him, and cut off all contact with Toby.

Thinking about his sons—how much Toby loved life, how much he missed Jason—turned his thoughts toward Madison Kaufman, and where she could have been. Why hadn't she turned up yet? How could no one have seen her out by herself?

No one, that is, but whoever did something with her. And that someone had done something with her, or to her, was now a conclusion impossible to avoid. This case had officially gone to hell. Now it was up to him to do something about it.

He held the bowl of food to his mouth and shoveled in the few remaining grains of cold rice. He went back into the kitchen and set it all in the sink, and went around the house turning off the few lights he had put on when he came home.

He went upstairs to step out of his clothes in the bathroom and stand under a shower that was so hot it made him gasp.

Then he wrapped himself in his robe and fell onto his bed and into a deep, dreamless sleep.

Madison Kaufman had been missing without her meds for over twenty-four hours.

Friday, November 7, 2008

15

At his desk early, Preuss read the case notes Cahill and Trombley had emailed him. On his way in he had stopped by the Tim Horton's doughnut shop on Woodward so he sipped coffee from a cardboard container and worked through an over-buttered bagel.

Cahill's report in particular caught his eye. It described her conversation with Sharon Kaufman's sister, Peggy Andrejewski, the evening before, after Preuss had spoken with her. The sister called the station looking for Preuss and got patched through to Cahill. Apparently Kenny turned up. He'd been in the pokey in Hamburg since Tuesday.

So not this uncle, Preuss thought.

Peggy also talked about a long-term relationship she claimed Sharon had been having with a man outside her marriage.

The sister knew enough to identify the man by name. She said the police should look in his direction if they wanted to find Madison. Apparently they started seeing each other in Buffalo.

He made a note to ask Cahill about that when they met.

His desk phone rang. Russo, summoning him.

He knew this would not go well.

The chief of detectives was in his shirtsleeves behind the impeccably neat desk he always kept. He held the copies of the reports from Cahill and Trombley, along with the one Preuss wrote late yesterday.

"So basically," Russo said, "we're at a standstill. That about right?"

Preuss had to admit it was.

"Here's what's going to happen. I'm calling in the Sheriff's Special Investigations Unit. From this point on they're in charge."

Before Preuss could protest, Russo lifted a hand and said, "Save it. You'll give them all the backup you can but they're going to take the lead. This isn't anything we can afford to look like fools on any more."

"You think we look like fools on this?"

"I think we look like fucking Andy Griffith and Barney Fife chasing our tails. Meantime there's a little girl out there with who knows what happening to her."

"Nick, the whole team's working around the clock."

"The fact is, we just can't move as fast on this as the Sheriff's squad can. We need more bodies than the department can spare. Or even has. That's true, and you know it."

"Agreed. But this is our case. She lives in our city. We should take the lead."

"Not going to happen. Cut Bellamy and Trombley loose to work on other things. Cahill's the primary contact from here."

Preuss took a deep breath before he replied. Trying to keep himself under control.

Before he could get anything out, Russo continued. "Cut 'em loose. With Tullio gone, we need them on other cases. You'll stay as part of the team the Sheriff's squad puts together."

"Not the best use of my people. And this isn't going to go down well with them. They've all got a commitment to this case."

Russo folded together the three reports he was reading and placed them carefully in the top drawer of his desk. His workspace was clean again.

"Objection noted," Russo said. "It's up to you to let your officers know about this decision. It's not up for debate. And then I want you and Cahill to report to the state squad as soon as you can. Have the other two write their final summary reports and get ready to take on new assignments. Understood?"

"Yes sir," Preuss said tightly.

"I'm not fucking around here."

"I can see that."

Russo gave him a fish-eyed stare. "Marty, I'd adjust my attitude, I were you. We're soldiers in the service of the greater good. We need to act like it."

"So what's your rationale for relieving me as lead investigator? Or even primary liaison?"

"Your job doesn't include questioning my decisions."

"I'm not questioning them, I'm asking for an explanation."

"You don't get that either," Russo spat. "Dismissed."

With that he picked up his phone and pressed a button. He asked his administrative assistant to get him the Oakland County Sheriff's Special Investigation Unit and avoided Preuss's eye until the detective gathered himself to return to his cubicle.

There he sat behind his desk and stared at the piles of folders and crime stat reports and containers of cold coffee.

"Bull *shit!*" Janey Cahill exploded.

"This is our case. We're working it the way we do. I don't have a problem with the county or even the state coming in, but dammit, you should be in charge, not them. This is our jurisdiction."

"I pointed that out. It cut no ice whatsoever."

"Fucking guy's still screwing you over because of Jeannette."

"I don't like it any more than you do. But we do need more help with this."

Trombley drained his Styrofoam coffee cup and tossed it toward the trash can in the corner of the small conference room. It hit the side and bounced away. "Tell you one thing," he said, "I'm not going to bail on this thing yet."

"Don't get yourself shitcanned because of this, okay?"

"Nobody's going to shitcan me."

Preuss said, "Look, let this thing play out the way it's going to. Russo can make things damn hard for you. Let Janey and me take this forward. If we need you, we'll bring you back in."

"This sucks. This is something you should take to your delegate."

"I'll survive. Meantime I don't want to see you do anything you'll regret. Will you do this for me?"

Trombley considered that for a few moments, then gave Preuss a humorless grin. "One loose end I want to tie up first."

16

At eleven a.m. Preuss and Cahill reported to the Oakland County Sheriff's Office at the sprawling county campus on North Telegraph Road in Pontiac.

There they learned Jim Cass would be lead investigator. Preuss knew of him. He had heard his reputation was good. A detective lieutenant with SIU, he was a big square faced man with a basso profundo voice.

His assistant was a detective sergeant named Emma Blalock, whom Preuss didn't know. She had straight dark brown hair pulled back from a high forehead and fashionable rimless glasses. She had a wide slash of mouth and her skin was the color of perfectly smooth milk chocolate.

Preuss spent an hour recapping the details of the case for them, with Cahill filling in as necessary. As it turned out, they got most of it thrown back at them for now. The Sheriff's unit would recanvas the neighborhood and liaison with the State on an Amber Alert and the Missing Child Clearinghouse, but Cass told Preuss and Cahill to keep working their leads.

A meeting was set for six that evening while Cass collected his team, which would include someone from the state police missing child unit.

"When we meet again, we'll parcel out the new tasks," Cass said in his deep rumble of a voice. "I'll also have had a chance to review the reports in detail."

When he stood, signaling the end of the meeting, Cahill told Preuss she's see him later and flew out of the office.

Emma Blalock stopped Preuss in the hallway. "Janey took off pretty fast," she said.

"She's not happy about giving up the lead on this investigation. You know her?"

"We had some training together. We keep in touch every once in a while. I suppose I wouldn't be happy either, my case got yanked. Wouldn't matter who got it."

"We're soldiers in the service of the greater good," Preuss intoned with mock solemnity.

"Very noble," she said with a smile.

"I'm quoting a great American public safety professional."

She reached out a hand on his arm, suddenly serious.

"Look, Marty. Something to remember for the both of you. Jim's a hardass when he feels like people are in his way."

Preuss looked deep into her brown eyes, trying without success to read her meaning. "Are you saying he thinks we're in his way?"

"No, not at all."

"What are you saying, then?"

She paused as though trying to figure that out for herself. "Jim doesn't like interference, no matter how well-intentioned. He likes people to do things his way."

"You're not warning me off this case, are you?"

"That's not what I'm saying."

"Good. Because I'm on your side. In fact, up until this morning this was my case. We all just want to bring this little girl home safely."

"I'm just saying, Jim's in charge. That's all. Remember that and things'll be fine."

He gave her another long look, and, still unable to figure out what she was getting at, he nodded goodbye and fled the building as fast as Cahill had.

17

"Hello? Anybody here?"

Preuss stood inside the doorway to a large airy corner space on the fifth floor of the Wells Building on Washington in Royal Oak. At first the office Roger Griswold Design Associates appeared to be only one room, a huge studio with a scattering of desks and several computer workstations. Hanging around the room were posters of design work, crisp and flashy graphics that overwhelmed the instantly forgettable products and services they were supposed to sell.

When a door opened along the left wall, Preuss realized offices were tucked on the perimeter of the space. A tall man who was all bones and angles peeked out. Black tee shirt and slick short black leather jacket and tight levis on long legs. He looked to be in his 50s, with a long hound's face and unkempt stringy grey hair.

He was followed by a younger, smaller, heavily made-up woman with shoulder-length dark brown hair and a baggy, shapeless brown knit sweater.

Preuss introduced himself and showed his badge. "Roger Griswold?"

"Yes."

"I have some questions I'd like to ask you. Is there someplace we can talk?"

"Come on back."

He beckoned Preuss into one of the side offices, cluttered from floor to ceiling with folders and magazines and boxes.

He pointed to the wire chairs surrounding a round wooden table. He took one and Preuss sat in another.

Before Preuss could begin, the young woman appeared in the doorway with a tray holding two cups of coffee. She set one coffee in front of Griswold and put another in front of Preuss.

Preuss shook his head but Griswold rolled his finger to indicate she should give him one anyway.

Preuss moved it aside and took out his notebook. "I'm here about a little girl named Madison Kaufman," he said.

Roger Griswold's face instantly darkened and Preuss knew this was the guy Sharon's sister had told Cahill about.

"You know who I'm talking about?"

"Of course."

"I understand you're a friend of the family."

"Well," Griswold admitted reluctantly, "that's a slight exaggeration."

"What is the nature of your relationship with them?"

"I used to be close with the family."

"Did you know Madison?"

"Sure."

"When was the last time you saw her?"

Griswold considered, then said, "I really don't remember."

"When did you stop being close with them?"

"Couple years now."

"Why was that?"

"No special reason. We used to have fun together, then we didn't. That's all. People change."

"How well do you know Sharon?"

Griswold bought time by taking a sip of his coffee. "I'm not sure what you're asking."

"I'm asking if you and she have an intimate relationship."

"Who told you that?"

"Is it true?"

"It's totally false. I categorically deny it."

"Mr. Griswold, I'm not the morals police. I don't care about your personal life. I just want to find Madison."

"You think I have her?"

"Do you?"

"If I knew where she was, don't you think I'd have told the Kaufmans by now?"

"I don't know you, sir. I don't know what you'd do."

"How is my personal life any business of yours?"

"If you and the mother of a missing child are involved, it's absolutely my business. Where were you on Wednesday night?"

"So now I'm a suspect in a kidnapping?"

"I didn't say she was kidnapped."

"But that's the implication, isn't it?"

"Answer my question," Preuss said testily. "Where were you on the night Madison disappeared?"

"I was here. Working."

"Anybody see you here?"

"Connie and I had a project go haywire with the printer earlier in the day and we were working late sorting it out. So she was here with me. Look, I don't know where Madison is, okay?"

"Have you seen Sharon Kaufman recently?"

Griswold shifted in his seat as though calculating how much Preuss knew.

"No," he said. Preuss was certain it was a lie.

"You knew each other in Buffalo?"

"Yes," he said. "That's where we met."

"And you continued your relationship once you moved to Michigan?"

"There's no relationship. We're friends. She helped me when I had problems with my son."

"What kind of problems?"

"The usual problems young people have. Drugs, property borrowed without permission. Like that."

"Property borrowed?"

"Sounds better than stolen cars."

Preuss considered that and passed his notebook and pen across the desk. "Write down his address for me, would you?"

The other man stared at the notebook, then at Preuss. "What do you want with him?"

"I'm only focused on Madison Kaufman's whereabouts, and if your son isn't involved in that, I'm not interested."

"What makes you think my son is involved?"

"Young guy who's scraping by, has a drug habit, dabbles in petty crime, it's not a big jump to think he might try to pry money out of the Kaufmans if he gets a chance."

"By kidnapping Madison?"

"Wouldn't be the first time something like that happened."

"It's been years since he's even lived in my house. I'm not sure he'd even know Madison if he saw her."

Preuss nudged the notebook a little closer to him, who breathed a sigh of annoyance but wrote down the information.

Preuss stood and passed one of his business cards across the desk. "If you think of anything that might help us find Madison, you'll let us know?"

Griswold said he would. He pocketed the card and walked Preuss to the front of the office. Walking beside him, Preuss noticed his exaggerated swagger, the walk of a bully.

Sitting at one of the workstations, Carol looked up and gave Preuss a cheerful wave.

Walking past her, he leaned over and said, "Where were you on Wednesday night?"

She blinked. "Here," she said, as though it would be ridiculous to think she might be anyplace else.

He nodded. "Good answer."

18

Buzz McMillan's Chevrolet Service Department in Royal Oak was a cacophony of air wrenches, hammers, and men's voices. Reg Trombley got The Look from a couple of the workers in filthy work shirts and pants. He gave it right back to them.

He asked one of the workers who was standing underneath a Suburban if he knew where Wayne White was.

"Who's looking for him?" the man asked. He was a wiry little guy with faded blue tattoos running up his ropey forearms and a cigarette hanging from the side of his mouth as he stood with his hands inside the car's undercarriage and avoided looking Trombley in the eye. A tough guy, Trombley thought.

He flashed his badge and kept it down so the little guy had to look his way.

Through the smoke from his cigarette he squinted with disinterest at the identification. "Ain't seen him lately." His mouth twisted in a mocking little grin.

"I thought smoking in the service area wasn't allowed," Trombley said.

"Gonna turn me in, are you?"

"Not too bright, either, smoking under the gas tank."

The man made a half-turn toward him but before they could get into it, a tall woman dressed in a cleaner version of the worker's outfit with a dealership jacket open and flapping over a striped shirt strode over to him.

"Excuse me?" she said loudly. "Sir? Customers aren't allowed in the service area."

"Not a customer," Trombley said. He identified himself and she examined his badge with harried, tired eyes.

"You're still not supposed to be out here. Insurance rules, okay? Let's go over here and talk."

She led him toward her desk past the service bays. Trombley thought he spied the extra-large form of a man tiptoeing up a set of stairs from the lower level and then breaking into a sort of run out an open bay door.

"Hey, Wayne!"

All work stopped and every head turned toward him.

Trombley took off in White's direction, thinking, the day I can't outrun an elephant like him is the day I hang it up.

Outside he saw White disappear around the service building and through the parking lot. He moved surprisingly fast for a big man, but Trombley knew he was quicker and took off after him.

The parking lot opened into a side street that dead-ended at a high rise senior residence on the left and a small pocket park on the right. White continued straight down the sidewalk that ran through the middle of the two and across a street and into a residential neighborhood.

He was slowing down as Trombley sped up. This chase would be over in five more seconds.

In almost exactly that time, Wayne White stopped running altogether and leaned against a tree, his chest heaving.

Trombley noted that he himself was more winded than he would have thought as he pulled up besides the big man. He resolved to start a running regimen again.

White looked at him out of the corner of his eye, still too winded to say anything.

"Hey, Wayne," Trombley said. "Where's the fire?"

White was too out of breath to speak.

"Not going to have a heart attack on me, are you, guy?"

The big man shook his head, but still couldn't catch his breath enough to say anything.

"Why you running, man? I just want to talk with you. Now I'm thinking you did something you shouldn't have."

In between huffs, White finally got out, "You mean . . . this isn't . . . you didn't . . ."

He couldn't finish because he came to the realization he had just said way too much.

"Oh, man!"

19

"When we braced him yesterday?" Trombley said. "And he was sitting on the couch the whole time? Know what he was doing?"

"No."

From behind the one-way mirror in the observation side room, they watched Wayne White slumped over the table with his big round head on his plump arms in the interview room.

"Turns out he was protecting the stash of child porn he keeps in a little compartment in the floor under the rug under the sofa. Mags, videos, the whole nine yards. Real filth, too, I'm telling you."

"Dumb shit." Preuss shook his head.

"When he saw me show up at the dealership, he assumed we know something about it. So he bolted. Insofar as a 300-pound man can bolt."

"And he admitted this to you freely?"

"More or less."

Preuss sighed. "Reg," he said, "don't do this to me."

"I didn't touch him. He told me of his own free will."

"He was just overcome with remorse?"

"There you go."

"You saw the stuff for yourself?"

"Took a uniform with me and we found it. He told me right where to look. Pretty ingenious, I'll give him that. He cut a square in the carpet under the sofa, and then he'd pulled up some floorboards and covered it all up with the carpet."

"How'd we miss it?"

"He had his big fat ass parked right where we needed to look. This hole, it's just five-six inches deep, a little compartment cut right between the floor joists. Big enough for what he shouldn't have had but nothing else."

"Well, good work. I'm not thrilled you're still following up on the Kaufman case, but you did well."

"I couldn't leave it without giving this guy one more go."

"You got him off the street. You're done now, right?"

"Maybe."

"Reg, don't mess around. Please. Walk away from it."

"I left an officer back at his house making another sweep, just in case."

The door to the observation room opened on Paul Horvath, the detective bureau line supervisor. "What's this fine citizen done?" he said.

"Parole violator," Reg said. "Sex offender caught with a stash of child pornography."

"Outstanding. Your bust?"

Trombley nodded.

"Nice work. Done with him? Got something else for you."

"A public servant's day is never done," Trombley said. He gave Preuss a quick wink and followed Horvath out.

Preuss entered the interview room. The big man picked his head off the table, laid it back down when he saw it was Preuss.

"Look at me, Wayne."

With great effort White picked his head up and gave a slack-jawed stare.

Preuss put the photo of Madison Kaufman down on the table and waited. White sat mouth-breathing for a full minute.

"Where is she?" Preuss said finally.

"Fuck if I know."

"I know you've seen her. I know her mother brought her to your dealership."

"So? Lots of people come there. Work there, too."

"Yeah, but lots of people don't have a thing for little girls. You do."

"Look, I give you my word of honor. I don't know where she is."

"Your word of honor."

"Yessir."

Preuss had to smile despite himself. "I'm sure I can take that to the bank."

White said nothing.

"I find out you're lying to me, Wayne, there's going to be hell to pay."

20

After forcing down a sloppy slice of pepperoni pizza and green salad at Como's on Woodward, he spent the rest of the afternoon at his desk going through the Calls for Service reports from the previous day to see if anything jumped out at him that might be related to Madison's disappearance.

Nothing did. Just the usual activity from the small but busy department. Larceny complaints, officer assists for the fire department, a neglect case of an elderly man called in by a neighbor, warrant arrests, fraud cases, traffic accident investigations, drunk driving violations, domestic violence arrests, stolen vehicle reports . . . and of course investigation of a missing child on West Woodland.

Nothing out of the ordinary, nothing that would lead to any understanding of what happened to the little girl who walked out of her family's home on a cold fall evening and then promptly fell off the face of the earth.

At 4:35 he fortified himself with a cup of coffee and rode by the Kaufman home before heading out to Pontiac for his meeting at the Sheriff's headquarters. He couldn't shake the feeling that if he kept returning to the spot where Madison had last been seen he would learn something about what happened to her. He would find something everyone had overlooked, or would be able to think himself into the girl's mind and sense where she was.

The Kaufman residence was hopping, with deputies moving in and out of the house carrying electronic equipment, and on the front stoop Jim Cass standing talking with Emma Blalock. One blue-and-white from Ferndale remained in front of the house, but the other cars were the royal blue SUVs with the Sheriff's six-pointed star and the round seal of the State of Michigan. Down the street, where the dog had found Madison's scent, and where yesterday his own techs from Evidence Collection had poured over the area, another batch of technicians was setting up equipment.

The pros from Dover.

He parked across the street from the Kaufman home and walked over to the two Sheriff's investigators.

"Preuss," Jim Cass said. "Anything shaking?"

"I was just getting ready to head out to our meeting."

Jim Cass exchanged a glance with Emma, then looked back at Preuss with hooded eyes. With a short nod at him, Cass disappeared up the front steps into the home.

"What was that about?" Preuss asked.

"What?"

"The Significant Glances."

After a long moment, Emma said, "The team already met." Her broad mouth angled with a sympathetic twist.

"I thought we were meeting at six."

"That was the original plan. Once we got the others together Jim decided to have a quick meet this afternoon to get started right away. We split up the tasks already."

"Why didn't you call me?"

"Jim wanted to get started and he couldn't get you."

Preuss reached into his coat pocket and pulled out his cell phone, which he examined with conspicuous care. "No calls," he said. "How'd you try, smoke signals?"

"You know, Martin," she said, moving closer to him on the front porch, "we talked about this. Jim's case is Jim's case."

"What's that have to do with going ahead without me?"

"I know. I'm sorry."

"Sorry doesn't mean anything to me, Emma. Was Janey there?"

"No."

"Couldn't get hold of her either?"

"Look, Jim, he runs roughshod over—."

"I don't give a fuck what Jim does. If I'm part of this investigation, I expect to be part of it. If I'm not part of it, I want to know that too so I don't waste my time."

She took him by the arm and led him around the corner of the house.

"Something you should know," she said when they were standing in the Kaufmans' driveway midway to the back yard. "Jim was told to keep you at arm's length."

"By who?"

She glanced back toward the front of the house.

"Who told him? Was it Nick Russo?"

"Yes."

He took a few steps away from her and struggled without much success to keep his anger in check.

"You didn't hear this from me," she said. "In fact, we never had this conversation."

"What for?"

When she hesitated, he said, "Tell me what you know."

"Jim said Russo told him you couldn't be trusted."

He snorted.

"That's all I know. Really. Martin, I'm telling you this as a favor. You're still on the case with us."

"But really you expect me to stick my thumb up my ass and stay out of the way."

"No," she said, "we expect you to keep working with us."

"How am I supposed to do that when I'm frozen out?"

She could say nothing in reply.

He made a throwaway, you-can-have-it gesture with both hands, and walked away.

Back in his car he called Russo's cell, but it went straight to voice mail.

He knew better than to leave a message in the state he was in.

21

"How you doing, my friend?"

When he opened his eyes to see Preuss looming over him, Tony Tullio gave a feeble grin and raised the hand attached to an IV line.

He was connected to some serious machinery in the cardiac ICU at Beaumont Hospital on Thirteen Mile and Woodward in Royal Oak. The equipment kept track of every bodily function. One machine pumped out the six-note riff from the Rolling Stones' "Ventilator Blues," along with whatever medicine it was pumping into him, laying on the bed staring into the ceiling.

"Got lucky," Tullio said. "Docs tell me it could have been a lot worse."

"This is luck, I'd hate to see misfortune. When you getting out?"

"No idea. Starting to like it in here, though. Three hots and a cot, just like the slam."

"People who take care of you here are nicer looking."

"You're flat on your back, you don't even notice."

Preuss forced a laugh and Tullio said, "Good to see you, Marty."

"Same here. We need you back."

"What's going on? Where are you with the missing girl?"

Preuss shook his head. "Nowhere."

"Still hasn't shown up?"

"Nope."

"Nuts."

"Looks like somebody snatched her off the street."

68

Tullio shook his head sadly. "Just what I was afraid of. Christ. So what's happening?"

"Tony, you don't want to hear about it, trust me on this one. Just work on feeling better and coming back."

"I want to know."

"It's just going to raise your blood pressure. Give you another heart attack."

"You don't tell me, I'll have one for sure and then you'll really feel like shit."

"I might be able to feel worse than I do now, but I'm not sure how."

"Never mind," Tullio said. "I can see it in your face. Russo pulled the investigation."

"This morning. Gave the county the lead, made Janey the liaison. Pulled it right out from under me."

"Guy doesn't like you. Never will."

"You think?"

Tullio writhed uncomfortably. "I've known for a while he wasn't your pal. Even when Jeanette was still alive."

"I didn't know he thinks I'm lousy police."

"Where'd you hear that from?"

"You know Emma Blalock? Sheriff's investigator, attractive, mid-forties?"

"Vaguely."

"From her."

"She reliable?"

"Seems like it. What do I know? Only one I trust nowadays is you. Guy in charge now is Jim Cass."

"I know him."

"She says Nick went out of his way to tell Cass to freeze me out."

"Want my advice?"

"Always."

"Go gracefully."

That rocked him.

"I don't know if I'm ready to retire yet, Tony."

"I don't mean quit the force, dumb ass. Just keep a low profile. Don't give Russo any more reasons to come after you. Work the
case on your own, and keep tabs through Janey."

Tullio lifted the hand tethered to the IV line again, and Preuss took it.

"This is gravy," Tullio said. "This kind of freedom of
movement doesn't come along often. Take it where you find it."

As Preuss stood their considering it, Tullio said, "I tell you
true, my brother."

Sitting in his SUV in the parking garage, Preuss let Cahill's cell ring
twice and then ended the call before she could answer. He decided
he didn't want to speak with her tonight until he calmed down, or at
least had the chance to think his way through to his next step. He
would talk to her in the morning.

Tony was right, he knew. This was a certain kind of freedom. He was officially assigned to the case, but unofficially not expected to take any part in it. If he wanted to, he could spend the
next few days playing his guitar and listening to Bob Seger CDs and
nobody would mind.

Until Russo sent his name through to Internal Affairs, or
cashiered him entirely.

The thing was, he wasn't entirely convinced that wouldn't
happen anyway. This could be Russo's chance to do something he
had wanted to do for years, get rid of Detective Martin Preuss in the
most damaging, embarrassing way possible.

And how had he felt back there when he thought Tony was
telling him to resign? He had been in the FPD his entire adult life.
What would he do if he had to find something else? Who would he
be if he wasn't Detective Preuss?

Maybe it was time to think about that, he told himself.

Maybe it was the natural and logical next step in rebuilding
the life he had left to him.

22

Toby was in his wheelchair in the living room of his house, parked on an angle next to the television set watching "American Idol," one of his favorite shows. Toby's vision was poor, and while it was hard to figure out exactly what he could see, everyone agreed his peripheral vision was best, so he watched TV from an oblique angle to the screen, and gave a sly, sideways look when people spoke to him.

Preuss loomed in front of him and said hello, and his heart lifted as his son's crooked smile lit up his face and he roared a happy greeting in his foghorn voice. Was there anything better than his son's smile?

He told Norma, the evening nurse on duty, he wanted to take Toby out for dinner. They determined he didn't need a change of diapers by peeking inside his pants, so Preuss rolled the wheelchair out to the SUV and, unbuckling his son's two seat belts, lifted him into the front seat.

The young man was getting heavier by the week, it seemed. Or else Preuss was getting older. Or both.

Preuss kept up a rolling patter of conversation as they drove to one of Toby's favorite restaurants, Joe's Crab Shack on Van Dyke in Sterling Heights. Toby loved Joe's because the waiters and waitresses burst into song periodically and danced around the restaurant. Up north they were more reticent about it than the servers at the Joe's Crab Shack in Myrtle Beach, where Preuss had taken Toby and the rest of the family for a vacation before the accident.

Back when they were a family.

That was when they discovered the attractions of Joe's Crab Shack for Toby, and ever since Preuss and Toby had a meal at their local franchise every month. By now the wait staff recognized them, and knew to aim their performances at Toby.

Now, as he watched the servers surround his son and sing "Heard it Through the Grapevine," and saw the boy beaming happily, Preuss could almost believe that all really was right with the world. He had often said Toby was the happiest person he knew, the most sociable, the most present in the moment, enjoying what he did and what was before him without regrets or remorse for what he couldn't do or didn't have. He still had so much to learn from the young man who sat at the table, who couldn't even enjoy the restaurant's food because he was fed a formula through a button in his belly because he couldn't chew or swallow normally.

Preuss reached out and grabbed Toby's hands, folding his fingers into his son's tight fists. Even though his muscles were cramped and twisted by his cerebral palsy, Toby had a remarkably strong grasp, and held onto his father's hands long after the music ended. Preuss gazed into the almost sightless brown eyes—his wife's eyes, a deep solid brown without any identifiable iris—and felt an upsurge of love for the boy that was almost unbearable.

After Preuss finished his shrimp scampi, he brought Toby back to his group home and helped the aide and nurse get him into bed and undressed. He bent down and kissed the side of his son's head, then held his cheek near Toby's mouth so the boy could give him a kiss. Toby couldn't control his mouth, but he knew what a kiss was, and he worked his lips and tongued his father's cheek in a wet and sloppy kiss that Preuss adored.

Preuss told his son he loved him, and would see him the next day. Toby smiled his lopsided grin, vocalized something that sounded like "Onion," and sang his high song of unmistakable happiness. He couldn't articulate words, but every so often he could make appropriate sounds like "uh-huh" and "uh-oh," and sometimes, like now, he could say "Onion."

By the time he pulled in to his own driveway, Preuss was at peace.

23

"You're going to be shit out of luck, dude," Brian Mobius said to Stevie Matuzik.

The two young men sat in Mobius's beater, an ancient Sunbird that stank of stale beer and tobacco but at least had a heater that took a little of the chill out of the air. And it saved Stevie from having to stand around stamping his feet until the girl finished her shift. They didn't like him hanging around on his nights off. They barely tolerated him when he worked.

"She ain't gonna give you a ride home, I'm telling you."

"She will," Stevie said.

"What if she don't?"

Stevie ignored him.

Mobius was silent for a few seconds. Then he pulled a plastic baggie out of his leather jacket and unzipped it and held it to his face and inhaled deeply. The sickening toxic smell of airplane glue filled the car. He held it out to Stevie, who knocked it away with his elbow.

Mobius shook his head as if the huff had popped his brain. "Mmm," he said. "It's good, and it's good for you."

"Got no use for that shit," Stevie said. "Shit'll rot your brain. If you had one."

Mobius zipped the baggy tight again and placed it carefully back in his jacket. "More for me," he said. Then, "Worried about you, man."

"Why's that?" Stevie asked absently, his eyes still on the front of the restaurant.

"This girl don't have feelings for you."

"You don't know what you're talking about."

"I'm telling you, I know ladies like this. She's playing you so you'll give her what she wants. They string you along and the first chance they get they'll give you the broom."

"There she is," Stevie said, and sat up straight. A bosomy young woman in a short levis jacket over a white dress shirt and black slacks walked out from under the portico of the restaurant, beside a short middle-aged man.

"Who's that guy with her?" Mobius asked, but Stevie didn't answer. He was too focused on the girl, how she leaned slightly backwards on her heels as she walked, how she seemed to cut the air with her breasts as she made her way forward.

He watched her walk toward the far end of the parking lot where the staff was supposed to park. They separated with a wave as they approached their cars and she continued to her Saturn, glowing a deep rich purple in the light from the towering poles.

Without saying goodbye, Stevie threw open the door to Mobius's car and trotted over in her direction.

He came up to her driver's side window and she looked up, startled, when he appeared, then gave him a big huge smile when she realized who it was.

Yes, Stevie thought when he saw it, yes yes yes.

Fuck you, Mobius. I know what I know.

She motioned him around the other side of the car and he walked around and slid into the passenger's seat.

"Hi!" she said. A high chirp that sounded like she was glad and surprised to see him. His heart warmed, lifted, sang.

"Hey yourself," he said. "Sup?"

Trying to be cool. Trying to be one of those guys who can take advantage of a situation like this. For once in his life.

She breathed a soft growl. "I am so tired!" she said. "My feet are like *killing* me."

Sitting so close to her, inhaling her sweet spicy scent and, beneath it, the slight sour tang of sweat from her night's work, he burned to take her into his arms.

Fuckit, he thought, it's now or never. He lunged toward her.

Taken by surprise, she flinched but then let herself be en-folded by him, though she turned her head away when he sought out her lips. He wound up kissing the side of her face. Which was okay with Stevie. Any kind of closeness with this girl was okay with him. He inhaled the dry, fruity fragrance of her makeup, the yeasti-ness of her skin. He tired to imprint the smells on his brain so he could call them up later.

He tried to keep holding her but she pushed him away. "That's enough."

He let himself be rebuffed.

"What are you doing here? I thought you were off tonight."

"I am. I came to see you."

"Aw, how sweet! How'd you get here?"

How sweet. Sweet.

"My buddy dropped me off. That's him over there."

Across the parking lot, Mobius's brake lights flared, then he peeled off and disappeared.

"Why's he leaving?"

"He's got this, like, thing he has to do tonight."

Okay.

"So I thought maybe I can hitch a ride with you?"

"Well, that depends," she said coyly. She gave him an up-from-under look with those dark eyes of hers. It brought a thrill to the pit of his stomach and a churning in his groin.

"On what?" Playing along, trying to stifle the shiteating grin.

"Whatcha got for me?"

He reached into his pants pocket and withdrew a handful of red, blue, and yellow pills, different sized capsules and caplets and tablets. It had taken most of his week's wages to score these, but he didn't care if it would get him closer to her.

"Yum," she said, and plucked a pair of white pills out of his hand. She reached beside her and withdrew an open can of Red Bull from the cup holder in between the two seats and washed the pills down with a long swallow.

She returned the can to the holder and sat back with her eyes closed. "Mmm," she said, "let's get busy."

Thinking she meant that as an invitation to him, Stevie leaned toward her to put his arms around her again and once more she half-turned in her seat and let herself be taken into his embrace with a soft sigh.

This time she let him kiss her full on her gluey, pillowy lips and even let his tongue probe her mouth a half-inch. He slobbered over her lips, then her face and neck, and mustered the courage to open enough buttons on her server's blouse to kiss the sweaty salty skin of her chest.

And she let him. She wanted him to.

Or so he thought.

Until he worked his way down and began to paw her breasts, when she pushed his hands away. "Don't."

"Why not?" he breathed.

"Just don't, that's all."

"But why?"

"Why do you think?"

"I don't know! That's why I'm fucking asking you!"

"I don't want you to."

She huffed out a sweet breath.

"Listen," she said, "I like you, I really do. But I'm seeing somebody."

"Who?"

"It doesn't matter."

"Was it the guy you were with the other night?"

She looked at him strangely. "What are you talking about?"

"The guy you were sitting in a car with. In front of your house."

"How do you know about that?"

"I saw you."

"How did you see me?"

"I came by your house."

"My *house*? What are you, fucking stalking me?"

"No," he began, but she said, "I don't want you coming to my house and watching me, Stevie."

He couldn't bring himself to say anything in reply. Suddenly this was all going terribly wrong.

"Anyways, I am seeing that guy. And what I do with him is none of your business."

"You know he doesn't love you as much as I do."

She said, "Okay, but, like, he's a grown man, Stevie, okay? With a job and everything. And you're what, a high school kid?"

With no words to refute her, or reason to persuade her that she was wrong, he could only reach for her again and after trying feebly to resist she gave up and let him climb over her, plastering her into her seat.

Suddenly, to his amazement she was letting him do whatever he wanted, so he pawed her and stuck his hand between her legs, until his erection grew like a pole in his pants. She rubbed it for a few seconds, extracting a moan from him.

And then abruptly she tried to push him away and he said, "No! Please! Come on! Come on!" in a harsh whisper but she succeeded in getting him off her and back in his seat.

"Please," he murmured, reaching out to her, "please," needing her to finish it and bring him off.

But she fended off his pleading arms and started the car and was backing out of the space, swinging the wheel around and tearing off from the parking lot.

He put his head against the seat back, dizzy from what had just happened, eyes burning with the anguish of the fullness of her body so near to his and the incredible sensation of her hand rubbing him.

And at the same time feeling so completely and totally abandoned.

Again.

Saturday, November 8, 2008

24

The address Roger Griswold gave Preuss turned out to be an empty lot on Cass Avenue in the heart of downtown Detroit, a part of the skid row end of the street that so far had been bypassed by the renewal projects that were, little by little, remaking downtown.

Preuss stood before the vacant, weed-filled and trash-strewn field shaking his head, thinking, Not smart, Roger. He called the station and asked for the last known of Michael Griswold, reasoning he'd be in the system somewhere. In thirty seconds the clerk gave him another address, 2315 Cass, which turned out to be more promising.

The building was a prewar apartment house that was all flaking paint on the clapboard siding and rotted floorboards on the porch. Preuss picked his way carefully into the entrance and saw in the inside foyer a bank of eight metal mailboxes that hung from the wall, all of them pried open. No sense in trying to find a name on them, or on the doors to the apartments that bore unintelligible tags from graffiti artists on the faded gloss of the moose-nose brown paint.

He started at the top, the fourth floor, and worked his way down. The grizzled faces of the black men who lived in the apartments stared out at him in hostility and fear from those few doors that cracked open before shutting in his face. On the second floor a young black girl, about twenty, swung the door to her apartment open and peered out at him with a beatific smile. She had a narrow, birdlike face with huge eyes like two black marbles. Her hair was fluffed around her head like a corona and she wore rings on her nose, lips, and ears, where a half dozen silver rings decorated the delicate shells of the helix of each ear. She wore a long black tee shirt that hung flat over her body, which seemed to have no perceptible curves, like a tee shirt on a hanger.

"Hello," Preuss said. When she didn't respond, he said, "I'm looking for Michael Griswold."

She still said nothing. "Hello?" Preuss said. He snapped his fingers in front of her face. "Miss? Are you feeling okay?"

She smiled sweetly and collapsed at his feet.

He made sure she was still breathing, then got an arm around her waist and the other under her knees and carried her into the living room of the apartment, kicking his way through piles of clothes and papers. Her bones were thin as a bird's under her clothes and she weighed less than a hundred pounds, he guessed. Almost the same as Toby. A feverish heat radiated from her torso through the thin tee shirt.

He eased her down on the sofa and went through the apartment to the kitchen, which was every bit as disgusting as he would have predicted. He saw no clean towels, or anything he cared to put against her skin, but on the counter was a roll of paper towels and he tore one off, soaked it in tepid water from the sink faucet, and took it back to the young woman. He mopped her face with it and folded it like a washcloth on her forehead.

She gave a small moan. She was still smiling.

He heard a shuffling through the debris on the floor and turned in time to see a young man swing a lamp base at his head.

Preuss put up an arm to deflect the blow, but the young man hadn't taken a full swing and the lamp glanced off his forearm.

The surprise of the attack knocked him backwards onto the sofa and the young man raised the lamp to take another swing but Preuss swept the kid's legs out from under him and he went over backwards. Preuss dove on top of him and his sudden weight swiftly took all the air, and the fight, out of the young guy.

Preuss grabbed the lamp base and threw it across the room. The young man remained prone, breathing hard. Preuss kept his weight on him.

"All right," the kid said with both hands raised in surrender, "all right." He was skinny to the point of emaciation. His hair was long and hung in lank strands over his face.

Preuss looked around. When he was satisfied no one else was coming for him, he said, "Michael Griswold, I presume?"

"Who the fuck are you?"

"Detective Martin Preuss, Ferndale Police. I'm looking for Michael Griswold and I'm thinking that would be you."

Preuss considered him. Roger Griswold had said his son was twenty-four, but this kid looked older, aged by his bad habits.

"Did my father send you?" the kid asked. "I wouldn't put it past the old prick to set the Ferndale heat on me."

Preuss smiled. "Can't remember the last time anybody called me 'the heat.' Or the first time, for that matter."

"Did he?"

"No." Preuss stood and let the kid get his breath back. He took the photo of Madison out of his pocket. "Know this girl?"

"Never saw her before."

"Stay there," Preuss said, and took a quick walk through the apartment, opening doors to empty closets and looking under the bed in the small second bedroom, which was set up as an artist's studio. No trace of Madison, or anybody else.

Back in the living room, Michael Griswold had boosted himself into a sitting position with his back against the sofa where his girlfriend still lay, dead to the world.

"I'm not here to make trouble for you, Michael," Preuss said. "I'm just looking for a little girl who's missing."

"Madison's missing?"

"Thought you didn't know her."

"Yeah, I know her," he admitted.

"We think somebody might have taken her off the street."

Preuss extended a hand to help him to his feet.

"Sorry about all that," Michael Griswold said, indicating with a flip of his head the drama of a few minutes ago. "I see a strange guy in my apartment in this neighborhood, only one way to react. Didn't know you were a cop."

"Forget it. So I take it you know Madison after all?"

"Yeah."

"Seen her recently?"

"Not for a couple years."

His girlfriend stirred uncomfortably. "Let's go into the kitchen and let her sleep," he said.

Preuss followed his narrow back into the kitchen, where they sat around the small table.

"I left home pretty young. Couldn't wait to get away from Rog. You met him, right?"

Preuss nodded.

"Before I left, every once in a great while Madison would come over with her mother. But I never had much to do with her."

"Your father told me he was friends of the family."

The young man smirked. "Is that what they're calling it now?"

"What do you mean?"

"He and Mrs. Kaufman were like going hot and heavy for years."

"Were? Past tense?"

"Couldn't tell you if they still are. I wouldn't be surprised, though. I'm not deeply not into Roger's life. But when my parents broke up, I wanted to live with him and I saw how he lived. After a while I realized what a shithead he was and wanted to live with my mother. But she didn't want me."

"Why not?"

"My mother hated his guts because of what he was doing with Mrs. Kaufman, and when I said I wanted to live with him, it was like I betrayed her too. I tried to tell her I was on her side, but she never believed me."

He shrugged. Parents. Go figure.

"So she'd tolerate me for vacations, but when vacation time was over it was back to Dad." He shook his head and gave a disparaging little laugh. "Ha. My 'dad.'"

"Where is she now?"

"Still in Buffalo."

"So the long and short of it is," Preuss said, "you haven't seen her for years and don't have any idea where Madison is."

"I just have no idea."

"All right. Thanks anyway. Sorry to bother you."

"yeah, hey, sorry again about the lamp."

"Don't mention it. What's the deal with all the art supplies?"

"I'm sure my father told you I'm just your basic druggie loser?"

"Something like that." Preuss was starting to like this kid, now that he wasn't trying to brain him with a lamp.

"I figured. I've made mistakes, don't get me wrong. But I'm really an artist."

"What kind of work do you do?"

"Oils, mostly. Watercolors occasionally. My studio's in the back. Want to see it?"

"Sure," Preuss said, and the kid led him through the filthy apartment to the second bedroom, where the smell of oil paints and turpentine was particularly strong. On a canvas on an easel was a portrait of the girl in the other room. It was a surprisingly sensitive rendering of her, capturing her fine, dark, expressive beauty.

"That's really excellent," Preuss said.

"Thanks."

"She's lovely. What's her name?"

"Vanessa."

"Have you sold anything?"

"I don't market my work. Art isn't about selling, it's about celebrating the beauty of the physical world."

"Still, plenty of people paint a whole lot worse than you and they make a good living."

"More power to them."

"If you ever decide to sell something, let me know."

Michael accepted the compliment awkwardly, with a dip of his head and faint smile. How little makes some people happy, Preuss thought. And how we withhold it, just because we can.

They went back out into the living room. Preuss looked down at the sleeping girl. The painting had made him look at her differently, had made him conscious of the way the light found the planes in her face, which Michael had caught so well. Her boney chest rose and fell in spurts under the tee shirt.

"So what's the deal with your girlfriend?"

She was breathing noisily.

"She's had a fever for a couple days."

"Been to the doctor?"

"No health insurance."

"Take her to Receiving, why don't you. At least get her looked at. Maybe there's something they can give her."

"We'll be there all day and night and they'll tell us there's nothing they can do. No thanks. We'll wait it out."

"Look," Preuss said, "this doesn't look good. Let me give you a lift over there, and I'll loan you cab fare to get home. They have to take you, whether you can pay or not. I know it's a pain in the ass, but she's all you have, right? You have to take care of her."

Michael finally agreed. Preuss helped him rouse Vanessa and get her downstairs to the Explorer, and drove them to the hospital. Together they got her out of the car at the Emergency entrance and Michael shook his hand. Preuss pressed three twenties onto him, along with his business card.

"You think of anything else, call me, all right?"

Michael grinned and took the stash, staring at the money as if he had never seen American currency before.

"Thanks, man."

"Pay me back when you start commodifying your art."

25

Janey Cahill said, "So one more dead end."

Preuss sat in the visitor's chair across from her at the Shanahan complex. He told her about his talk with Michael Griswold.

"Interesting kid. Nothing like what his father led me to expect."

"Yeah," she said with a wink, "fathers. What do they know? It's a wise father knows his own kid."

"He did tell me he thought Sharon and his old man might still be an item. Griswold claimed there wasn't anything going on between them anymore. Probably lying."

"I'm shocked."

"Not surprised he lied about that. Gave me the wrong address for the kid, too."

"Maybe we should put somebody on his house."

"Not a bad idea. Have a car watch him for a day. At the least it'll let him know we have our eye on him."

"What happens when you lie to the police. I'll get Cass on it."

"So what are you up to?"

"Working on progress notes. I'll copy you on them. Emma called earlier and told me what they're doing."

"Which is?"

"Basically everything we've already done. Your redundant tax dollars at work."

"That's okay," he said. "If we missed anything, they'll find it. Meantime I'm trying to move things forward on my own. Better to do that without having to answer to a team."

"They're also going to set up a traffic stop on Pinecrest with pictures of Madison, see if anything surfaces that way. Cass is talking about flooding the neighborhood with deputies."

"What you can do with warm bodies. Russo was right there."

"How are you doing?"

"Fine," he assured her. "I'm going to work for another hour or so and then take off."

"Big plans for the night?"

"Oh yeah. Sky's the limit in my super-playboy lifestyle."

"You know my feelings on that subject."

He gave her a head shake and went to his cubicle. She had been urging him to start dating again and he always shrugged her off. He had not seen anyone since Jeanette died. He was lonely, sure, but he was comfortable with his loneliness, and saw no need to open himself to the tension and anxieties of a close relationship with anyone other than Toby. Maybe that would change if he met someone, but for now he was happily unattached.

Just as he settled in to work his cell phone rang.

Ed Blair.

"Something happened today you might want to know about," Blair said. "Free for a coffee?"

"Tell her what you told me," Preuss said.

Sgt. Edmund Blair pulled a chair from one of the other detective's cubicles and sat astride it in the doorway to Janey Cahill's space. His knees stuck up from his legs like the angles kids use in geometry class.

He always reminded Preuss of Buddy Ebsen, all gangly arms and skyscraper long legs. He wore a walrus mustache below a sharp nose and keen grey eyes. He was well-known and liked in the department, from a celebrated police family. One of the big parks nearby was named Blair Park in honor of his father, who used to be chief.

"Earlier today I responded to a call at the home of one Walter Szymanski," Blair said. "On West Woodland."

"Madison's street," Cahill said.

"A meter reader for the gas company called 911 because this guy Szymanski went after him with a baseball bat," the tall man went on. "The responding officer was Gail Crimmonds. She called me in when she saw it was more complicated than it looked."

"Walk her through the story," Preuss said. "What's his name, the gas man?" He checked the copy of the incident report he was holding. "D'Andre Watkins."

"When he showed up at Szymanski's house," Blair said, "he rang the side bell. It's one of the older homes where the gas meter's still in the basement, so he needed access to it. No answer, so he starts to knock. Then pound. Said he thought the homeowner was sleeping so he lays on the door pretty heavy."

"Did he know Szymanski?" Preuss asked.

"No. This isn't his usual route. Never saw him before. Said this was a special reading. He wanted to make sure he got in to get the numbers."

"Special reading," Preuss said, "what's that mean?"

"There was a request from the homeowner to read the meter."

"Walter Szymanski asked him to come out and read the meter and then chased him away?"

"No, Watkins told me it was a relative that called. Szymanski's cousin. The gas company hadn't done a reading in a while and she wanted them to come out. She pays the bills."

"Why can't Szymanski pay his own bills?" Cahill asked.

"Just wait," Blair said. As though expressing her impatience, she sat on her hands.

"So Watkins keeps knocking and finally Szymanski throws it open and comes after him with a baseball bat."

"Just opens the door and comes out swinging," Preuss said. "Did he say anything, or just come roaring out?"

"Watkins said he's yelling, 'Get out of here, you can't come in, they won't let you in, you can't see her.'"

Cahill looked at Preuss. "Dude," she said. "Holy crap."

"That's what I'm saying," Preuss said.

"It sounded like he was hearing voices," Blair said. "But 'you can't see her' got my attention too."

"He's charging out of the house because he's hearing voices telling him to clock the meter reader with a baseball bat because 'they' won't let him in and he 'can't see her'? See who? Could it possibly be Madison?"

"What Watkins said happened was, this guy comes out, takes a swing at him, then stands still as if he's listening to something, then says all that shit and comes at him again. This time he pops him on the shoulder. Watkins runs back to his truck and calls 911. Then he drives the hell out of harm's way and waits for an officer to show up."

"Have you talked with the cousin?" Cahill asked. "Are there people staying at his house?"

"I have not talked to her," Blair said. "By the time I got to the scene, Szymanski had totally calmed down and was standing on the stoop by the side door. I talked to him for a couple of minutes, getting his information from him. It was clear he's got some problems but he was totally rational."

"What kind of problems are we talking about here?"

"Mental, looks like to me. First I thought it was a racial attack: Watkins black, Szymanski white. Once I talked to the guy I realized he was just confused and disoriented."

"There's confused, and there's being a danger," Cahill said.

"He calmed down right away," Blair went on. "I followed the ambulance to Beaumont in case Watkins needed a ride back, and while we were sitting there I sort of talked him out of going through with the complaint. I figured it wasn't something that was going to happen again. This guy Szymanski seems like he's got enough problems without having the law on his ass."

"Maybe so," said Preuss. "On the other hand, if he's attacking people who come to his door, he can't just roam free."

"I made a judgment call," Blair said. "He'd calmed down enough so I didn't think he was a danger. When I left him, he was talking normally, apologizing, feeling remorse."

"Nobody's faulting that," Preuss said.

"So afterwards I started to think it was peculiar it's the same street as that little girl that went missing, and it seemed funny to me he wouldn't let the gas man in the house. And all that shit about 'you can't see her.' I had a feeling about it."

"I agree," said Preuss. "I think we should go see him."

"How about we find his cousin first," Cahill said. "Maybe she can help us get in."

"Do we know what the cousin's name is?"

"I got it from Watkins," Blair said. "You want, I can give her a call."

"Do that," Preuss said. "But I'm not waiting for her. If you can't get her to meet us there within the hour, we're going to move."

26

Claudia Zarneki was a plump woman with a harried look and a put-upon set to her mouth. She was not happy about having her day disturbed for her cousin and made sure they knew it.

Claudia used her key to open the door for the three police, then Cahill put a hand on her shoulder to pull her back gently from the doorway so she and Preuss and Blair could enter the home at the corner of West Woodland and Livernois.

Szymanski was fast, amazingly fast, as he burst from the kitchen with a bread knife raised high above his head the instant the front door opened.

He raced full tilt boogie down the long hallway from the kitchen to the front door with the knife raised and ready to slash the first person he could reach.

Which, unfortunately, was his cousin Claudia.

Immediately Cahill reached out to grab the older woman by her jacket to pull her out of Szymanski's way.

That saved her life, but didn't prevent a bloody wound. Cahill pulled her back but not before Szymanski slashed the knife down and into Claudia's left shoulder. The blade tore through her coat and into her flesh.

Claudia howled in pain and fainted.

Szymanski's momentum kept him going, and he bowled over the three standing on his stoop. Edmund Blair was on the front walk, and he neatly stepped aside as Cahill, Preuss, and Claudia came tumbling backward off the steps.

Szymanski lost his footing and fell atop the three who were now on the ground. Before he could get the knife up to strike again randomly, blindly, at any body beneath him, Blair stepped in quickly and wrapped his own long arm around Szymanski's knife hand and twisted it backwards with a quick jerk rough enough to fling the knife away.

It went sailing off and Blair pulled Szymanski up and in seconds had him separated from the others and face down on the leaves covering the lawn.

Blair cuffed his arms behind him and it was over.

Except Claudia's clothes were soaked with her blood.

Cahill ripped off her windbreaker and pressed it to the wound as Preuss was already on his cell requesting an ambulance.

The call made, the wound pressed, Szymanski cuffed, the three stood in the sudden stillness and looked at each other.

"Just your basic Saturday afternoon in Friendly Ferndale," Blair said, and shook a pants leg down over his running shoe.

Claudia came around as the paramedics were patching her up for the trip to Providence Hospital.

Her wound was not as bad as it looked. No major arteries were damaged, but the fleshy part of her shoulder bore a nasty diagonal cut. One of the EMTs, a young man with red curly hair and the makings of a red goatee, said she was incredibly lucky. They all knew it.

Blair went with her while Preuss called for a cruiser. When it arrived, the officer, a veteran named Vollmer, put Szymanski in the back seat and the cruiser took off with him to the psychiatric emergency center at Beaumont Hospital.

In the doorway to Szymanski's house, Cahill said, "We don't have a warrant for this."

"Exigent circumstances. If Madison's here, she might be in danger," said Preuss. "I'm not going to wait. Are you?"

She shook her head and they separated as they entered the house. It was dim and close with a strong smell of dirty socks. Preuss took the basement and Cahill the first floor.

Downstairs the basement was one large area, empty except for a washer and dryer at one end and the furnace and hot water heater at the other. Suddenly Preuss's head spun and he had a strong and upsetting sense of déjà vu, as if he had been in this house before, in a dream that ended tragically.

He shook himself out of the sense of doom and noticed a small room built out from the far end of the basement. It looked hand built but not new. He wished he had thought to bring a pair of latex gloves with him, but decided not to bother going back to the SUV, where he kept some in an evidence case.

He steeled himself and swung the door open.

It was a cedar closet. The rich, sweet smell of cedar escaped from a small room packed with a woman's clothes wrapped in clear plastic and hanging on a pole. He whisked through the clothes, searched the floor, tapped the walls. Nothing there.

On the way back upstairs he paused on the landing that led to the kitchen, and looked out the window of the outside door. He could see three-quarters of the way up West Woodland. Could Szymanski have been watching out this window when Madison went for the walk she never returned from?

In the kitchen he met up with Cahill, who hadn't found anything either. Together they went up to the second floor. They went through each room, starting with the bathroom. They found no evidence of anybody living here besides Szymanski. His hair brush, electric razor, and deodorant were on a shelf in the medicine cabinet, along with a half-dozen bottles of prescription medicines that were all in his name.

One of the bath towels was damp and a wet washcloth had been squeezed out and hung over the tub faucet. They went into the master bedroom, a neat, almost sparse room, and pawed through the closet. Still nothing.

In the second bedroom there was a single bed, and on the single bed was a small bundle exactly the size of a seven-year-old girl hunched under the blanket.

Preuss and Cahill caught their breaths and froze.

27

"Madison?" Cahill called.

They entered the room and Cahill whipped the blanket back.

Under it was a pillow, rolled and held in its shape by a blue striped terrycloth towel and topped with another towel rolled into the size of a seven-year-old's head, then all of it covered with a sheet and blanket.

Nice and cozy. But no girl was there.

"What the hell?" Cahill said.

They sat silently on the drive back to the station in the SUV, their urge to talk about what they had found in the tiny bedroom overwhelmed, for now, by the intensity of what they had just gone through.

After changing out of their bloody clothes into FPD sweatshirts and sweatpants they sat over coffee in the station canteen. They were starting to come down from the dual adrenaline rushes of the attack and the almost-discovery of Madison Kaufman, and now were starting to get shaky. The coffee wouldn't help that, but they needed something hot and comforting.

Preuss broke the silence. "Nice reflexes back there."

"A tad faster and I could have gotten her out of the way completely."

"I think she'll forgive you. You saved her life."

Silence.

Then Cahill said, "My heart stopped for a second when I saw that bundle on the bed."

"What do you suppose was up with that?"

"I don't know. Fucking eerie, it was. It was almost like he was trying to make it look like Madison."

"Think that was the 'she' the gas man wasn't supposed to see?"

"I don't know. But why? What was it?"

"Maybe there's some other reason for it we don't know."

She considered that. "So it didn't have to be Madison?"

"Right. We've got Madison on the brain, but maybe there's something going on with him and little kids we don't know yet. Is he on the Sex Registry?"

"I'll have to check with Reggie to be sure, but I'd say no. I'm sure Reggie would have zoned in on him, considering he lives right down the street. I never ran into him before today. I'll run a check for priors anyway."

"Meantime, I want to go to the hospital and see if I can talk to him. That thing on the bed bothers me."

"Yeah, good luck with that."

"What's up?" Preuss asked.

Szymanski was sitting in an observation room at the emergency psychiatric unit at Beaumont Hospital. Officer Vollmer was outside the door, working on his report.

"He's waiting to be seen," said Vollmer. Preuss peeked through the window in the door and saw Szymanski slouching, head down, in a hard chair at a table in the center of the small room. Preuss tried the door. Locked.

Preuss went off looking for someone to talk to. He found the psych emergency intake nurse, a thin dark-skinned young man with an identification card pinned to his shirt pocket. His name was Samuel Piper and he was finishing up a phone conversation.

When he hung up, Preuss introduced himself. "I'm here about Walter Szymanski," he said.

"Yes," Piper said, "he came in a little while ago."

"I was in the brouhaha that brought him here."

"I heard it was a rough one. Are you all right?"

"Fine. It was all over in a few seconds."

"All it takes."

"How's he doing?"

"He's calm. But he's going to be staying with us." The nurse's voice was low and soothing. "At least until we get him back on an even keel with his meds."

"The thing is, I need to talk with him right away."

Piper shook his head. "Not going to happen tonight. Sorry."

"It's urgent," Preuss pressed. "It has to do with that girl missing in Ferndale. You've heard about that?"

"You think he's involved?"

"He may know something about it. Is he able to talk? I just need a few minutes with him."

"I'm afraid you won't get much out of him. He's pretty wasted. When he comes in like this it's because he's been off his meds for a while. He'll need to be restabilized."

"He's been here before?"

"Never with this kind of violence. I can't really say much more about him."

"How about this: How about I try to talk with him for a few minutes, and if it looks like it's going to be a waste of time, or it looks like it's getting him agitated, I'll stop."

"I'm going to have to say no, detective. You've got to let us do our jobs here. The shape he's in now, you wouldn't get anything. Or anything you could trust. When they get like this, they're in their own worlds inside their heads. We're going to give him something that'll make him sleep and when he wakes up we'll see how he is. When he's back on his meds, he usually shapes up pretty fast."

Preuss nodded reluctantly.

"Let's see how he is in the morning, and take it from there," Samuel Piper said.

Preuss gave him his card and asked him to call with news of any change. "Otherwise I'll check back tomorrow," he said.

Out in the corridor, Preuss told Vollmer what was going to happen. "What do you want to charge him with?" Vollmer asked.

"Let's start with aggravated assault for now," Preuss said. "I'll talk with the ADA about anything else. He's going to be safe in here for a while."

Vollmer nodded and told him he was going to get some information for his report before he took off.

Outside the hospital entrance, he remembered he wanted to stop in and see Tony Tullio while he was here but it was too late; visiting hours were over.

Instead he went to see Toby.

Preuss greeted his son with a kiss on top of his head. He inhaled his scent, a combination of fragrant apple shampoo and Toby's own natural scent, a yeasty odor that smelled more and more like a man. He also carried a tang of urine on his skin, which he got when he needed to have his diaper changed.

"And what's up with you?" he asked Toby. "Keeping everybody on their toes?"

Toby turned his brown eyes on his father and gave him one of his crooked smiles. He said, "Num num num."

"Num num num," Preuss replied.

He sat holding Toby's hand for the next hour and chatted with him. As he stood to go, Toby had a seizure. They were mostly controlled by medication, but every so often he had a bad one. They passed over him like a cloudburst, and his eyes rolled upward and his arms and legs stiffened. Sometimes before it was over he started to smile. When that happened, Preuss asked him if it hit his funny button because that's what it looked like.

Most often, like now, the boy just needed to be comforted until the cloudburst passed. Preuss held him and urged him to return—"Come back, Toby, come on back"—until finally Toby's muscle tone relaxed and the boy signaled the end by coughing.

Preuss patted his shoulder and told him he would see him the next day. Toby favored him with a loving smile.

He remembered he had never asked Sharon Kaufman what kind of seizures her daughter had. He wanted to find that out.

Back home he made himself a plate of scrambled eggs with toast and orange juice, which he devoured standing at the kitchen counter. Afterwards he lay down on the sofa in the living room with Emmylou Harris's *Red Dirt Girl* on the CD player.

He didn't even make it to the title cut before he was out for the night.

28

"Can't pick you up after work," said Mobius when he dropped Stevie off.

"Why not?"

"Got a job tonight."

Stevie understood that to mean he was breaking into a house, the stupid motherfucker bragging as usual about things he wouldn't possibly dare to do, Stevie thought. So Stevie would have to get himself home from work.

During the evening he worked up the courage to ask her if she could give him another ride home.

He cornered her while she was picking up a food order and her eyes sparkled and she gave him a big smile when he asked her. And she said right away, "I'd *love* to."

He replayed her voice in his head for the hour afterwards.

I'd love to.

Love to.

Love.

He wanted to stop her from rushing around the restaurant to tell her that she was the most beautiful girl he had ever seen and he would do anything for her, anything at all, but she was moving too fast for him. And besides, he just wanted to hear those words in his head for as long as he could hold them there.

Love.

Love to.

Love you.

For the rest of the night he was flying, clearing tables quickly and hauling the bins of dirty plates and glasses as though they were weightless, congratulating himself for being so cool as to get up the nerve to ask her. Now he had a date with her . . . because that's what it was, a date. And he had some primo weed to share with her. She'd appreciate that, no doubt, and maybe show her gratitude in any number of ways. And then who knew where the night would end? Where the date would go?

When their shifts were over and all the tip money was distributed and their dirty aprons were thrown in the laundry baskets in the staff lounge, Stevie waited for her out front, rocking back and forth from foot to foot, too juiced to stand still. In fact, while he was waiting he lit up some of the good Columbian, not only to calm his nerves but also to have something ready to offer her right away when she came out.

She was late getting out, and when he saw her walking out the door she was deep in conversation with somebody on her cell. She continued walking past him. She must be too far into whoever she was talking with to know where she was, he thought, so he followed her. He couldn't pick up any of her words, but he got the tone, intimate and wheedling. He did hear her say a name over and over again: Ronnie did this, Ronnie said that.

When she snapped the phone closed in annoyance, he double-timed up beside her in the parking lot.

"Hey!" he said.

"Hey yourself."

"Smoke?"

He offered her the weed right off the bat. It was now close to a roach since he had smoked most of it down.

"Excellent," she said, pausing to grab it eagerly. She took a deep toke, burning the stub almost down to the end where she held it daintily between slender thumb and forefinger. Her hands, like the rest of her, were fabulous.

She held in the smoke and closed her eyes. "Mmmm," she said, "sweet," as though it were the tastiest thing ever, and held the smoke in as she leaned toward him.

He thought she was going to kiss him.

Instead she said, "Hey didn't you ask me for a ride?" As she spoke the smoke came out of her mouth in puffs.

"Um, yeah, I did. My buddy can't make it to pick me up. So, you know, I was wondering," thinking to himself, *do it, do it, do it,* "do you want to go grab something to eat first?"

"Aww," she said, and lifted a warm and lemony fragrant hand to palm his cheek. "You're so sweet. But I can't," she drawled, drawing out the sound with regret.

"You can't?"

"No. My friend, she just called me, and she's like, 'Dude, you've <u>got</u> to come to this party. It's da bomb!'"

"Maybe I can come too."

"Aww," she said again, "you're so sweet! But I can't just, you know, invite anybody I want. It's not my party. Though it would really rock if you could come."

"No," he said, "I'll come, it'll be cool."

"No, you can't. But hey, I'll see you tomorrow, okay? Nighty-night!"

She flounced off to her car and was gone.

He stood rooted to the spot and watched her taillights flare. Then she patched out of the parking lot in a long squeal of tires. She beeped the horn twice for his benefit.

Sweet.

So sweet.

Love to.

Love you.

His head spinning in the confusion of his feelings for her—anger at being dumped, blind, total love for everything about her, her smell, her feel, the feel of her body against his own that he craved—he set off walking in the darkness of Twelve Mile Road to the John R SMART bus stop. The busses didn't run very often at this time of night on this route, but it was his only option for getting home. Unless he walked. Or hitched.

He hated hitchhiking. He hated how girls in expensive cars sailed by, flipping him the bird as they whipped by in their laughter like the wind. Hitching just made him feel everything he was afraid of being and knew he was: poor, without the freedom everyone else in the world seemed to have, abandoned by those whose job it was to care for him, alone in the world.

No, he would ride the bus instead. At least then he could sit and let his thoughts wander in the anonymity of mass transit.

As he walked along, his dreamy state of love for that girl soured more and more with each step, like milk kept too long on the counter, and gradually a rage built inside him. First she said she would give him a ride home. He heard her say she would love to give him a ride. Love to! Then she said she couldn't. She could if she wanted to, but the thing was, she didn't want to!

What's up with that? Nobody who would Love To give you a ride would turn around and say (and here he mimicked her voice cruelly in his mind), "Awwww, you're so *sweet*, but I just *can't* tonight, I just *caaaan't!*" Stretching it out in bitter mockery.

But I love you, he screamed at her in his mind. I love you, how can you not love me? I love every part of you. How can you not love me at all?

In his present state, he knew he would not have the patience to wait for a bus, so he started walking down John R. He lived north of Eight Mile. It was only about four miles to home. He could walk this easy. It didn't matter it was so late, and he was too juiced to stand still until the bus showed up.

Walking along, he needed a physical release of his confused feelings, so he shouted out to the street, "I love you!" His voice rang between the strip malls along John R. "I love you!"

The release seemed to work: as he walked in the cold night air he began to calm down again.

It wasn't her fault, he told himself. It was him, whoever was on the other end of the line. And he knew her caller was male. The person who invited her to party was male, no doubt about it, even if she had said "she." His rival, who probably had a car and nice clothes and money and everything he, Stevie, didn't have. No, it wasn't her fault at all but that guy's, whoever he was. Maybe that was Ronnie.

Probably the guy she was with in the car the other night.

Suddenly he was convinced of it.

He had edged Stevie out one more time.

His rage began to erupt again, but this time it didn't focus on her but on the guy, who in his imagination was one of those rich pricks, somebody whose family had money and whose family's family had money too.

His breath came quickly now, not from the exertion of the walk but from the fury that rose in his gullet toward Ronnie, in fact toward all the Ronnies of the world, rising like burning vomit in his throat to be choked down and swallowed, only to ascend again like all the Ronnies whose mothers never left them and whose fathers never wound up behind bars. No, those other mothers and fathers loved their sons and took care of them and had hopes for them and made sure they had hopes for themselves. Unlike those two losers who called themselves Stevie's parents. If it wasn't for his uncle, who took Stevie in when his father was sent to Jackson, he wouldn't have anybody. He'd be homeless. His uncle wasn't much, but he was all Stevie had.

He imagined Ronnie's face, and saw himself beating it to a pulp, blood flying, bones crunching, pleas to stop unheeded in his rage.

He walked faster through the dark, empty, cold night, toward the bed in his uncle's dark, empty, cold home.

Monday, November 10, 2008

29

Preuss awoke shortly after 4 a.m.

He lay with his thoughts a muddle of all the hospital rooms he had been in the past years, rooms with dim lights and rooms with bright shadowless fluorescents, rooms with the smells of death and medication, rooms with the air heavy with artificially fresh disinfectants. Rooms where people walked out healthy, and rooms where people were carried out feet first.

And other kinds of rooms, all those where he and Toby had spent time. Toby's life had been an endless circle of hospital rooms and doctor's offices, and Preuss roused himself before he revisited in his mind every doctor, nurse, PT and OT, speech therapist, vision therapist, and other medical professional who had ministered to Toby. It would have been a small army.

He arose, stiff and dizzy. He showered, shaved, and dressed, and, too impatient to eat anything, was at the station before six.

Two bleary-eyed uniformed officers from the night patrol were in the lounge finishing their coffees in green cups from the all-night National Coney Island in Royal Oak. Preuss grabbed a cup of thick, dark coffee from the pot that had most likely been warming all night. Nothing was left in the Dunkin' Donuts box beside the coffee maker so he trudged back to his cubicle to work on his case report while it was still quiet.

By mid-morning, he had gone as far with it as he could for the time being. He was also getting antsy to talk with Walter Szymanski, so he drove out to Beaumont on the chance he could make contact with him. If Szymanski was in good enough shape.

The inpatient psych unit was on the third floor of the hospital, a lockdown wing that Preuss gained entry to by flashing his badge to the security guard behind a desk at the entrance.

The administrator on duty was not any keener on Preuss's plan than Samuel Piper had been the day before. He was a big soft man with a mustache-less ragged beard that outlined the bottom half of his round face. His name was Joe McClatchy, said the ID card clipped to his shirt pocket.

He shook his head without waiting for Preuss to finish.

"Joe," Preuss began again, but McClatchy held up a palm like a traffic cop.

"I understand your point of view. Really I do."

"No, I don't think you do. This is an investigation of a missing seven-year-old girl. She's been gone since Wednesday night. That's five days. Do you know what can happen to a little girl in five days in the wrong hands?"

McClatchy's objections stopped as he considered Preuss's point.

"I wouldn't push this if I didn't think it was so crucial."

"I understand that."

"Is he coherent today?"

"He seems much better than he was when they brought him in. He's not talking about hearing voices anymore."

"The thing is, he may be able to help us find this girl. If there's any way I can sit down with him for even five minutes?"

McClatchy mulled that over briefly, and said, "This isn't a decision I can make. I'll have to ask the attending psychiatrist. She has to give her okay."

Preuss gave him a double thumbs-up. "Is she around?"

"She's on call in the building. It'll take a minute to track her down. How about you have a seat in the family lounge while I find her?"

"Joe, thanks a million. You're doing a good thing here."

Preuss went to sit in the lounge, a big open area with a TV at one end and tables and chairs all around. It was empty of staff or patients. The TV was off.

In fifteen minutes McClatchy came out looking for him. "Okay," he said. He sat on the plastic chair beside Preuss's. "I got hold of Dr. Prakash and told her what you want. She says you can try your questions, but not about anything he might have done, or anything that might have legal implications for him."

"No problem. I'm not here to get him in trouble. I just want to know what he knows about the girl."

"You're sure he can tell you something?"

"Virtually certain."

"Okay. If it starts to get him agitated, you have to stop."

"Fine."

"Dr. Prakash also wants me to sit in on the conversation."

"Not a problem." It would be good to have a witness there anyway.

"And one last thing. She wants to make sure he understands you're a policeman."

Preuss nodded his concurrence. He could live with all these. Just as long as he got to ask his questions, and get some answers that had at least a ring of sanity. And truth. He hoped this wasn't too much to ask. So far Preuss's only interaction with Szymanski had been to get out of the way of the knife he came charging after them with.

Preuss followed McClatchy down the hall to the patient rooms. All the doors were closed, though behind some of them he could hear voices, both male and female, moaning or talking loudly. One woman asked, "Where do I go? Where do I go?"

McClatchy used a key on a long retractable fob attached to his belt to open the door to the room where Walter Szymanski was lying on his left side on the bed. It was a standard-sized hospital room, painted in institutional beige and sparsely furnished, like a cell, with a single hospital bed and two chairs and a closet at one end of the room.

At the opening of the door, Szymanski eyeballed the two men with a complete lack of interest.

"Walter," McClatchy said, a little too loudly for the room, "it's Joe. How are you feeling?"

Szymanski raised his shoulder an inch. He kept his eyes on Preuss, eyes that may have been dulled with drugs but that had a definite spark of intelligence behind them. A good sign.

"Walter, this is Detective Preuss," McClatchy said. "He's a policeman. Do you understand me? A policeman?"

A nod.

"He wants to ask you some questions. Is that all right?"

Szymanski gave no sign of acceptance or refusal.

"I'm going to be sitting in with you. If you want to stop at any time, you just let me know, all right?"

When Szymanski didn't say anything, McClatchy said, "Walter, how about you sit up? You might be able to focus on the conversation better if you're sitting up. How about that?"

Walter reluctantly hauled himself upright onto the side of the bed. He had been washed and the acrid smell of his body odor was gone.

"How are you feeling, Walter?" Preuss asked. Szymanski remained silent. "So Walter, there's a little girl who lives on your street who's lost. Have you heard about her?"

Szymanski looked at him without expression and Preuss went on. "You didn't have a little girl staying in your house, did you, Walter?"

"Careful, Detective," McClatchy said, but then Szymanski said, "No." His voice was soft, almost apologetic.

"Okay," Preuss continued. "That's good. Do you know why I'm asking you?" Szymanski shook his head. "Because inside your house there's a little bundle up on the bed in one of your bedrooms that's made up to look like it might be a child. Like when we're little and we make a bundle in our bed to fool our parents. Do you re-member making that bundle in your bedroom?"

Szymanski blinked a few times. "You were in my house?"

"Yes. Yesterday. I and another detective."

"What for?" Not angry, but curious.

Preuss ignored the question—best not to get into that—and instead said, "Walter, you need to tell me, do you remember making up a little bundle of towels and pillows on the bed in one of your rooms?"

"Yes."

"Can you tell me why you did that?"

Szymanski didn't answer immediately. He seemed to be trying to decode the questions from a language he didn't quite understand, though he seemed alert enough.

"It's for," he started to say, but the words trailed off, as though he lost the thread of his thought.

Preuss decided to try a different approach. "Walter," he said, "this little girl? She's been missing from the neighborhood for the past few days."

"She was on the news."

"That's right. Everybody's very concerned about what happened to her."

"I saw it on TV."

"That's good. This little girl, her name is Madison Kaufman. She lives down the street from you. Do you know who she is? A little seven-year-old girl who lives down in the middle of the next block?"

Szymanski thought for a few long moments, then said, "Yes. I know Madison."

Preuss wasn't convinced Szymanski knew who she was. He exchanged a look with McClatchy, who apparently had the same doubts as he monitored the exchange.

"You know who I'm talking about?" Preuss asked.

"Yes," Szymanski said, and this time his voice had more authority. "I know Madison."

"How do you know her?"

"I've seen her."

"Where?"

"She rides her bike. And plays outside."

"Has she ever been inside your house?"

McClatchy shook his head, but Szymanski said, "No."

"She wandered away from her house on Wednesday night. She's missing. Her parents are very worried about her. Do you know what day this is today, Walter?"

"Sure."

"What day?"

"Sunday."

When neither Preuss nor McClatchy said anything, Szymanski quickly said, "Monday, I mean. It's Monday."

"Yes, that's right," Preuss said with an encouraging nod. "That means Madison's been missing for five days. Five days is a long time for a little girl to be away from her parents."

Szymanski blinked several times. "I know," he said.

"Have you seen her lately, Walter?" Preuss took his photo of Madison out of the pocket of his leather coat and placed it on the bed next to the man. "Here's her picture."

Szymanski's gaze wavered, then focused on the photo. He took it and held it up in front of his eyes.

The silence stretched. Preuss was starting to think this wasn't going to work after all.

He reached his hand out for the photograph. "Okay, Walter. I won't take any more of your time. Thanks for helping."

Then Szymanski said, "Yes," and moved the photo out of Preuss's reach.

"Yes what?"

"I saw her."

Preuss was suddenly alert. "You saw her? When? Since Wednesday?"

"No. Not since."

"Then when?"

Szymanski gazed off at nothing on the wall opposite where he sat. Stay with me, Preuss silently pleaded. "Walter, when did you see her?"

"What day did you say she got lost?" Szymanski asked.

"Wednesday night."

"Maybe it was Wednesday, then."

"You saw her Wednesday?"

"Yes."

"What time on Wednesday?"

"It was dark. Don't remember the time for sure."

"Okay, Walter, I just want to get this straight. You're telling me you saw her last Wednesday night for sure?"

"Yes. Wednesday night," he said without hesitation.

"How did you see her?"

"I was looking out the window in my side door."

"Looking up West Woodland?"

"Yes."

Exactly where Preuss had stood when he and Cahill searched the house for Madison.

"And how about Madison? What was she doing when you saw her?"

"She was walking down the street."

Preuss leaned forward. Yes. Yes. This was what he needed. Stay with me.

"Woodland?"

Szymanski nodded.

"She was just walking along? Toward Livernois?"

"Yes."

"You're absolutely sure this was Wednesday night?"

"Yes."

"Was she by herself?"

"Yes."

"So she was alone on Woodland."

"Yes. To begin with."

"To begin with. Then she went somewhere else?"

"Then she turned on Livernois."

"Which direction did she turn?"

"Right. She turned right."

"Toward Nine Mile?"

"Yes. But then when she turned onto Livernois she wasn't alone anymore."

"What do you mean?"

"There was somebody behind her."

"Did you see who it was?"

"Yes."

Preuss waited, then said, "Walter, who was it?"

"I don't know who it was. I just saw the person walking behind her."

"Like, following her?"

"Yes."

"Can you describe this person? Was it a man?"

"Yes. I didn't see his face because it was dark. But I could tell it was a man."

"Do you remember anything about him?"

"I remember he was big. He was a big man."

"What do you mean, a big man?"

"A fat man. You know, tall and very heavy."

Wayne White, Preuss thought coldly.

Then: I'll kill that motherfucker and his word of honor with my bare hands.

"He was walking behind her?"

"Yes."

"Did it seem like he was going to talk with her?"

"I couldn't tell. It was right before she fell."

"She fell?"

Preuss could feel Madison's presence in the room with them.

"What do you mean, she fell?"

"She fell down," Walter insisted. "She was walking along and all of a sudden she fell down."

"She was just walking down the street and she fell over?"

"Yes."

"Was the fat man near her when she fell? Could he have pushed her down?"

"Not when she fell, no. He wasn't near her."

"What happened after she fell down?"

"After she fell, right as she fell, someone came driving down the street and stopped. He got out and looked at her."

"And what did the fat man do?"

"He ran away. Up Woodland."

"So what did the man who stopped do?"

"He picked her up and put her in his car."

Preuss had trouble keeping himself calm now.

"You're telling me someone was driving down the street and when she fell he stopped and picked her up and put her in his car?"

Walter nodded. "Yes."

Preuss stood up and walked to the window just to be doing something with the trembling that had struck his body. The window looked out over one of the hospital parking lots.

He turned back toward Walter. "And this person who stopped, he picked her up and put her in the car? You're absolutely certain you saw that happen?"

"Yes."

"Did you see who it was who stopped?"

"I saw somebody stop, but I couldn't tell who it was."

"Was it a man or a woman?"

"A man."

"How do you know?"

"I could see a bald head."

"How could you see a bald head?"

"I saw it in the streetlight. Shining, like."

"Completely bald or just a little bald?"

"You know, bald like with a little fringe around the side."

"But you didn't recognize the man?"

"No."

"Would you know him if you saw him again?"

"I don't know."

"What about the car? Did you see what kind of car it was?"

"Yes." Walter screwed up his features. "But I'm not good with cars."

"That's okay. Maybe if we showed you some pictures of cars you could tell us what kind it was?"

"No. It wasn't really a car. It was a truck. One of those big pickup trucks."

"Could you tell the color? Or anything else about it?"

"No. It was a dark color, that's all I could tell. But I did see it had a trailer attached to it."

"What kind of trailer?"

"One of those open metal trailers. With a big ramp sticking up in the air. And some kind of machine on the back."

"What kind?"

"I couldn't see for sure."

"Did you see anyone else around on the street? Anybody walking their dog, for example?"

"Not that I remember."

Walter lowered his head. Preuss couldn't tell if he was just taking a break to think, or had lost consciousness, or had fallen asleep.

"Detective," McClatchy said, "I think maybe that's all."

"But we're close, Joe. A few more questions?"

But there was nothing more coming. Preuss waited, asked another question, and then nodded reluctantly. This was all he was going to get for the time being.

But this was big. This was huge. This was what they had been waiting for.

Szymanski suddenly picked his head up and said, "Madison."

Preuss froze. "What about her?"

"In my house. That little bed. That was for Madison."

"The bundle under the covers on the bed was for Madison?"

"Yes."

"Walter, I don't know what you're saying. Did Madison stay in that bed?"

"No. But I made a place for her. To help her get better. I thought if she had a place to sleep, she would get better."

"So you made a safe place for her to help her after you saw her fall down."

"A safe place, yeah. So she wouldn't be so tired."

So tired that she fell over, Preuss thought. The sympathetic magic might work after all. He wanted to reach out and put a hand on Szymanski's shoulder, but didn't know if Szymanski would appreciate it or jump through the ceiling.

"Walter," Preuss said, "I can't tell you how helpful you've been. But I have one question for you. Are you still with me?"

Szymanski looked at him with eyes that grew less focused by the second. He was fading fast.

"Did you see which direction the truck went? Walter, stay with me, this is important. Where did the truck go after the driver picked up Madison?"

But Szymanski could only shake his head. Slowly he lay back down on his bed and rested his head, eyes closed, on his pillow.

30

"He saw her get taken," Cahill said.

She was standing in front of her pickup truck cupping a cigarette in her hand in front of the Kaufman home when he drove up. A Sheriff's car was parked in front of the house.

"He couldn't give me a good description of the guy who took her. But it explains why the traces of her disappeared."

"And that fat fuck White. Lied right to our faces."

"Only dumb luck somebody else came along, or he would have been on her like stink on shit."

They walked down the street and crossed Livernois to stand at the side door of Szymanski's home. On the stoop of the side door, Preuss turned so he would see exactly what Szymanski had seen that night.

He pointed to the southwest corner and said, "That's where it happened. According to him, she fell right there."

"That's just where the dog said her trail ended."

"And then someone came along at exactly that moment and stopped and lifted her into a truck."

"So she was never inside Walter's house."

"No. That little trick on his bed was his way of trying to keep her safe. Like sympathetic magic."

"But she never showed up at any of the hospitals in the area," she said.

"No. I'm wondering what the fall was. A seizure?"

"That's what I'm thinking. It would explain how she was just walking along and fell."

"I never did ask her mother what kind of seizures she had."

"Let's go talk to them. Afterwards I'll call Cass."

"I were him, I'd want a crime scene team down here to see what they can find around where Madison was last seen."

"Last seen," Cahill said, and he nodded in full awareness of the implications of the phrase.

"No, I can't say any of that sounds familiar at all," Sharon Kaufman said.

She was sitting in the living room, trying to take in what Preuss had just told her. Her husband was at work. Cahill was in the dining room, trying to call Cass.

"Nothing about it? Not the description of the man who picked her up, or the truck?"

"Nothing. You'll have to ask my husband if it means anything to him."

In the other room Cahill snapped her phone shut and stood in the archway. She nodded to Preuss. Cass was notified.

"What kind of seizures does your daughter have?" Preuss finally remembered to ask.

"Petit mal."

When he nodded, she asked, "Do you know about them?"

"They're also called absence seizures. My son has them sometimes. Some people call them stare seizures. The kids look like they're just staring into space. Did she ever have more serious seizures that would cause her to fall down?"

With that question, Sharon put her hand over her mouth and broke down. She sobbed so hard she covered her face with both hands and her shoulders heaved spasmodically.

Sharon stood and rushed into the kitchen. The sliding door to the bathroom off the kitchen closed with a *thunk!* They heard the sound of retching.

Preuss and Cahill were momentarily alone in the soup of misery that was this family's life. Now was the best and worst time of an investigation, when the outlines of the case were taking shape, but the shape was confirming their worst fears.

And it was all complicated by another concern: had Szymanski told Preuss the truth, or a tale fabricated by the voices in his head? It would be good to corroborate what he said. For now it was all they had to guide them toward Madison.

In another five minutes they heard the sliding door to the bathroom open and Sharon returned to the living room.

Preuss said, "We know this is hard for you. But we have some information here that may be critical and you really need to try and help us."

She took a deep breath and said, "No, my daughter's seizures aren't that severe. They're controlled anyway. She takes Dilantin."

"She wasn't feeling sick on Wednesday?"

"No. She seemed fine when I saw her."

After they left her, Preuss sat with Cahill in her truck while she called Stanley Kaufman. She put the cell on speakerphone so Preuss could hear the conversation.

"Not when I picked her up from school," Kaufman said. His tone emphasized how he was the custodial parent on that day. The clear implication was that if his wife had done her job as she was supposed to, none of this would be happening now.

"You know," Cahill said in her calming voice, "I've seen a lot of families go through times like this. And I know two things. The first is, you have to stick together if you're going to get through it. And the second is, sometimes it helps if there's someone you can talk to."

Kaufman snorted derisively. "More counseling? No thanks."

"No, but are there friends or family you can talk with?"

Kaufman responded with a dismissive huff.

31

"Cass is on his way," she said. "I'll fill him in on what they said. Maybe they'll remember something if he has another go at them."

"Couple of real charmers," Preuss offered.

"I'd say this whole thing is exposing the problems in their relationship neither one wanted to face."

"Thank you, Dr. Phil over here."

She shrugged. "You could be an expert on relationships, too, if you had any. So what now?"

"I'm assuming someone on Cass's team will jump on the DMV database and look for the pickup and utility trailer. I'm going to go at this from another direction."

"Which would be?"

"Tell you when I think of it."

"Keep in touch."

On the way back to the station he considered his next move.

The best thing to do at this point, he decided, would be to write up the notes to his interview with Walter Szymanski. It took him a couple of hours sitting in his cubicle writing and remembering everything Szymanski had told him. It was the key interview so far.

Preuss printed out his case notes. They still had a lot to do before they found Madison.

So much here was new. Madison's falling down, and the man picking her up and putting her in the truck were the most important bits of information so far. Though Wayne White's presence—assuming it was him—was also a problem. He would need to talk with the fat man.

A quick check of White's file on the computer told Preuss he had been transferred to the Oakland County lockup already.

Cass's team would try to locate the truck and trailer, but without any other descriptors it wouldn't be easy. What else was there that Szymanski had told him that could narrow down the search for the truck? It might not even be registered in Michigan. There had to be some other way to narrow the search.

He read through the notes again. Szymanski couldn't remember if there was anybody else in the street, but that didn't mean there weren't others around, walking dogs or taking evening constitutionals.

That was a lot to ask for, but that was the way cases were closed: somebody saw something, and then that somebody came forward or was found and the new information joined the old information and it all realigned and clicked into place in the pattern they were waiting to find.

He sat back and turned off the lamp on his desk. Was there anything more he could do tonight?

He tried to remember if Toby had anything tonight. He called the group home and the nurse told him the aide took Toby and Charlie to the new James Bond movie. Good for him. That boy had a busier social calendar than his old man.

Preuss took an inventory of his body and discovered what he really needed to do was go straight home and grab some dinner.

Before he did, he drove around the Kaufman's neighborhood in northwest Ferndale. He thought he would just take a quick swing up and down the streets around West Woodland, but wound up cruising around for over an hour. He examined the cars in the street, those parked at the curb, and those in the driveways, searching for a pickup and trailer.

The upscale neighborhood around the Kaufman home had few pickups, but as he expanded his circle he found more. He noted the addresses and plates so he could check them in the morning.

Nothing matched the pickup-trailer combination Szymanski told him about, though.

When his eyesight started to blur, he called it off and went home.

There he fried a hamburger from his freezer and afterwards sat in his living room with his wine red Gibson Les Paul Classic plugged into an amp and a set of headphones and for the rest of the night wailed on every Rolling Stones song he knew (and he knew most of them) until his head buzzed and his ears rang. He didn't sing the songs, but every so often made sounds that were more like cries of pain than lyrics.

After an hour he unplugged the guitar, placed it back in its plush case in the corner of the living room, and trudged up the stairs to his bedroom. He fell into bed without the energy to take anything off but his shoes. He felt as though he had fallen into a world of cotton batten where every sound was muted.

In that muffled state, he slept.

Until his cell phone woke him from a sound sleep.

Shelley Larkin.

32

"Media inquiries go through the Sheriff's team," he reminded her. He was groggy and confused. He tried to make his head clear.

"I know," she said. "I spoke to them today. I figured I'd try you and get the true facts."

When he didn't say anything, she said, "Hello? Still there?"

"What makes you think I have them?"

"I'm guessing I have a better chance with you than with the others. Where are you now?"

"At home. It's late."

"Were you asleep?"

"Yes."

"Are you in Ferndale?"

"Yes."

"I'm heading south on 75. I can be there in twenty minutes. Is there someplace we can meet?"

"I don't have anything more to add to what you probably heard today. I'm not as close to the center of the case as I was when I was running it."

"It'll be worth your while. Trust me on this one."

The waitress placed a Brawny Lad in front of Shelley Larkin at the Big Boy on the service drive of I-75 south of Nine in Hazel Park. She scooped it up and took a huge bite.

Preuss watched her with his hands around a cup of coffee, warming them up. He had forgotten his gloves at home and his fingers were purple and stinging with cold.

She swallowed and smacked her lips. "You have no idea how much I love these. Whoever invented the Brawny Lad deserves a Nobel Prize."

She gave her short black hair an ironic shake and set the sandwich down on her plate. She wore a short black leather jacket with an Indian style scarf wrapped twice around her neck. She smelled of the cold outside. Her dark eyes flashed.

"Sure you don't want one?" she asked.

"Thanks. I ate earlier."

"What did you have?"

"A hamburger, as it happens."

"Aha," she said. "Two minds with but a single thought."

When he didn't rise to the flirtation, she grew serious.

"Okay," she said, "here's the deal. So remember that story I was working on? The treatment of minorities by the media?"

"Sure."

"The thing is, it's on hold."

"Editor spike it?"

"No, but as I was thinking about that little girl who's missing, I realized there's a story there all on its own."

She took another huge bite out of the Brawny Lad and daintily wiped her lips with her napkin.

"You know, little girl missing, who speaks for her, that type of thing."

"Uh-huh."

"What's the matter?"

Already he was beginning to regret agreeing to this. Why was he here? Because she had shown up Russo and this was part of his revenge on what his boss had done to him? Or because she was an attractive young woman who called him on a night when the house seemed especially empty?

That was part of it, he had to admit.

"It just seems to me you're doing exactly what you were going to criticize in your first story. You're going to give this little privileged suburban white girl the kind of media attention minorities get denied."

"Mmm," she said, holding up a finger till she finished chewing the last mouthful of the Brawny Lad. She could eat. He noticed her fingernails were painted black. Her hands were strong and supple and ringless as she collected the crumbs and sesame seeds left over from the sandwich into a pile that she pinched into her mouth.

"If you feel like licking the plate, don't let me stop you," Preuss said.

She smiled and immediately put a hand up to shield her teeth. Then she swallowed and shook her head. "I can see how you might think how I'm giving her more media attention. But here's the thing. My piece is going to go way beyond that."

"Uh-huh."

"No, really. I'm going to be looking at this little girl as an oppressed minority."

"A little white girl who lives in the Gold Coast of Ferndale is an oppressed minority?" He shrugged. "Hey, knock yourself out."

"No." Now she grew animated. "Hear me out. Girls her age are an oppressed minority in our culture. Look how sexualized and commodified childhood is these days. Have you ever actually watched *Hanna Montana*? Or anything on Nickelodeon or the Disney Channel? You'd be appalled, I guarantee it. Come on, detective, there really is no such thing as childhood in this kind of culture, which turns everything—what kids buy, what they wear, what they eat, the toys they play with, everything—into a commodity."

"Including the articles you write about them?"

She held a hand out as though that demonstrated her point exactly.

"But," she said, "*but*—the article is going to bring the plight of this girl to the public's attention. And by extension, the plight of every lost child. The fact she's lost is a metaphor for what our culture has done to the childhood of girls."

The waitress came by with a refill on his coffee. When she was gone, Preuss said, "Unfortunately, I don't have the luxury of seeing her as a metaphor. To me she's a little girl who needs to be found."

"I'm not saying she's a metaphor. I'm saying her situation is a metaphor. There's a difference."

"Whatever."

"Don't play the 'Aw shucks, ma'am, I'm just a dumb cop' routine with me." Her dead-on imitation of a hayseed made him shout with laughter despite himself. "I know you get exactly what I'm saying."

"Even so, what do you want with me? My formal role in the investigation is limited."

"Limited? What's that mean? What did you fuck up?"

"It's a long story," he said. "One I would prefer not to go into at the moment."

She smiled at him. He smiled back. She was very easy to look at. Maybe she wasn't as young as he thought. In the restaurant lighting he now pegged her as being somewhere in her thirties. The crinkles around her eyes, the smile lines at either side of her mouth, those were not part of a young woman's face.

"When I talked to him today Cass said they're 'pursuing new leads' in the case." She made air quotes with her fingers to show her disdain for the cliché. "Do you guys think we don't see through that bullshit? Anyway, I want to know if there's anything more going on that you can talk about."

"And if there were, I would tell you because—?"

"Because I can feature you prominently in my story. Heroic cop, never say die, keeps fighting the good fight? People would eat it up."

"Which would go over big with the department. Single me out for the media attention I so richly deserve."

"Just a thought. There's a larger social issue here I know you care about. Or would if I could just make you understand it."

"If I wasn't such a dumb cop?"

"Detective Preuss . . . can I call you Martin? I know you're not a dumb cop."

"Maybe not, but it's still not clear to me where the offer comes in. You know, the one I can't refuse?"

"Maybe that was a bit of an exaggeration. I wanted to ask what else is going in that the big cheese isn't talking about. And also I wanted to see you."

She paused to let that sink in. He stared into her black eyes for a few moments, trying to decide if he could trust her.

As if reading his mind, she said, "You can trust me. You know something, don't you?"

Preuss said, "If I tell you anything, it positively has to be off the record. Okay?"

When she didn't answer right away, he said, "If you're not okay with that, I'll stop. The people I answer to have strong opinions about things like this, and I'm way over the line here."

"Fine. You don't have to worry about anything you tell me."

"We're now virtually certain she isn't just lost. We're pretty sure she was snatched off the street in Ferndale."

She sat back. "No way."

"Yes way."

"You're pretty sure about this? What does that mean?"

"Ninety-five percent certain. The source is a little hinky but I trust it. There's corroboration." He thought of what the dog found.

"How long have you known?"

"We've suspected for a few days. Today we made a huge breakthrough."

She sat in silence for a few moments.

"So this is a little more serious than revealing the commodifications of childhood," he said. "Her life is at stake."

She was quiet for a bit longer. "That poor girl," she finally murmured.

Then she surprised him by saying, "What can I do?"

"What do you mean?"

"What can I do to help you find her? Forget the story. What can I do? This is a genuine offer. I might have access to resources you don't. I want to help you find her."

"I appreciate that, but the best thing you can do is just give us space to do our jobs. Without having to worry about what information comes out in the papers."

She leaned forward over her folded arms on the table. "You and I are not natural enemies, you know."

"Maybe not, but we have different agendas."

She reached out to lay a hand on his arm. "Can I tell you something, Martin?"

He opened his hands by way of invitation, and in so doing nudged away her grip.

"You may not believe this, but I know exactly what this family is going through."

He waited for her to explain. "Twenty years ago my little brother disappeared," she said. "He was ten. I was twelve. It was summertime and my parents took us on a vacation to New York City. We were at the Metropolitan Museum of Art. David wandered off when all our backs were turned. He had a history of running away, so that was the first thing the police thought happened. But we all knew he wouldn't do that, not in New York City. He hated it there. They closed down the museum, and the police finally decided he must have been lured away from us. It's not an unusual thing to happen in crowded public spaces. You probably know more about that than I do. Anyway, he was never found."

She pushed the empty plate away from her. "It was a major trauma, as you might expect. I don't think my father ever really recovered." She ran a black-tipped hand through her short hair. "So this kind of situation really speaks to me. I'll ask again. How can I help?"

He watched her for a few seconds more. Then he said, "You're good."

"What do you mean?"

"Can I call you Martin? Can I tell you something? The sad story . . . oh, you're good."

"What are you saying?"

"It seems a tad too convenient for the situation, don't you think?"

"It's the truth."

"Right. As soon as I find Madison, I'll look for your brother."

The instant he said that, the look on her face—stricken and furious at the same time—made him regret it. With tight, angry gestures she reached into the motorcycle messenger bag she used as her pursue and pulled out her wallet. She extracted a twenty and tossed it on the table. "All due respect, fuck you, detective," she said, and slid out of the bench seat and headed for the door.

He jumped up to follow her and caught her arm in the parking lot. She pulled it out of his grip. "Let me alone, I'll call a real cop."

She continued to her car, a silver Honda. She clicked it open and tossed her bag on the passenger seat and got in.

"Wait," Preuss said, tapping on the driver's side window. "Shelley, wait. I'm sorry."

She sat staring straight ahead, then moved her pursue so he could get into the car.

He went around to the other side and fell into the passenger seat. He had to slide the seat back to give him more legroom, and said again, "I'm sorry. I didn't mean to insult you. But you have to admit it sounded pretty expedient."

"Why would I make up a lie about a lost child?"

"Look, I don't know you. I've been told every lie you could possibly imagine, for every reason under the sun. My first instinct is to disbelieve what I'm told. It's an occupational hazard. So my first thought was that you might be using a tragedy like this to advance your own career, or sell papers."

"My paper is free."

"Whatever. It was a little distressing. But I shouldn't have said that. It makes me sound like somebody I'm not. I'm sorry."

Without saying anything she pulled her wallet out of her messenger and handed him a photo of a smiling, dark-haired, gap-toothed young boy.

"That's him. David. The last photo my parents ever took of him. The morning he disappeared." Behind the child Preuss could see a vast staircase filled with people. Banners hung overhead. Preuss froze when he realized the photo was taken in New York City on the steps of the Metropolitan Museum of Art shortly before he disappeared.

As he examined it, she said, "David Larkin. If you don't believe me, you can check the *New York Times* and the *New York Post* for July 10, 1988. The day after he disappeared. I can also give you my mother's number and you can check my story with her."

He handed the photo back to her. "I don't want to call your mother."

"I thought we were on the same page here."

"I'm sorry I doubted you."

She raised her shoulders and kept them high for a few seconds, staring off into the crowded parking lot. When she relaxed with a huff of breath, her anger seemed to dissipate, though a curtain seemed to fall between them, which he was surprised to realize pained him.

"You're right," she said. "You don't know me. I could be telling you anything. Don't worry about it."

"But this doesn't change anything. Madison's disappearance is a police matter. I told you the truth: just give us the space to look for her without having to worry about the newspapers."

"Us? I thought you were off the investigation."

"I'm on it informally."

She stared at him for a few seconds, as though his mind, transparent to her a few minutes ago, were now opaque.

"So maybe you really are the heroic, never say die, fighting on when all seems lost kind of cop after all."

"I lost one of my sons," he said. "He ran away a few years ago and he's been out of touch ever since. I don't want to fail another lost child."

She considered that. "Okay," she said. "I won't publish my story until you find her. How's that?"

"That'll work."

"But can you tell me what's happening? Do you have anything?"

"Off the record, still?"

She agreed and he told her about the pickup truck and trailer, and the runner Walter Szymanski had seen. He knew he shouldn't be telling her so much, but he felt the need to make it up to her. "Right now that's what we have."

"You trust this Walter guy?"

"I know there's a big risk, considering his mental state. But yeah, I believe him. I don't think these things are figments of his imagination."

She put her hands on the steering wheel and tapped the black nails. "Okay," she said. "But you have to keep me in the loop. And I can file the story after you find her."

"All right."

She stuck out a hand, which he took. "I'll be in touch," she said. "Thanks for meeting me. And trusting me with the information. You won't be sorry."

He got out of the car and began to walk over to where he had left his car.

She started the Honda and lowered the window on the passenger side. "Hey," she shouted after him. He came back and she leaned across the front seat. "Sometime I want to hear about your son."

"Sure. I have another son, too. He lives around here."

"Do you ever see him?"

"As often as possible."

Without thinking he reached a hand into the car and now she took it.

"I'd like to meet your son."

"Deal."

They shook and held it for a few seconds before she squeezed his hand and they said goodnight.

He returned to the SUV. He watched her brake lights disappear out of the parking lot and onto the service drive of I-75, and wondered what was starting here.

The thought was replaced by the image of the little seven-year-old in her school photo. Where are you? he silently implored.

Madison Kaufman had been missing for six days.

Tuesday, November 11, 2008

33

Wayne White sat staring at Preuss with the same dull gaze he had the last time they encountered each other: hooded eyes, mouth slightly open, breath raspy in his throat. A dumb look.

The look of a guy who couldn't possibly be that dumb.

"I dunno what you're talking about," White said.

Preuss stared back at his with his own look, a fish-eyed glare that bored right through the man on the other side of the desk in the interview room at the Oakland County Sheriff's lockup. Bored right into his lying heart.

Preuss allowed himself a small smile. "Here's the thing, Wayne," he began. "We have an eyewitness who saw you . . . who saw you . . . follow Madison on the night she disappeared."

"It's a fucking lie."

"It's the fucking truth, Wayne, and you know it. And it's only a matter of time before we find hard evidence that places you at the scene on the night the girl was taken."

White regarded him with stupid suspicious eyes. "Yeah? What kind of evidence?"

"An oak leaf with your DNA on it, for example," Preuss said, riffing and wishing Janey could have been there to see the sudden look of suspicion on this guy's face.

"All we have to do is find an oak leaf with your DNA that places you at the scene and your ass is grass, my friend. We got you for accessory to kidnapping a minor. Your record, you'll never see the light of day again."

"Hey, whoa, time out." White made a time-out sign with his pudgy hands.

"I'm just telling you the facts, Wayne."

"What can you do for me if I tell you what I know."

"I can put in a word with the ADA."

White thought about that for a few moments.

"For real?"

"Word of honor," Preuss said.

I'll tell him to lock you up and throw away the key, you moron, he thought. That's the word I'll put in.

"So you were there that night? Following Madison?"

"Yeah. Do I have to say what I was following her for?"

"No, I think we can figure that out for ourselves. I just want to know what happened."

Wayne White proceeded to corroborate Walter Szymanski's story. With a few key details that Szymanski didn't know.

"I dint see the name of the company on the truck," he said. I just remember it was a landscaping company."

"You're sure about that?"

"Positive. There was like a big lawn mower thing on the trailer. When I saw the truck pull over I ran off but I stopped a little ways up the street. Just to see what was going to happen."

"And make sure the little girl was safe and sound, no doubt. So what happened after the guy picked Madison up and put her in his truck?"

"I saw him turn into a driveway a little ways up the street."

Preuss asked him to repeat that to make sure he understood.

He did. White couldn't remember what house, exactly, but he knew it was on the north side of the street.

Madison might still be on West Woodland.

From his Explorer in the parking lot he called Reg Trombley, who was at his desk at the Shanahan building. Preuss asked him to find a pick-up truck or trailer registered to a landscaper on West Woodland. In less than ten minutes.

Five minutes later Trombley called back. He checked the DMV registry and got the plate number of a Ford F250 registered to the Nu-Life Landscaping Company at an address on Woodland. The name at the address was George Schenk.

Preuss caught Cahill on her cell on the way to Pontiac for a meeting with the task force.

"Forget that and turn around," he said. "Meet me at this address."

"What's up?" she asked.

"I think I might have found her."

34

Preuss tore across Nine Mile and up Livernois to the Schenk residence.

Fuming the whole time: about George Schenk and whatever he had done to Madison. About Wayne White and what he had in mind for her.

Maybe Shelley Larkin was right. Madison Kaufman was an oppressed minority.

The Schenk home was a large tidy Tudor with a picture window overlooking West Woodland. The curtains were closed, like a lid drawn over an eye.

The Explorer bounced up onto the curb. He jumped out and looked down the street to the Kaufman home in the middle of the block. Had someone from this house been watching Madison? Were they waiting for the chance to snatch the girl who lived there? What had happened here?

These questions could wait. The most important thing now was to find her.

The driveway was empty. He pounded on the door and rang the bell. When nobody answered he rattled the storm door, but it was locked tight. He jumped off the porch into the bushes and tried to peer through the front windows but couldn't see anything through the curtains, either through the wide picture window or the sidelights at either side of it.

He trotted up the driveway to the back of the house, and went through the same routine with the back door and back windows. Nothing there either, though he could see into the kitchen. Nobody around.

He sat in the Explorer, growing more anxious by the minute until Cahill showed up.

"We've got to get in there," he told her.

"Hold it, hold it, hold it," she said. "Want to tell me what's going on?"

He gave her a shortened version of what he learned earlier. "We need a warrant," he said. "Madison might be in here."

"I'll work through Cass."

"Fine, whatever. Just hurry."

She pulled out her phone and walked back to her truck. Preuss did not care who got the warrant as long as they got inside that house as soon as possible. He stepped back to take in the placid brick exterior of the home. He walked around to the back of the house again to see if he could get into the oversized garage but found no way to get inside besides the big overhead door, which wouldn't budge.

Around front, Cahill held her cell phone out to Preuss. "Cass wants to talk to you."

He took the phone. "Preuss."

In his deep rumbling voice, slowly and ponderously, as if he owned the whole world and nothing could happen without his okay, Cass asked, "What do you have?"

"We're standing in front of a house in northwest Ferndale down the street from the Kaufmans that belongs to the people who might have taken Madison. I got this from an eyewitness. She might be inside. We need a warrant to enter immediately."

"Catch your breath for a second," Cass began, but Preuss waved it away as though Cass were standing right in front of him.

"We don't have time for this bullshit." He explained what he suspected. "We have to get inside. I want to know if that little girl is here, or if she ever was here."

"Are you sure about probable cause?" Cass asked.

"As sure as we can be. This is the strongest lead we have and I don't want to lose it. If you don't get a warrant to enter this residence, I'm going to break a window myself and climb the fuck inside."

"You definitely don't want to do that," Cass said.

"Well, then?"

"I'll get working on it and be out with it soon as I can. Preuss, don't you go inside that house until I get there, do you hear me?"

Preuss snapped off the phone.

This was going to take too long. He needed to find George Schenk. He wasn't going to have the patience to wait around until Cass found an ADA and then a judge to get this moving. He looked in his notebook for the Nu-Life Landscape Maintenance phone number and called.

Amazingly, someone answered.

The male voice that announced the company name sounded like a young man.

"This is Detective Martin Preuss of the Ferndale Police Department. Who am I speaking with?"

After a brief hesitation, the voice said, "Jerry Schenk."

"Jerry, are you the owner of this company?"

"Part owner."

"Who owns the other part?"

"That would be my father."

"George Schenk?"

"Yeah."

"Does he drive a Ford pickup with this license plate?" He read off the plate number.

"Yeah, that's his. Look, what's the problem here? Was he in an accident or something?"

"Who owns the house on West Woodland?"

"That's my dad's house."

"Where is he right now?"

"Is everything all right with him?" the young man demanded.

"I need to know where your father is right now, Jerry. How about you tell me?"

"Well, can I ask what this is in reference to?"

"What you can do is tell me where to find your father."

"He's out on a job."

"Where?"

Jerry hesitated again. "I'm not sure."

Preuss gripped the phone until the plastic creaked. No point now in even trying to hold his temper.

"Jerry," he said, and began to pace with the phone and gesture as though Jerry were standing in front of him, "here's what's going to happen. You're going to tell me where your father is in the next five seconds or I'm going to charge you as an accessory to kidnapping."

"Kidnapping? Are you serious?"

"You have three seconds."

"All right, all right. I'm sure there's some mistake here."

"Tell me where your father is and we'll sort it out later," Preuss shouted into the phone.

"Hang on, I'll find the address."

In a few moments Jerry Schenk gave Preuss the address of an office building on Telegraph Road in Southfield. "He's working on the grounds. He'll be outside someplace."

"Jerry," Preuss said, "I'm going to instruct you to not tell him we're on our way, do you understand what I'm saying?"

Jerry Schenk promised he wouldn't alert his father.

But by the time Preuss arrived at the office complex on Telegraph a half hour later, all Preuss saw was an empty utility trailer with its yoke hanging dejectedly on the parking lot and a bulky teenager with a shaved head driving a small tractor over the expanse of lawn in front of the office building. The tractor was towing a trailer filled with fallen leaves.

Preuss flagged him down when he came near and drew a hand across his throat to signify he wanted silence. The boy shut off the tractor's engine and the air went still. Words were tattooed on the side of the boy's neck in gothic lettering, but the writing was too fancy for Preuss to make out.

The kid said he had no idea where his boss had gone. He took off in his pickup about fifteen minutes ago.

"Let me guess," Preuss said, "right after he got a call."

"You got it," the kid said.

35

In minutes the description and license number of George Schenk's pickup truck was broadcast to police agencies throughout the area, as well as Ohio and the Ontario Provincial Police in Canada across the Detroit River.

Preuss returned to West Woodland, where a half dozen Ferndale police and Oakland County Sheriff's cars were now parked around the Schenk home. A news van from Channel 7 was down the street with its antenna extended. Knots of neighbors were gathered up and down the sidewalks.

This is certainly inconspicuous, he thought as he double-parked in front of the house. Schenk wouldn't suspect a thing.

They were all still waiting for Cass to show up with the warrant. "This is unacceptable," Preuss fumed, but Cahill took him by the arm and led him away from the group of police and deputies who were standing in front of the Schenk house.

"Relax, okay? This is what we have to do. You know that."

"I'm losing my patience and I want somebody to pick up Jerry Schenk."

"Who's that?"

"The son. He tipped his father off and now the father's de-camped." He gave her the son's phone number and she called it into the Ferndale dispatcher.

"Done," she said. "Come here, sit in my truck for a few minutes till Cass gets here. And block the impulse to jump through the dining room window and fuck up the whole case."

He climbed into the passenger seat of her pickup, first brushing away empty Happy Meal boxes and a plastic Happy Meal toy that was already broken.

Preuss watched the silent house for a minute, then said, "Mrs. Schenk."

"What about her?"

"Exactly. What do we know about her?"

"Marty, what do we know about *him*?"

"That's what I'm saying. Is there a Mrs. Schenk? Where is she? We need to find out about her while we're waiting. She might be as involved in this as he is."

"Let's talk to the neighbors," she said. He nodded and they climbed out of the truck.

They started with the neighbor to the left of the Schenk house, but nobody was home there. On the right, an older woman with white hair came to the door. She was tiny and looked to be in her late seventies. She looked up at Preuss and Cahill with sparse querulous eyebrows as they asked about the Schenks. In the background classical violin music was playing. She told them her name was Grace Lukasik.

"Yes," she said, "I know them well. Carolyn and George."

"Carolyn," Preuss said, "that's Mrs. Schenk?"

"Yes. Is she in some trouble?"

Cahill said, "We just need to ask her some questions."

Grace Lukasik leaned around Janey to eyeball the battalion of police cars in the street. "Is this all about Madison?"

"Yes, ma'am," Preuss said. "Do you know the Schenks well?"

"Oh, yes," she said. "We've all lived here for years."

She looked from one to the other with bright blue eyes. "George is a very good man. Very hard-working. He has his own landscaping business. Keeps the house up, as you can see. Oh, and religious . . . very religious. They're both very religious. Wonderful people. They're not in any trouble, are they?"

"Have you seen Madison around here the last few days, Mrs. Lukasik?" Cahill asked. "This is very important."

"I've seen her play down the street, but not around here."

"Do you know the Kaufmans?"

"Only by sight."

"Have you seen Carolyn and George lately?" Preuss asked.

"George I've seen. Now that you mention it, I haven't seen Carolyn for a few days."

"Since when?"

"Last week sometime. Midweek, I guess."

"Is that unusual, not to see her for that long?"

"Usually I see them every day."

Preuss and Cahill exchanged a glance, a terrible certainty growing between them.

36

The crowd of law enforcement officials had grown around the Schenk house, as had the neighbors milling outside their homes and the news vans broadcasting live video of it all. Jim Cass still had not arrived with the warrant.

"I think there are almost enough police around there to executive a search warrant when it gets here," he told Cahill. "I can't just stand around. I'll be back in a while."

"Where are you going?"

Without answering he jumped into the Explorer and gunned it down to Woodward, where he made a Michigan left and swung north to jump on 696 west. It was closing in on rush hour but this would still be the fastest way.

Traffic was thick but he made it out to Telegraph in good time. He squealed into the blacktopped parking lot of the office building where the skinhead kid had been collecting leaves earlier that day just as a big guy was connecting the trailer, now carrying the tractor, to a green Dodge Ram.

Preuss pulled up in front of the truck and stepped out with his badge already out.

"Jerry Schenk?"

The young man straightened and gave Preuss a dark look without responding.

Preuss identified himself and asked, "Are you Jerry Schenk?"

"That's right."

"I'm arresting you on suspicion of kidnapping."

"You gotta be kidding."

"Oh no, I'm not," Preuss said.

And to prove it he read Jerry Schenk his rights.

Jerry Schenk sat in the interview room at the Shanahan building with Preuss and Cahill across the table from him. Jim Cass and Emma Blalock showed up at the Schenk home with a locksmith who got them inside and they were executing the warrant as the younger Schenk sat glaring at the two detectives. He had refused a lawyer.

"I don't have anything to say about any of this," he insisted. He was big and husky, like a Viking with blonde eyelashes and almost white hair cut short. He looked to be in his mid-twenties. He wore a Nu-Life Landscape Maintenance sweatshirt with a rising sun logo. His hands were filthy, with a build-up of dirt underneath his fingernails that looked like it would never come clean.

"After we spoke on the phone," Preuss said, "did you call your father and let him know I was coming for him?"

When he didn't answer, Preuss said, "If you don't cooperate, Jerry, it's going to go that much harder."

"Yeah," the young man finally admitted. "I did."

"Why did you do that?"

"I wanted him to know you were looking for him, that's all. I didn't think he'd take off. Wouldn't you call your father and let him know the cops were looking for him?"

"No, as a matter of fact, I wouldn't, if a police officer told me not to. Do you know where he is now?"

"Did you check his house?"

"There are roughly forty-seven police officers and Sheriff's deputies walking around inside his house as we speak. Any other suggestions?"

Schenk shrugged.

"I'd like a list of all your relatives, with addresses and phone numbers."

"Whatever."

"Is there an office for Nu-Life? Besides the house on Woodland?"

"No. We work out of there. We keep most of our equipment in his garage. Some in mine."

"By the morning we'll have a warrant to search your house, too."

"What are you looking for there?"

"Your father, for one thing."

"I'll save you the trouble. You won't find him there."

"Where will we find him?"

"I don't know. But I know he isn't there."

That wasn't worth responding to. "We're looking for Madison Kaufman," Preuss said. "The little girl we suspect your father of kidnapping."

Jerry Schenk blew out a small puff of air.

"We have a witness who tells us he saw your father drive away with Madison Kaufman in his truck on the evening of Wednesday, November 4, and come to this address."

Schenk was quiet for a moment. "Who told you that?"

Preuss pulled the photo of Madison from his jacket pocket and laid it on the table.

"That's your witness? A little girl?"

"That's Madison Kaufman. Are you seriously telling me you've never seen her? Even though she lives down the block from the house where you grew up?"

Before Schenk could answer, Preuss leaned forward. "Jerry," he said in a low voice, "you're getting on my last nerve. You want to tell me where your father is so we can get this little girl back home?"

Schenk sat back and folded his arms. "I don't know where my father is. And I don't know where that little girl is. I don't have anything else to say." He looked off into the corner.

Preuss nodded to Cahill and the two stood up. Preuss passed a pad of yellow legal paper to Schenk along with a pencil, saying, "Names and numbers for those relatives," and opened the door to call in an officer who was waiting outside. "Soon as he's done, take him away for processing," Preuss said.

"He'll be out by the morning," Cahill said in the hallway. "That charge is sort of bogus."

"Maybe so," Preuss said. "At least we'll keep him out of play for the night."

She said she was going back to the Schenk home, and Preuss said he would meet her there in a little while. Before he left his cubicle, he called Edmund Blair at home.

Blair answered after the third ring. "Hey," Preuss said. "What are you doing right now?"

"Finishing dinner. What's up?"

"I want to know if you can do a little surveillance work." Preuss gave him the address on Republic in Oak Park where Jerry Schenk lived and asked him to get over there as fast as he could. Blair lived off Hilton on the east side of Ferndale, and said he could get there in fifteen minutes.

"Good." Preuss filled him in on what was going on. "I want to know if anybody enters or leaves that house tonight."

"What do you want me to do if I see anything?"

"Call me and we'll decide."

37

At the Schenk home, the preliminary search was completed without finding Madison Kaufman.

The house was immaculate. It was after ten o'clock at night and Jim Cass, Emma Blalock, Cahill, and Preuss stood conferring over the hood of Cass's car. The neighbors had all gone in for the night, and once it became clear there would be no surprise discoveries the news vans returned to their stations.

"Where are the techs?" Cass said in annoyance. "I want them in there."

"On their way," said Emma.

Preuss told them about his interview with the younger Schenk. "He's not going to give up his father," he said. "That's pretty clear."

"Do you think the son's involved?" Cass asked.

"I think he knows something. Here's a list of their relatives." He handed the paper to Cass, who glanced at it and passed it straight over to Emma. She took it and walked a little distance away to get on her cell to request deputies to visit their homes.

"All right," said Cass, "Preuss arranged to hold him over till tomorrow so we can go at him again in the morning. In the meantime, where the hell are these people?"

"When we find them, we'll find Madison," Preuss said.

"I hope to Christ you're right," Cass rumbled.

Preuss left them in the street to hash over their next moves and went into the Schenk house.

It smelled of Pine Sol. As he moved from room to room he took in the layout and décor. Just the perfect little castle, everything tidy and organized. No artwork hung on the walls except for paintings of a sad-eyed Jesus in the dining room and an arrangement of photos of the family along the long wall of the living room. The man whom Preuss assumed was George Schenk was bald with a fringe of hair, just as Walter Szymanski had said. Preuss saw just the one Schenk child, Jerry, and a woman Preuss assumed was his wife, a young woman with a perfectly round face, and two chubby little boys.

Preuss didn't think the Schenks would be at their son's house, and probably not at the relatives', either, which would be the first places they would expect the police to look if they were on the run. And with them having suddenly dropped from sight, Preuss was convinced they had Madison.

But why? What could they possibly want with her? Grace Lukasik had talked about how religious they were. Was that part of it? In Preuss's experience, the more religion people claimed for themselves, the more hypocritically they acted. Could an ultra-religious couple have taken this girl for reasons Preuss couldn't even bear to think about? Was that really conceivable?

In the kitchen he stood and looked around. Like the rest of the house, the room was orderly and neat, with clean clear counters and another print of Jesus attached to the refrigerator with a magnet to bless the food. Bless our daily bread.

And the little girl we're holding captive, too.

On closer inspection, under the picture of Jesus was a prayer about blessing the family. According to the publication information at the bottom of the sheet, it had been printed by the New Life Church of God.

New Life.

Nu-Life?

As in Nu-Life Landscaping?

As if some connection had been made, his cell rang. Blair.

"Got some action here," he said. "A woman's on the move."

"Alone?"

"Yeah. She just this minute trundled two little boys next door and then she took off. What do you want me to do?"

"Can you follow her?"

"Got it. In pursuit."

Preuss heard the motor of Blair's car. "Where is she now?"

"Heading out toward Hilton."

"Keep her in your sights. Let me know where she goes."

Out on the street, Cass, Cahill, and Emma Blalock were still talking things over next to his car. The techs from the Sheriff's Office had arrived and were unpacking their equipment to go about their business of collecting evidence that would determine whether Madison had been in the house. Preuss told them what Blair was up to and Cass grunted his approval.

In another fifteen minutes Preuss heard from Blair again. "Now we're on Eight Mile, headed west. We just crossed the Greenfield overpass."

Twenty minutes later another call from Blair came through. "She landed."

"Where?"

"Little church in Livonia."

"The New Life Church of God."

"Damn. That must be why you're the detective."

"Did she go inside?"

"First she drove past it and parked in a driveway on the side street next to the church. Then she walked back and went inside in the back door."

"Where are you?"

"In a Kroger parking lot directly across the street from the church. There's a low berm with trees partly blocking the view of the street, so I'm pretty well hidden. But I've got my eye on the front and the back."

"You're an ace," Preuss said. "Stay put and I'll be there as soon as I can. What's the address?"

Preuss took down the location and told the others what he had just learned. "I'm going out there," he said.

"Keep me posted," Cass said. "Let me know right away if you need backup"

"Wouldn't be a bad idea to liaze with the locals, let them know what we're up to."

Cass made a face.

"If you find something worth following up on, I'll make a call. Till then keep a low profile."

Preuss waved a hand and was off.

38

The church was on Five Mile Road in Livonia. He took Eight Mile west to Merriman, where he turned left and drove south to Five. He paused at the light at Five and Merriman, not certain which way to turn, and chanced a right. The numbers were going in the wrong direction so he made a U-turn and went the other way.

The New Life Church of God was a new-looking brick building on the south side of Five Mile, a freestanding, plain Protestant house of worship with a cross in front. A signboard on the lawn throwing light out into the darkness read:

C H ** C H
What's Missing?

The building was completely dark, surrounded by a sprawling dark empty parking lot.

Preuss drove past it, then took a slow turn around the next block. Schenk's pickup was nowhere in sight. He parked in the lot across the street from the church, where Edmund Blair was sitting inside his Suburban. He was parked in a spot where he could see the front of the church, the side entrance, and the rear door. No one could get in or out without him noticing.

The two of them exited their cars and walked across the empty street to the church. Preuss regretted Cass's decision not to warn the local police department they were out here tonight. He understood the wish to keep them out of their hair, but this was their city. He wouldn't want Livonia cops on his turf without someone knowing about it. Still, that was not his battle.

Preuss tried the wide double front doors of the church. Both were locked. The two men separated and walked around opposite sides of the church, checking all the windows for light reflected from inside and pulling on the doors for any way in. All the stained glass windows along the side of the church were dark, though Preuss thought he could pick up a glow coming from a light somewhere inside.

He knelt down on his hands and knees towards the rear of the side wall but couldn't see into the window, which had been blocked up from the inside with wood.

If Jerry Schenk's wife was in there, it's a good bet the others would be too, he thought. With Madison.

They reconnected at the back of the building. "If anybody's in here," Preuss said, "the problem is going to be getting a warrant to search a church." Blair regarded him, working his big mustache. "We'd have a hard time convincing a judge to sign a search warrant for anything based on what we have now."

He ran his hand along the brick of the church wall as if trying to feel for the vibrations of whatever was going on inside. But the brick was cold and still and secretive.

"What do you think?" Blair asked.

"I think Madison Kaufman is inside this building."

They walked back around to the front. "Let's see if we can get hold of the reverend." On the front door was a card with an emergency number on it, and the reverend's name, Rev. Norman Burkus. Preuss punched the number in on his cell phone and waited for three rings before the line was answered by a man with a soft and saccharine voice.

"It's a beautiful night!" the man said instead of hello.

Preuss identified himself and asked for Reverend Burkus.

"This is," the man said.

Preuss explained he was looking for Madison Kaufman and had reason to believe the girl was inside the Livonia church.

The man on the other end of the line was silent for a few moments, then said, "Why, detective, what makes you think there's a girl inside my church at this hour of the night?"

"Are George and Carolyn Schenk parishioners?"

"Yes, they are."

"Have you seen them recently?"

"They were at church on Sunday."

"Reverend, I would like to take a look inside the church. Could you come down and meet me there?"

The clergyman seemed to choose his words very carefully. "I'm afraid I can't do that."

"A child's life may be at stake."

"The church is a sanctuary, and I will not allow the police to invade its sacred space. You'll have to take my word that there's no child inside whom you need to see."

The careful formulation convinced him Madison was inside.

"I will get a search warrant, Reverend, if you won't cooperate."

"That's what you'll have to do. I'll say good night, sir."

At that, Reverend Burkus hung up.

"Fuck you, too," said Preuss to the dead line.

"Nothing?" Blair asked.

"No. He claimed Madison isn't there and refused us entry."

"Not very Christian of him. What now?"

Preuss thought about that. "Let's sit on it for a while," he said. "See if anything happens. We can try for a search warrant in the morning."

"Won't be easy."

"Maybe not."

Staking it out inconspicuously wouldn't be easy, either. They weren't in their jurisdiction, so he hoped they would get lucky and the patrols were busy elsewhere because things would get funky if a curious Livonia patrol car showed up.

"Both of us don't need to sit here in the cold all night," Preuss said. "Why don't we do it in shifts?"

"Fine with me. I might as well take the first watch."

Preuss glanced at his watch. "It's 10:30. How about we do two five-hour shifts? You start from now till 2:30, and I'll spell you and go till 8:30. If something doesn't happen by then, it should be easier to get inside during the day."

Blair said, "Give me fifteen minutes to tap a kidney and get some coffee and I'll be good to go."

"I'll stay here."

Blair loped back across the street to his car and took off in the direction Preuss had come from, toward a late-night Wendy's drive-through on Merriman.

Preuss took a final look around, then went back across the street to his SUV. He called Janey Cahill to tell her what was going to happen, then she said, "Hold it, let me relay that," and listened to her, then to Emma Blalock's voice for a few seconds. Preuss couldn't tell what she was saying, but then Cahill said to Emma, "Okay, hold on. Let me tell him."

She came back on the line and said, "The techs are still working. Cass and Emma are going to hang around for a while. Afterwards he's going to post a car near the house."

"Okay."

"Hang on again, Martin," she said. Emma's voice. Cahill listened for a while longer. In the tinny sound going into his ear, Preuss thought he heard what sounded like "blood."

Away from the receiver, Cahill said, "Hold on, let me tell him."

Then to Preuss: "She said they just this second got a hit on blood traces in the second floor bathroom."

"Whereabouts?"

"Drain in the sink."

A shiver went down his spine. "Anyplace else? Any spatter?"

She asked that question of Emma, then said to Preuss, "Not so far. They're taking samples. Hold it." After another murmured monologue from Emma, she said to Preuss, "Nothing else. Take a little while to type and match it."

"This changes everything," Preuss said. Now they were going to go over the house with everything they had.

"Emma's going to tell Cass about the situation you have there and see if we can get inside the church in the morning."

"This should be enough for a warrant. Soon as Ed gets back, I'm going to take off. Need me to swing by the house?"

"Everything's under control, and it's going to be a long night. We'll call you if we need you. I were you, I'd try to get some sleep."

"Yeah, right." Like that would happen.

They said goodbye and he settled himself behind the wheel and his cell rang at once.

Cahill again.

"Almost forgot," she said. "Emma told me to tell you. There's a meeting in the morning, nine a.m. in Pontiac. Cass wants you there."

"You mean I finally worked my way into the elite inner circle?"

"Save your sarcasm for those who appreciate it, okay? I'm just the messenger."

"I'd be better off staying out here and seeing how things look in the morning."

"I'll let him know. Hey, Marty, one more thing . . . what did you say that clergyman's name was?"

"Burkus. Why? Ring a bell?"

"Yeah. A year or so ago his church came under some heavy scrutiny for making threats against an abortion provider in Birmingham. It was a right around the time of the murder of that doc in Kansas and everybody was pretty tense."

"Anything come of it?"

"Not as I recall. He got hauled in but they only found some shaky connections with some of the more violent anti-abortion groups. Couldn't make anything stick on him, though. I remembered because I was doing my anti-terrorism training at the time. For what it's worth."

"Thanks," he said grimly, and snapped his phone shut.

After ten minutes Blair returned, and Preuss drove home.

Wednesday, November 12, 2008

39

As he suspected, sleep never came.

His mind wouldn't stop working. Too many things to think about: how to get into the church, what he would find there, where George Schenk was, what the anti-abortion link meant, what was going to happen to Preuss's career once this was over, how to renegotiate his relationship with Russo . . .

From there his thoughts cycled out even further, to his constant worry about Toby and what was going to happen to him, to all his regrets over the way his life had gone, how he had made a mess of everything, all his skills and talents and possibilities, how all of his potential was gone, wasted, squandered in his poor stewardship of his own life.

Was this the sum total of that life? Another sleepless night in a solitary bed? In an empty house, too big for him and rumbling with voices that were gone forever? A child lost somewhere in the world? A dead wife? A dead-end career protecting a society that he was not sure deserved or wanted his protection?

And a disabled child whom he couldn't take care of himself, but whom he loved with whatever was left of his battered heart and who enjoyed himself more in one minute of his life than he, Preuss, did in a year?

This child indeed is father to this man, so far ahead of Preuss in everything that mattered.

He roused himself and changed his clothes. No sense letting these thoughts eat at him. Most often he kept them at bay, but the early morning hours like this were the worst, when nothing could help him shove them in a closet and bar the door, no other activities to turn his attention to. And right now they only distracted him from what he needed to be thinking about.

Downstairs he made himself some eggs and coffee, and stood in the kitchen eating and drinking. He doused his eggs in salsa and forked them over a piece of toast in the silence of the middle of the night in his large, still house.

At 2 a.m. he called Edmund Blair, who told him all was quiet. He got back into the Explorer with a travel mug of coffee and drove past the Schenk home. The crime scene techs were still methodically processing the entire house, but Cass and everyone else had gone home except a lone deputy who sat in a Sheriff's car and gave Preuss the hairy eyeball as he drove by.

Further up the street, the Kaufman house was dark.

He eased the Explorer to Pinecrest, and went south to Eight. From there he breezed west to Merriman, and found Blair awake and alert in the parking lot across from the church.

He pulled up beside Blair's Suburban and slipped inside. The car was warm and the air heavy with coffee.

"All quiet," Blair said. "Nobody in or out."

"Why don't you get going? Anything happens, I'll give you a ring. Thanks a million, man."

"The pleasure was all mine," Blair said. They shook hands and Preuss jumped back in his Explorer.

Blair pulled away and left Preuss alone again with his thoughts.

The worst part of being alone was living so much in his own head. Now that he was engaged in doing something, however, he could keep his thoughts more disciplined. He tried to work his way through all of the possible permutations of reasons for Madison Kaufman being inside the New Life Church of God.

He was now convinced she was inside. But who knew what was going on in there? Being a completely irreligious man, he had no particular affection for church-going people, nor any automatic respect for their moral character. But he would not be surprised to find they had stumbled on a den of child molesters.

What other reasons would they have for taking her, and keeping her hidden? He assumed Kaufman was a Jewish name; why would a group of Evangelicals be hiding a little Jewish girl? Conversion, as if this were the middle ages? No, the only reason he could think of now was molestation.

He thought of Shelley Larkin and her article. Her brother, taken years ago for who knew what kind of terrible life. Molestation had always been in the forefront of his concerns for Toby. Being so completely vulnerable to his environment, Toby was at grave risk for mistreatment, not only sexual mistreatment but improper care in general, in getting his medication incorrectly, in not being kept clean, in not getting his diapers changed regularly . . . Back in the early days when Toby was living at home with him, Preuss used to chat with the nurses who were his respite care workers and they would tell him horror stories of profoundly disabled children they took care of, who lived with families who mistreated them criminally, who made them sit in their dirty diapers all day, never spoke to them or interacted with the children from morning till night.

His mind roved in these ways for an hour, then he got out of the car and relieved himself in the bushes of the berm that was his cover, and got back in the Explorer to watch some more. Traffic along Five Mile had stopped entirely for the night. A few patrol cars had passed, putting him instantly on edge, but they kept going without stopping and now even they had disappeared.

At some point, despite his best efforts to stay awake, he dozed.

40

It might have been the faintest of vibrations that reached his car and gave the Explorer an infinitesimally small shake.

Or the noise of voices that reached across the street and let him know something was happening.

Or a light from a pair of car headlights that cut through the gloom of the cold fall evening and raked his face from the parking lot across the street from where he sat.

Whatever it was, he popped awake and looked around dumbly, for an instant not knowing where he was or what he was doing. Then he remembered with a shock, and looked across the street to see a minivan parked behind the rear door to the church.

Shaking his head wildly to clear it, Preuss took his binoculars from the glove compartment and focused on the car. It was a dark Pontiac Montana, but no one was around it. He turned the dome light off and stepped out of the SUV and slipped up to the berm so he could get a better view of the back door of the church. He watched for another twenty minutes before seeing a slice of light escape from the doorway in the rear of the church as the back door opened and a figure in a puffy parka exited.

The slice of light collapsed immediately as the door closed without any sound floating across the empty street. The dome light of the minivan flashed briefly on and through the binoculars Preuss made out a woman who looked to be older than Jerry Schenk's wife would be. Possibly it was Carolyn Schenk. He tried to remember what she looked like from the photos in her house, but couldn't conjure up her face.

He could make out no other passengers in the van besides the woman. Thanks to his incredible stupidity in falling asleep, it was possible Madison Kaufman had been loaded into the car and was stuffed in a heap on the back seat. He was furious with himself.

Whoever it was, the woman was in a big damn hurry. She peeled away from the back door and around the side of the church toward the parking lot exit that gave onto Five Mile. Preuss heard the squeal of her tires as she rolled into the street and he decided it must be Carolyn Schenk.

And he had to stop her.

He ran back to his Explorer. As she headed east toward Merriman, Preuss followed.

She drove fast up Merriman to Eight Mile, then turned right and accelerated.

Heading back to Ferndale? Did she know what was happening at her house, or would that be a surprise? An unpleasant surprise to find yellow crime scene tape hanging across her door and a deputy in front, awaiting her return?

But where was Madison? He thought of the possibility of her being in the car, and he knew he had to intervene. He was miles from his jurisdiction but with no alternative.

He lowered his driver's side window and attached the flashing gumball light onto the roof and sped up until he was immediately behind her van.

The woman drove for another block, watching him in her rear view mirror. From the look on her face, he knew she was trying to decide what to do. Pull over? Continue on? Call for help?

Fortunately she made the right choice. She pulled over and he skidded to a stop in front of her. He stepped out of his car with a flashlight he kept under the seat and came up to the driver's side of the other vehicle. The woman had collapsed over the steering wheel, her back heaving in great sobs.

He thought he could recognize the words, "Thank God. Oh thank God," repeated over and over.

He shone the light around the rest of the vehicle. Empty.

He knocked on the driver's window and she pulled herself together enough to lower it. "Carolyn Schenk?" he asked.

She nodded.

"Step out of the car."

She threw the door open and burst from the car and into his arms, still sobbing.

Only now she said, "I'm sorry, I'm sorry, I'm sorry."

And then: "God forgive me."

41

He led her into the passenger seat of his Explorer and came around to sit behind the wheel. He waited until she calmed down enough to speak. She was trembling with anxiety and relief, a thick-set woman who looked to be in her middle sixties, with long graying hair that had been wrapped in a neat braid pinned to the back of her head.

"Mrs. Schenk, do you know where Madison Kaufman is?"

She nodded.

"Is she at the church?"

Another nod.

"Is she all right?"

She looked at him with a look of such sadness that it made his insides drop. He fought down nausea and forced himself to ask, "Is she alive?"

She nodded.

"What's the matter with her?" he demanded.

She shook her head, unable to speak about it.

She began to sob again, this time into her hands.

He called the Ferndale police dispatcher and told her where he was and what he was going to do. He told the dispatcher to get hold of Janey Cahill and Jim Cass with the Oakland Sheriff and tell them what was happening, and not to worry about the time.

He wanted to ask her to bring in the Marines, and the Grand Army of the Republic, too.

And after that he wanted to call in artillery on this church, and then he wanted to take a pickaxe and with his own hands demolish what was left brick by brick until it was only a steaming pile of rubble.

When he snapped his phone shut, he asked the woman sitting next to him, "Where were you going?"

"To get help."

"For Madison?"

She nodded. "She's not doing well," the woman whispered.

He forced himself to say, "Did you people hurt her?"

She shook her head. "We would never . . ."

He swallowed the burning nausea that rose again in his throat. He knew he should wait for someone to join him, but now, after getting so close to the little girl and learning she was hurt, he did not have the patience to wait. He needed to act.

"She needs help," she continued. "I couldn't just stand by any more and watch her fail . . . so I left to get help."

"Where were you going to go?"

"To get the midwife and bring her back here."

"What midwife?"

"There's a midwife who belongs to our congregation. She's been helping us out."

"With Madison?"

She nodded.

"Why didn't you just call an ambulance? Or put her in the car and take her to the hospital?"

"They said they didn't want me to do that."

For a moment Preuss heard an echo of what Walter Szymanski had said about what *they* didn't want him to do, the authoritarian *they* that directed so much of our lives.

"Who's *they*?"

"The others."

"What others?"

"Reverend Burkus and the congregation. And my husband."

"Reverend Burkus is involved, too?"

"Of course."

"Where is he?"

"Back at the church."

Then he lost it. "Goddamn it to hell!" he exploded. He reached out and grabbed a handful of her puffy coat. "We're going back to the church and you're going to get me inside," he said through clenched teeth, "and then I'm going to get Madison and walk out with her. Are we clear?"

"Yes."

"And I'm going to shoot anybody who tries to stop me."

"Nobody will," she hastily assured him. The crazy angry part of him almost wished somebody would try.

"Now call Burkus and tell him you forgot something and you need to get back inside. I'll take it from there."

He made a U-turn on Eight Mile and started back to the church.

His cell rang.

Cahill.

"She's here," he said. "At the church."

"What shape is she in?"

"Not good, but I don't know the specifics. We're going to need an ambulance."

"Are you still outside?"

"Yes. Mrs. Schenk's going to get me in."

"Why don't you wait for help?"

"We've lost too much time already. Mrs. Schenk tells me Madison's in bad shape. We can't wait any longer."

"I'll call the ambulance and come right over. Be careful, Martin, all right?"

42

He maneuvered the SUV behind the church with the driver's side near the back door but out of the door's sight line. Preuss nodded to her and she made the call on her own cell.

"Norman?" she said when the call was answered. "It's Carolyn. I need to get in again. Yes," she said, and looked at Preuss next to her. "I forgot something. I'm right outside."

She disconnected and got out of the Explorer. Preuss slipped out from his side, leaving the door hanging open, and stood beside her and drew his gun from his belt holster and held it behind his back, then nodded and she pounded on the door.

When the door opened and the slice of light from inside extended, he pushed her aside and entered a corridor that ran the width of the back of the church. He pointed his gun straight at the chest of the doughy, middle-aged man who looked at him with amazement and shock.

To Preuss's equal amazement, the man immediately threw his arms up and fell to his knees and with his eyes squeezed shut and, face upraised, began to pray in a thin, fast, quiet voice.

He was beseeching Jesus to help him in his hour of need.

Preuss turned to Carolyn Schenk standing behind him. "Where is she?"

He holstered his weapon, thinking if it was out he would be too inclined to use it.

They stepped around the praying man and she led him through the corridor to a set of stairs down to a lower level, under the chapel. Before they took the stairs he looked inside the chapel and saw it was dark and empty and plain.

At the bottom of the stairs another hallway led into a large windowless community room, brightly lit but empty of people. She led him slowly through the room and into another hallway lined with posters from overseas missions of the church. Leading off from that was a tiny overheated room where George Schenk, whom Preuss recognized from his DMV photo, a younger woman Preuss guessed was Jerry Schenk's wife, and an older woman stood crowded around a small portable cot.

On the corner of the desk next to the cot was an array of bandages and bottles of alcohol and hydrogen peroxide. When they heard Preuss and Carolyn Schenk approach, they silently parted as on a signal.

On the cot, bundled in blankets, was Madison Kaufman.

43

Her eyes were closed and her fine blonde hair stuck to her flushed forehead. If she was still breathing, her respirations were so shallow as to be imperceivable. Preuss could not believe he had found her, nor that she was in such bad shape.

It was so close in the room he could smell the sour breath and body odor of the adults, and another, putrid smell coming from the girl on the bed.

He stepped forward, shouldering himself between the people in the room, which he now saw was an office that had been arranged as a makeshift sickroom, and bent over the small and wasted body. He placed a hand on her head and felt she was burning up. Fever was good. A sign of life.

He straightened and turned to stare at the people watching him with blank expressions. He wanted to shoot them all where they stood, drop them one right after the other.

Instead he demanded, "What's happening here?"

When nobody answered, he raised his fists at them in fury. "What have you done to this child?"

As though in reply, they dropped to their knees, one by one, starting with George Schenk, and began to pray the same way the man upstairs had done, with their eyes closed and their hands held high above their heads, their lips moving in rapid and silent entreaty to some god who had long ago abandoned this world to the likes of them.

Fortunately, at that moment he heard sirens converge outside. He retraced his steps and met two paramedics at the back door. He led them through the maze of the church to the small office.

"Get on your feet and get out of here," Preuss ordered the supplicants, who were still on their knees, and they helped each other up. He roughly pushed them from the office.

The paramedics took their places. They immediately set to work on the girl in the cot. As he watched them he realized she was not wearing the clothes she had gone missing in, but was in a pair of pajamas they must have gotten for her.

She was also holding a small stuffed animal close to her small body. It was a bunny, a new-looking, floppy-eared plush toy whose fuzzy velveteen skin was damp with sweat.

Once the EMTs got her loaded into the ambulance they rushed her to the nearest hospital, St. Mary Mercy, which was not far down Five Mile Road east of the church.

But her injuries were too severe and she was too weak. She died in the emergency department of sepsis resulting from an untreated gunshot wound to the abdomen.

The bullet was still in her. It was a .22 caliber, according to the emergency physician who extracted it.

If she had been taken to the hospital at the time she sustained her wound, she would have survived, the doctor said.

But she wasn't taken to the hospital, she went to the church instead.

And she didn't survive.

Madison was already dead by the time Janey Cahill could get the Kaufmans to the hospital. They had to make a formal identification of Madison, which they did in a private room in the emergency department. Preuss and Cahill stood behind them while the husband and wife gazed down at their daughter's body, covered up to her neck by a sheet. The resident physician stood, head down, on the other side of the bed.

"Why?" Sharon Kaufman wailed.

She collapsed sobbing on a chair in the room. For his part, her husband could only stare mutely at Madison's face, now waxen with the pallor of death. Preuss could not even be sure he had processed what was happening.

"Why?" Sharon cried again. Neither Preuss nor Cahill could give an answer that made sense. When it was clear Stanley was not going to move, Cahill knelt beside Sharon and let the grieving mother sob into her shoulder.

At some point soon they needed to find out if the Kaufmans owned a gun, and if they were the ones who shot her. And that demanded an extraordinary degree of tact. Cahill was the only one Preuss knew who could pull that off.

Without a word spoken between her and Preuss, they left the parents to say goodbye to their daughter in private.

Afterwards, seated together in an interview room in the emergency department, Cahill laid a hand on Sharon's arm. "The details of the injury aren't known yet," she said gently, "but it looks like Madison had been shot with a gun."

Both husband and wife gazed at her, stupid in their grief.

"Forgive me for asking this, but I have to do it, and there's no good time. Is there a gun in your house somebody could have gotten hold of?"

Both Kaufmans denied owning a weapon. Or even knowing anyone who did.

44

Though Madison died in their city, the Livonia district attorney had no problem with Ferndale taking over the prosecution. Sitting in the large interview room at the Shanahan Complex on Friday afternoon, Preuss, Janey Cahill, Jim Cass, and Emma Blalock stared at George Schenk sitting next to his lawyer, none of the investigators knowing quite how to proceed with this man who caused the death of the child they had been searching for during the past week.

Yet he sat in perfect tranquility, stiff-necked and with features squeezed together like the face of a doll made of a dried apple.

Finally, Jim Cass asked the question on everyone's mind. In his rumbling voice, he said, "Why?" He opened his hands in a gesture of bafflement. "That's all I want to know."

Watched carefully by his lawyer, a member of their congregation named Clarence Lundquist with heavy jowls, a brown combover, and a blue business suit, Schenk said nothing for several seconds. He sat with his eyes closed and his hands clasped on the table in front of him.

Praying, no doubt, Preuss thought. Asking the blessings of his Lord for ending Madison Kaufman's life.

Finally Cass sighed heavily and said, "Well, if he's not going to tell me why, at the very least I would like to know what happened here. And how a little girl is dead and your client seems to be at fault."

Lundquist said, "We reject that assignment of blame and I repeat that my client will not make a statement of any kind."

Cass stared at Lundquist with a glum distaste. "I've been a law enforcement officer for most of my adult life and I have never seen anything like this before."

Schenk's eyes snapped open and he said, "You wouldn't understand," in a voice that tried not to be patronizing but failed.

"That's for damn sure," Cass said.

Schenk was about to say something else but Lundquist said, "That's enough," with a restraining hand on his client's arm.

Preuss leaned over and whispered something in Cass's ear. Cass considered briefly, then nodded. "All right, Mr. Schenk. We're done for now."

"What's going on?" Lundquist asked.

"We're finished," Cass said. "For the time being."

The four rose and left the room. What Preuss had whispered to him was that he was certain they would have more success with Carolyn, who was waiting for them in the next room.

Lundquist was also representing Carolyn Schenk. When they were all settled in that room, including Lundquist, Cass began the conversation by growling, "Mrs. Schenk, I highly recommend you get your own attorney. It's not a good idea for you to have the same lawyer who's representing your husband."

"My client is comfortable with the present arrangement," Lundquist said.

"Does she understand the implications?"

"Yes. Let's proceed. The faster we get this over with, the faster my clients can go home."

"I just want to be clear," Cass said. "We're going to get into some things that might not be good for your husband, and I want you to be aware we'll run into issues of conflict of interest."

"My client will not be making any statements to the police," Lundquist said. But Carolyn nodded her understanding of what Jim Cass had just called her attention to.

"I would like to know how this little girl wound up inside your church," Cass asked.

Carolyn gripped her hands together on the table. For a moment Preuss expected her to start praying like her husband, but she was just trying to hold herself together, as though she would fly off in different pieces around the room otherwise.

"I am so very sorry," Carolyn began, and Lundquist said, "Carolyn," but she continued over whatever objections he was going to raise. "No, I have to say this."

"This is against my advice," Lundquist said to Carolyn.

"I am so very sorry," she began again, ignoring the lawyer. "I can't begin to tell you how badly I feel." She started to cry. Cahill materialized a box of tissues, which Cass placed in front of her.

"We all do," Cass said, with as much gentleness in his tone as he could muster. "That's why you need to walk me through how this happened. I'm sure you didn't mean for that little girl to die."

"My client has no comment to make about the events leading up to that tragic death," Lundquist said.

"No," Carolyn said, "I have to get this off my chest. Please, Clarence."

"Let's start with Wednesday night," Cass said. "The first night Madison went missing. Did you see her then?"

"Yes."

"Where and when?"

"I was home," Carolyn began. "Waiting for George to come back from a late job."

"What time was this?"

"Sometime before eight-thirty. He came in about quarter to nine."

"Did he have Madison with him?"

She opened her mouth to say something and Lundquist interrupted at once.

"This conversation is finished. Carolyn," Lundquist said, standing, "we're done here."

"No," she insisted, "I need to make them understand."

"Well, that's not going to happen." Lundquist said.

"Yes," she said, loudly and with more steel in her voice than Preuss had seen before now, "it is."

Lundquist looked at her. It took him by surprise, too.

"I can't carry this around with me for the rest of my life."

To the detectives, the lawyer said, "Give us a minute, would you?"

They stood and filed out of the room.

"Asshole," Cass muttered when they were in the hall. "The fuck'd he think was going to happen when she started to talk?"

In fifteen minutes, Lundquist came out of the room.

"I'm going to withdraw from her case. Carolyn is getting separate counsel."

"How soon can you get new counsel here?" Cass asked.

"I just made a call. My associate is on her way in."

"Carolyn," Emma Blalock said. "You started to tell us what happened on that night."

The detectives were back in the room with Carolyn Schenk, this time with her new counsel, a woman named Cecile Dutka, who looked like Lindquist's twin except for some additional padding around the bust and hips. She sat silently, taking notes.

"I was waiting for George to get home from work. Before he got there, he found Madison on the sidewalk."

"This is all hearsay," Carolyn's lawyer pointed out. "My client only knows this because her husband told her. She has no first-hand knowledge of this event."

Sitting beside Blalock, Cass broke in. "Agreed. Go on."

"I was sitting in the kitchen reading and he came in the back door with Madison in his arms."

"Did you know who it was?" Emma asked.

"Of course."

"What did he say happened?"

"He said he was driving along on his way home and saw her out by herself, then just as he was passing she fell down and he stopped to see what the matter was."

"Did he say where this was?"

"No. He said he thought she just tripped out on the sidewalk and he stopped to see if he could help her. But he saw there seemed to be something wrong with her. So he picked her up and put her in his truck."

"Why would your husband pick up a little girl who was hurt and put her in his truck and bring her to your house instead of taking her home to her parents? Or the hospital? Or calling an ambulance?" Cass asked.

"We didn't know she was hurt, at first."

"You just said you knew who she was, didn't you? You knew who her parents were, didn't you? Why didn't you call them?"

"We did."

"Excuse me?" Cass said.

"The first thing he did was call her parents."

"Your husband called the Kaufmans?"

"Yes," she said. "And spoke to her father."

"Your husband talked with Stanley Kaufman?"

"Yes. And told him his daughter was with us."

Cass sat back, exchanged a dumbstruck look with the equally amazed Preuss, and said, "I'll be dipped in shit."

45

While the others were speechless, Emma Blalock plunged ahead.

"And what did Stanley Kaufman do?"

"He came over to our house."

"And what happened then?"

"We had taken Madison into the living room and laid her down on the sofa. At first we didn't know what the matter with her was. We thought she might have the flu or something. She was moaning as if something was hurting her."

"What did Stanley do when he got there?"

"None of us could figure out what the matter with her was."

"Did anybody think to take her to the hospital?"

"No. And Stanley didn't want to take her home."

"Why not?"

"He said something about wanting her to get better care than her mother would give her."

"So Stanley Kaufman was there and said he didn't want her to come home."

"Yes."

"What happened then?"

"We told him we would get medical attention for her."

"And what did you mean by that?"

"There's a midwife who's a member of our congregation. George called her."

"Carolyn," Emma continued, "did Stanley know you were talking about a midwife when you said you'd call for someone to look at her?"

"I don't know."

"You really don't know? Did your husband mention the midwife?"

"I don't think so."

"What happened then, Carolyn," Blalock prompted.

"George convinced Stanley that we would get good care for her. And then he left."

"So Stanley Kaufman left his daughter in your care?" Cass asked.

"Yes. Remember, we still didn't know what the matter with her was."

To the others he said, "And he filed a missing persons report about his daughter, knowing she wasn't missing."

"And swore to us he didn't know where she was," Preuss said.

"I can't believe his wife knew about this," said Cahill. "I just can't believe her upset was faked."

"Pick him up," said Cass to Blalock.

She left the interview room to order the arrest of Stanley Kaufman.

"Mrs. Schenk," Cass said, "you didn't think there was something wrong about this? Keeping a sick little girl away from her mother?"

Carolyn pursed her lips, as though trying to keep the words inside. Then she said, "We know her mother is not a good woman."

"That's really not your business, is it?" Cass said.

"Wait," Preuss said. "What do you mean by that?"

"We know how that woman carries on with other men."

"How do you know that?"

"We see her out on the street, walking her dog with other men than her husband. We see other men coming to that house. We know what she does in the privacy of her home. Everyone on the street knows."

She was silent for a moment. Then she said, "Besides, my son was close friends with the son of the man she carries on with. They went through school together. And this boy told Jerry all about his father and that woman."

"Is your son's friend Michael Griswold?" Preuss asked.

The other detectives stared at him.

"Yes," she said. "My husband and I didn't want to send that little girl back to such a wicked family."

"And you're telling her father didn't want to his daughter home?" Blalock asked.

"Yes. He said he thought she would be better off out of that household. I know this doesn't make any sense to you people," Carolyn Schenk said, her eyes moving from stony face to stony face in the interview room. "But my husband and I, we have strong beliefs about what we're seeing all around us in Ferndale today. We're seeing values that are perverted and dangerous. And those values are polluting our entire culture."

They all sat still, the group a bit stunned by her revelations.

"Those people are violating God's commandments," she continued. "They're terrible parents, both her and her husband. They let that girl run around by herself at all hours of the day and night. None of this," and here she indicated all of them, implicating them in this mess, "would have come to pass if they were good parents and knew where she was."

Her face was bright red in indignation.

"None of us wanted any harm to come to Madison," she continued. "Just the opposite. George just wanted her to be safe from those people. That's all. We didn't know what was wrong with her."

"But you didn't call an ambulance," Blalock pointed out. "You didn't take her to the hospital, or call the police. Wouldn't those be the responsible things to do if you wanted to help her? Instead you called a midwife, of all people."

"Why didn't you call the police?" Blalock asked.

"The police would have taken her back to her mother. Even her father didn't want that to happen."

The others in the room looked at each other, trying to figure out if anybody else was getting this.

"So what did you do when you saw the blood?" Blalock asked.

"My husband took her up to our spare bedroom and I tried to make her comfortable. At first I didn't know she was bleeding."

"You didn't realize this child was shot?" Cass demanded.

"No. My husband had wrapped her up in a blanket from his truck. But when we got her upstairs I unwrapped her and saw she had blood on her shirt. The first thing I thought of was that her mother had stabbed her with something. And that's why she was out by herself at that hour of the night."

"And then what happened?" Blalock's voice, soft and cooing, unlike Cass's, trying to get Carolyn to unfold the entire story to a roomful of increasingly horrified police.

"So I cleaned her up as best I could. We bundled her up and took her to the church, where the midwife met us."

"Did Stanley Kaufman know she was bleeding?" Blalock asked.

"I don't think so. He had left by then. We didn't notice it till we got her unwrapped from the blanket upstairs."

"This midwife, is she an RN?" Blalock asked.

"No. She's a homeopathist, though."

"What the hell is a homeopathist?" Cass asked.

When Carolyn didn't respond to his gruff question, Preuss said, "It's a form of alternative medicine."

"What's it do?"

"You probably don't really want to know."

"Carolyn, go on," Emma said.

"She cleaned the wound and put a poultice on it."

A poultice, Preuss thought sadly. Like we're living in the middle ages. A poultice of dogbane and pig shit, no doubt.

"And the others in the congregation would pray for her," Carolyn continued. "We took her to the church where the midwife cleaned the wound and we left her to recuperate in peace, though the power of our prayer."

"So this little girl didn't get her seizure medicine because you put a poultice on her and were praying over her?" Preuss asked.

"Her father brought us her medicine. We gave her one dose but the midwife had something else she gave her."

"And you're seriously telling us you didn't know she had been shot?" Cass asked.

"I told you, I thought she'd been stabbed."

"Your midwife doesn't know the difference between a gun-shot wound and a stab wound?" Cass demanded.

Carolyn shook her head.

"When did you do this?" Emma asked.

"That same night we found her."

"Wednesday night?"

"Yes."

"And you took her to the church when?"

"Later that same night."

Cass said, "So when you saw all the police activity over the course of the next few days, and you knew this girl was missing, you didn't think to mention to anyone that you had her?"

"I didn't know what was happening. I was staying with her at the church. We thought she needed rest and spiritual renewal."

"Carolyn," Blalock's soft voice said, "didn't you know you had to do something more to help her? You personally, now. Not the congregation, not your husband. You. Didn't you realize the personal responsibility you had for this little girl?"

The older woman considered the question for several long moments.

Finally she said, "Reverend prayed with us for the wisdom to do the right thing. Which we thought we were doing."

Jim Cass buried his head inside his large hands.

"This isn't easy for you to understand," Carolyn said.

Cass's head snapped up. "You think?" he exploded.

"Carolyn," Preuss said, "I think I speak for all of us when I say we're all having a hard time seeing how you could have let this happen. You're obviously a religious person. But all your actions led to the death of a little girl."

Torn between defending the actions of herself and her husband, the obligations of her faith, and the horror these brought into being, she could only sit mutely and stare at her tightly clasped hands on the table in front of her.

46

They left the interview room and reconvened in a conference room down the hall.

"I never heard of anything like this in all my life," Cass said. "Of all the sick, stupid reasons for a little kid dying, this one takes the cake."

"We now know where Madison's been all this time," Preuss said. "And how she got there. We might not understand it all, but we have a basic sense of what happened."

"Assuming she's telling the truth," Cass put in.

"Sure. Which has to be determined. If she is, the next question is, how did she get shot?"

They agreed that question framed the next stage in the investigation, and spent the next three-quarters of an hour constructing a timeline of events of the case on the whiteboard in the conference room, from the time Madison Kaufman left her house to the minute Martin Preuss discovered her in the church.

Cass said he wanted to go back into the interview room and go over the timeline with Carolyn Schenk to see if she could fill in the events they didn't know yet. Preuss said he wanted to follow up on the shooting aspect. Janey Cahill excused herself to take care of a situation at the high school, so Emma Blalock went back into the interview room with Cass.

Preuss returned to his cubicle. Some events they still didn't know about. Not only who shot her, but precisely when did Schenk find her, and when did they take her to the church? And what happened after she got there?

And why on earth would her father agree to let these nut-jobs take charge of her?

And why did he claim he didn't know where she was?

The thought of them patching her up with the bullet still inside made him want to weep.

He turned away from that thought. For him now the biggest unknown was where that bullet came from, so that's what he tried to concentrate on. This was a whole other mystery. It seemed unlikely that either Schenk could provide any answers.

Now that Madison had been found, Cass's crew would start to back off and the case would return to Ferndale. The child was going to be autopsied, and once they performed ballistics tests on the bullet the emergency doc extracted, they could begin to narrow the search for the gun. And find whoever pulled the trigger.

And answer the other question, why someone would shoot a seven-year-old on the streets of Ferndale's best neighborhood.

He spent the rest of the afternoon writing up a report of the events of the previous night and early morning. At a little after five Emma Blalock came to tell him both Schenks were going to be bound over to the Oakland County Circuit Court on preliminary charges of negligent homicide, depraved indifference to human life, and unlawful restraint.

"For starters," she said. "They'll be held overnight and we'll bring them up for arraignment in the morning. Carnahan's considering charges for the parishioners."

"What about Stanley Kaufman?"

"Cass's throwing the book at him. Filing a false police report, for starters. We're investigating other charges."

She sat in the chair across from his desk. "Makes me sick to think she was in that church this whole time, dying."

He nodded and an uncomfortable silence settled between them, which he did nothing to alleviate. He couldn't help but have bad feelings about her even though he knew the decision to freeze him out earlier had not been hers. She was the messenger, and he held it against her, as unfair as that was.

Finally she said, "You did some good work on this."

"Too little, too late."

"Those poor people are going to have to live with this for the rest of their lives."

"At least they'll have lives. They're ahead of Madison."

"It's so sad."

"Religion gives you funny ideas about how right you are and how wrong everyone else is. And a little girl had to pay for it."

"I'm not sure religion was their whole problem."

"I was in the same room as you were back there. You heard what I heard."

"But I also heard something you didn't," she said. "While Jim was in there with them this afternoon and you were working over here, I slipped out and did some checking on them. Did you know they lost a daughter a few years back?"

"No."

"Freak accident. They were at a park somewhere in the west of the state and some kids were goofing around, playing baseball with tennis rackets and lawn chairs and like that. Evidently somebody took an umbrella and swung it like a baseball bat and the top separated from the base and flew off and caught their daughter right in the eye. It was one of those umbrellas with a pointy tip. Died instantly. Eleven years old."

"How'd you find that out?"

"A deputy brought their church pastor in."

"Ah, the famous Reverend Burkus."

"You met him?"

"If by 'met' you mean he lied to me and then fell to his knees and commenced praying up a storm the instant he saw me last night, then yes, I've had the pleasure."

"I sat with him for a while to get some background on the Schenks and he filled me in. Makes it a little easier to understand why they thought they could save Madison," she reflected. "Or felt like they had to try, anyway."

"Maybe for you. Nothing can explain this away as far as I'm concerned."

She nodded sadly. "I'm just saying, that's all."

With that she stood and started to leave, but paused in the doorway to his cubicle.

"We're putting together a news conference in a little while to announce this. Jim would like you there."

"No thanks."

"You broke the case, Martin. Besides, it might do you some good around your department, if you know what I mean."

"I appreciate the thought. But I'll let you and Cass take the glory. I still have an interview to do before I pack it in."

She pressed her lips together. "See you later, then."

As she turned and walked away, a great weariness settled over him. He had been up for two days straight with only a short nap when he fell asleep on his stakeout. But he needed to keep it together until he made one more visit tonight. He would just be wasting his time at the news conference.

Unless one of the reporters was going to be Shelley Larkin.

He thought of her reaching out to him from her car the other night, and had an immediate urge to see her. Tonight. Right now.

He shook the thought out of his head.

47

"Walter, remember me?"

Walter Szymanski was sitting in the television lounge in the inpatient psychiatric center watching a thin young blonde on "American Idol" screeching at the top of her lungs and calling it singing. Preuss had watched this show with Toby, who enjoyed the hysterics. The singers cracked Preuss up when they referred to themselves as "artists" in the interviews.

When Preuss sat in the empty chair beside him, Szymanski looked away from the screen at him and Preuss knew immediately he was feeling better. Amazing what the right meds could do. Szymanski's eyes were still dark-ringed, but he seemed more of this earth than previously. His eyes connected with Preuss's, instead of skipping away as they had the last time.

Szymanski nodded. "Can't remember your name, though."

Preuss told him and said, "How are you feeling?"

"Better."

"You look a lot better than the last time we talked."

Szymanski was distracted by the television, but he tried to keep a portion of his attention on Preuss.

"I was thinking about what you told me when we had our talk, and I just wanted to let you know how helpful you were."

"That's good."

"Thanks to what you told me, we found that little girl. Remember I asked you about her?"

"That's good, isn't it?" Preuss nodded. Then Szymanski said, "Her parents must be glad."

Preuss didn't mention the shape she was in when they found her, or how shattered the parents were.

"I've been thinking about one of the things you told me and I wanted to ask you about it," Preuss went on. "Can we talk?"

"Sure."

"You told me you were looking out the window and you saw that little girl fall down."

Szymanski nodded.

"And you saw someone put her in a pickup truck. You remember telling me that?"

A great commotion on the television show distracted Szymanski. Preuss reached up and turned the TV off. "I'll turn it on when we're done, okay? So Walter, here's my question. Why were you looking out the window in the first place? Was something happening outside that made you look?"

"I don't know," Szymanski said.

"Because something must have made you decide to look outside. Unless you always just keep an eye on what's going on in the street?"

Szymanski shook his head. "That night it was the voices."

He looked sheepishly at Preuss. "Sometimes I hear voices in my head. And they tell me to do things."

"They told you to go to the window?"

"Yes."

"Was something happening the voices wanted you to see?"

Szymanski thought for a minute and shook his head as though to clear the reception in his brain. "There were noises. Noises outside I was supposed to listen to."

"What kind of noises?"

"Popping sounds."

"Like the sounds of guns going off?"

"Yes. And voices, too."

"Different from the voices telling you to look outside?"

"Yes. Voices from outside."

"What were they saying?"

"I couldn't make out any words."

"Did they sound angry, like they were fighting?"

"I don't think so."

"You definitely heard popping sounds and voices."

"Yes."

"In that order? Popping sounds, then voices?"

"No, first the voices, then the popping."

Preuss considered that. "Could you tell how many voices there were?"

"No."

"Could you tell how close they were?"

He shook his head. Well, Preuss thought, he wouldn't know; on a cold night all the windows and doors would have been closed.

"Anything else you can remember about that night?"

"Voices yelling, then popping sounds . . . then a scream."

"A scream like somebody makes when they get hurt? Like maybe the popping sounds hurt somebody?"

"No, it was more like the sound you make when you feel bad. When you want to cry your eyes out about something."

As it happens, Preuss thought, I know that sound very well.

"That's very helpful, Walter. Is there anything else you can think of?"

Szymanski shook his head. Then he said, "My cousin."

"Claudia?"

Walter rubbed his face with both hands. It appeared to be some kind of ritualized tic. When he was finished, he said, "I think I did something to her."

"I'm afraid you did."

"Is she okay?"

Preuss assured him she was fine, and would come to see him soon. Szymanski sighed and the tension seemed to evaporate from his body.

Preuss turned "American Idol" back on and left him to his program.

48

Stevie Matuzik lay on the couch in his uncle's living room sucking down a Red Bull and clicking through the channels of the television for something to watch. A hundred rotten bullshit channels, he thought, and there's still nothing on.

And it was the worse TV set in the world, an old model somebody gave his uncle once when theirs broke.

He scanned past the infomercials for 1960s music and cooking shows with dumb shits in high chef's hats, and came to the front of the dial again. Looking for something to occupy his mind after his shift at work. *She* had been on, too, but spent most of the night avoiding him.

It pained him deeply.

Glassy-eyed and disinterested, he paused on Channel 2 when he saw a beautiful news reporter, a young black woman who was all big eyes and long straight black hair, doing a report. On screen were her name and the word "Ferndale."

While he waited, he heard her say West Woodland. It caught his attention at once.

That was the street *she* lived on.

He heard the reporter say "died" and "killed. "

He sat up.

Somebody got killed on her street in Ferndale?

On the street where they just were? Near where she lived?

As he watched, the camera moved away from the reporter and panned across the street. He saw her house in the background.

Now Stevie really tried to tune into the reporter, literally tune in her voice, resolve the blather that poured from her mouth into intelligible words the way a static-ridden radio station turned into a clear signal. It was not easy. His own mind was a competing station tuned to a different channel.

She was talking about a little girl who lived on that street. Stevie had trouble understanding her, but it seemed to concern this girl who disappeared off the street near her house at around the same time on the day he and Mobius were there. Who was missing and had just been found. Who had been shot.

And now was dead.

Shot.

And now dead.

The police said the little girl had been shot, then picked up off the street by a neighbor. And then she died. A police detective had found her that day, but it was too late.

As she went on, the television showed scenes outside a hospital, then some images of people milling around West Woodland.

Stevie thought about what he just heard. Shot, and then dead, a couple days after he and Mobius were there.

A terrible fear held him. This was bad. This was very bad.

What should he do? Was there anyone he could talk to? His uncle, maybe?

Could he really trust his uncle enough to talk to him about this?

He thought about that for a full minute, then decided he couldn't. His uncle would go apeshit on his ass, and Stevie didn't want him to know about what he had been up to.

No, there really was nobody to talk to at all about this.

The reporter concluded her report with, "Police are continuing their investigation of how this poor child met with a bullet on that dark November night almost two weeks ago. Denise Wiggins, Channel 2 news, reporting from Ferndale."

He turned the set off and stared into the dead dark screen, unable to form a clear thought about any of this.

Except for a single one, repeated over and over again, chiming in his head like a bell: *shit shit shit shit shit.*

The buzz from the Red Bull merged with his distress at what he had just heard to keep him awake all night. He was already muddled and confused by the events of the past ten days.

By the time he heard his uncle banging around in the morning, Stevie was in an uncontrollable state of sleepless agony.

Thursday, November 13, 2008

49

Gunshots.

Preuss woke up at 9:30 to the sounds of gunfire.

He jumped up and ran to the window before realizing the gunfire was only in his head, the remnant of a dream that was fading even as he thought about it.

As he showered, he reflected on hearing phantom sounds, like the voices Walter Szymanski heard. From everything Preuss knew about hearing voices, the voices Szymanski heard were not phantoms but were real. Scientists had even identified the spot in the brain where the voices originated, he once read. Thanks to the voices in Szymanski's head, they had been able to find Madison, even though it had been too late to save her.

Too late.

Well, that wasn't Szymanski's fault. Without him they might never have found her at all. Who knew what the people at the church would have done with her if Preuss hadn't shown up when he did. Maybe wrap her up and leave her on the doorstep of the hospital in a reed basket.

Or bury her in an unmarked grave in someone's backyard.

If only he had gotten to her even a few hours earlier, he told himself, she could have survived. The doctors might have been able to save her. They said so themselves.

But that meant he would have had to be even sharper, faster, quicker to figure it out. It was only the smallest of consolations that she was still breathing when he walked into the putrid little office, ready to shoot the whole lot of them standing around her cot. Szymanski's tiny effigy had not helped her much, unless it had somehow planted the vision in Preuss's head that led him to her.

He had to keep telling himself he was not the one who fired the gun that shot her. He was not the one who plucked her off the street and then never called for help.

Downstairs after dressing, he ate a bowl of Honey Nut Cheerios standing at the kitchen counter, looking out at the back yard. He had not had a chance to rake the leaves out to the curb for the Monday pickup. Now he was a week behind and the leaves would be harder to move out front.

He rinsed out the cereal bowl and placed it in the dishwasher along with the spoon.

Thus his morning was filled with small thoughts and acts as he tried to come to terms with the loss of Madison Kaufman. And his own inability to save her.

It was late morning by the time he made it in to the station. He knew he would need to speak with Russo at some point, but couldn't face it now. He wasn't as tired as he had been yesterday, but still a great fatigue in his bones deterred him from talking to the chief of detectives.

Settled into his cubicle, he called Cahill's cell but went straight to her voicemail. He asked her to call and walked down to the canteen to fill his coffee cup. There he saw a day shift patrol officer sitting filling out a report. Preuss nodded to him and accepted his "Nice work" as gracefully as he could, knowing his work was not nice. It was too slow and too plodding, and a child died as a result. It was not good police work.

He said thanks anyway.

After lunch he returned to West Woodland, where a contingent of deputies lingered at the Schenk house. No official cars around the Kaufman home. They would still need to speak with them to rule them out as the people who shot their daughter, but Cahill was convinced neither parent was involved, despite the monumentally bad decisions Stanley had made, and Preuss agreed. The answer had to be elsewhere.

He parked further up West Woodland from the Kaufman home and walked down the south side of the street, retracing Madison's steps. He turned right on Livernois and stopped at the point where her trace disappeared, knowing here was where Walter Szymanski, Wayne White, and George Schenk saw her fall.

He stood at approximately the spot where she would have stood, and got down on his knees so he would see what she would see. The cold of the sidewalk pressed through his knees and he was struck by the sensations the frightened, cold, hurt little girl must have felt, out by herself in the dark.

From that perspective, it was a bigger and more dangerous world than the child could have imagined in her too-short life.

He had to swallow the anger that burned in his chest at the thought she could have been saved. Preuss knew in his heart she was not dead because of him; she was dead because her father and George and Carolyn Schenk did not call 911. If that had happened, she would be playing on this spot today.

And more: if the person who fired the shot that tore into her had been standing on some other street, or had not had access to a firearm, she would also still be alive.

Again he thought of Szymanski and the popping sounds, which Preuss assumed was gunfire.

Was it reasonable to assume those sounds were gunfire, and if so the bullet that dropped Madison came from that flurry of shots?

But why would she be targeted? Preuss had not been able to find anyone with enough of a grudge against the Kaufmans to make them want to kidnap their daughter, so why would someone have wanted to hurt her that much?

If somebody had not wanted to kill her deliberately, then either she was shot accidentally or she was shot randomly. So she got in the way of a bullet meant for someone else, or someone passing by had been looking for a target and found her. Either way she was the unluckiest girl in town.

Regardless, this would be extraordinarily hard to solve. In the past few days, the Sheriff's traffic stops had not found anyone who knew anything about Madison, so he wasn't hopeful another canvas of the street would show anything. Still, what else did they have? They would have to ask different questions, and maybe they would get the different answers that would let them reconstruct that evening.

He took a sheet of paper from his notebook inside his coat pocket and made a sketch of the street and the houses. He drew squares to represent houses, and inside the squares he drew the names of the people he could remember off the top of his head. He would have to go to the reports to discover the names of the others who lived around the scene and fill in the diagram later.

He stood, brushing leaves from his pants, and took off his jacket and placed it in a heap on the ground where he had been standing, where Madison last stood. He walked across Livernois to Walter Szymanski's house. He stood on the side stoop so he could see what Szymanski would have seen that night when the voices told him to look outside.

He studied the scene up Woodland and down Livernois from that angle. He wished there could have been a ballistics report; they would never know exactly how Madison had been standing when she was shot and went down, but it would have been helpful to get a feel for the wound ballistics so they would have a notion of where the shot that killed her might have been fired from.

Maybe the medical examiner could give him that when she did the autopsy: the angle of the shot. They might get an idea of where the shooter had been standing when he or she fired the fatal shot. Unless the Schenks and their accomplices had monkeyed with the wound enough to ruin any evidence they could glean from that, too, as they had discarded the girl's clothes.

He caught himself.

No fatal shot had been fired because the shot didn't kill her.

What killed her was the Schenks' criminal effort to "save" her from her parents, or from the larger culture, or, at some deeper level of George Schenk's consciousness, to go back in time to save his daughter from the awful thing that happened to her.

He held his crude map up before him and tried to factor in Szymanski's sight lines, a guess on the ballistics from the gun, and

Madison's last position, and hoped that it would all add up a tentative theory of what happened. Was he missing something?

Stupid question.

What wasn't he missing?

As he walked up and down Woodland he tried to put together the few facts he had. From the emergency department doc he knew there was one entrance wound, in her abdomen. So Madison was shot from the front with a .22. It would be very hard to know how far away from her the shooter was standing. Her clothes were gone, so there would be no way of knowing if scorch marks or powder burns would indicate a close-up shooter. Maybe the M.E. could figure out from the depth of the wound how far away the gun might have been. Though if Walter Szymanski did not see anyone standing near her when she went down, except for Wayne White, who was behind her, that would mean the shot had to have come from some distance, out of Szymanski's sight. It would have needed a high-powered load to travel that far.

He walked back down Livernois and climbed onto Walter Szymanski's back stoop and surveyed the scene again.

He stared at the pile his coat made across Livernois marking the spot where Schenk had picked up Madison. What if she had not been walking straight down the sidewalk when she was shot? What if she stopped in front of the house cattycorner to Szymanski's, perhaps if someone there called her name, and she turned toward the house and was shot from that angle? Szymanski had not mentioned anything about that, but maybe he hadn't been able to tell them the whole story?

If several shots had been fired, and Madison had been standing in that position, where were the other bullets?

From the porch he looked over the house across the street, in fact the houses to the right of the one across the street and the houses to the left, all the way across Livernois. He walked up to each one and looked as carefully as he could in every window, in the cedar shingles and brick and vinyl siding of each of the houses, but saw no indication of any damage or holes that might have been made by a bullet.

No, this was wrong. Szymanski would have known if Madison had been shot while standing facing his house. He seemed clear enough that she had been walking straight south down the street. That would mean she had been shot by someone in front of her, not to the side. It had to be someone further south on Livernois.

He walked down Livernois in that direction. He tried to examine the area, but by now the late afternoon light was too uncertain for him to see much of anything. He would have to come back in the morning.

He retrieved his coat from the sidewalk and returned to the station. He tore a large sheet of paper from a chart in the conference room and taped it to the glass half-wall in his cubicle. He reproduced the sketch he had drawn of West Woodland, and got the names of the other neighbors who had been interviewed in the earlier canvases and wrote in as many as he could. Some empty boxes still remained, which meant people had not been home for the officers to question.

He added it to the list in his notebook. He would leave a copy of the diagram for the administrative assistant and ask her to check the city records department to fill in the blank boxes when she came in the next morning.

He would leave this scene till then.

Friday, November 14, 2008

50

Paul Horvath cornered him before he could get started on West Woodland in the morning. A woman on Flowerdale south of Nine Mile had called in a complaint, Horvath explained. She said her neighbor was videotaping her as she showered in her home, and Horvath wanted Preuss on it.

After talking with the woman who had made the complaint, Preuss went to speak with the man next door, who wasn't home. The woman said the man worked as an electrician at Providence Hospital in Southfield. Preuss located him and spoke with him in an empty office at the hospital.

To his surprise, the suspect folded immediately and confessed what he had been up to.

Once when she was called out of town unexpectedly, the woman next door had given him a key so he could feed her cat while she was gone, he told Preuss, and he used the opportunity to enter her home and plant a wireless camera in her bathroom.

Preuss put him under arrest and they went back to his house, where the detective seized the man's computer. It turned out to contain videos of the woman showering and using the bathroom. He had uploaded these to the Internet.

By the time he got the guy processed there were still a few hours of daylight left, so he drove over to West Woodland. He sat in his car going over his small diagram of the scene, which the admin had filled in for him while he was busy with the peeping Tom. Then he walked up one side of Woodland from Livernois to Pinecrest and down the other side. He tried out scenarios in his mind, locating the shooter in different places.

Then he walked down Livernois all the way to where it ended at Breckenridge, just before it entered a shopping center. He walked up the other side, playing his attention over the homes and Episcopal and Ukrainian churches that lined the street.

He paused again at the location where Madison had been picked up by Schenk, which was presumably where she had taken the bullet, too. He gazed all the way south on Livernois, still running over possibilities in his mind. The shots must have come from down the street, there was no other way to imagine it. So where would they have originated?

He walked down the street again, stopping the dog walkers and asking them if they remembered being out on the Wednesday a little over ten days ago when Madison was hit. It was a stretch, and nobody could remember hearing gunfire that long ago.

He stood at the end of the block on the same side of the street as Madison had been, then crossed over the grassy median in the middle of Livernois to the other side of the street and looked back at where she would have been standing when she fell. Then he went down another block and did the same thing: looked back at where Madison would have been standing, and crossed over to the other side of the street, zig-zagging to get different perspectives on the scene as he worked his way down the street.

At one point, in the middle of one of the blocks down Livernois and the same side of the street as Madison had stood, he noticed a street sign that read Deaf Child Area. It looked wrong. The top was bent backward. He came up close underneath it and saw a small channel in the metal. As he studied it he realized it was the kind of mark a bullet might.

He stood back and raised his hand to sight an imaginary weapon at the sign. He stood underneath to check its angle. But the angle wasn't right for someone to stand underneath and fire, so he moved further south on Livernois and kept sighting his handgun.

He discovered with a cold shock that someone standing at one spot could have fired at that sign and, if the shooter had missed, or moved the gun slightly, the bullet would have gone right to where Madison Kaufman had been standing.

He lowered his hand and stared at the scene, every element of which seemed to have clicked into place in a way that changed the entire landscape. Everything took on an intense clarity, even in the gathering dusk.

He shifted his gaze slightly, still staring from the perspective that he had assumed, and realized if the person shooting the gun had shifted it a little to the right, another bullet could have been fired right into the house directly across the street from Walter Szymanski.

He studied his diagram. He extended the lines that represented Livernois on the paper, and starred the location where he was standing. Here's where it happened.

X marked the spot where the bullet that hit Madison Kaufman originated.

Looking down the street, he thought there might be four possible targets. Someone was trying to shoot at Madison, which he couldn't imagine, or the Deaf Children sign, the house across from Szymanski, or at someone or something unknown that was in the sightlines.

Turning the corner on her walk, Madison Kaufman had blundered into the wrongest place at the worst time, just as a bullet had been fired directly at her.

Dumb, stupid, fatal bad luck meant the girl would never have a chance to live her life. If her mother had come home on time, or the argument between Sharon and Stanley had taken place on a slightly different schedule, or not at all, or if Madison herself had decided to slip away ten seconds earlier or later, none of this would have happened. Madison Kaufman would be at home now, playing in her bunny room.

Reflecting on that, he searched his pockets and came up with a mechanical pencil that was out of lead. He placed it on the ground with the point facing up the street and walked up to the house across from Szymanski's. Maybe he would get lucky and find the homeowner waiting for him.

He rang the bell, but got no answer. He stepped back and examined the exterior carefully, front and side, top to bottom. The exterior was completely clad in a cream-colored vinyl siding, out of place in the arts-and-crafts architecture of the rest of the block. Under the siding was probably clapboard, like several of the houses further up the street. Preuss could see no obvious holes or other defects that could have been caused by a bullet.

But he did notice what appeared to be a small hole in one of the windows on the top floor. Imperceptible unless you were looking for it, like maybe a .22 had found its way through the window? A Tot Finder fire safety decal was stuck on the pane of glass, and the bullet hole—if that's what it was—went right through it. That would be what saved the glass from shattering.

If a bullet had made the hole, it was likely still in the house, he reflected, lodged in the ceiling or the wall, depending on the angle of its trajectory.

What else could it have been if not a bullet? Preuss felt certain it would be from the same gun that shot Madison Kaufman. Jim Cass's techs would need to comb through the upstairs to prove the connection, but he felt in his gut it would match.

He walked back down the street, retracing his steps and turning every few feet to check on his theory about what direction the bullet came from. Back where he left his pencil to mark the spot, the ground was covered with bright red and yellow maple leaves from a massive tree in the side yard of the house he stood next to. Starting from where he thought the shooter might have stood, he sifted through the leaves in widening circles.

After forty-five minutes the darkness settled in and he gave up. Cass's tech crew might have better luck in finding a spent shell casing. He was mostly interested in having his theory of the shooting proven, not identifying a shooter. Besides, getting usable fingerprints from a spent shell casing was almost impossible because the hot shell burns off the oils and acids that aid identification.

Back at the nearly empty police complex he did a computer search of the property. That was more important at this moment. Whoever lived there, or even the home itself, might have been the target for the bullet that instead found Madison Kaufman.

51

The owner of the house on West Woodland was listed as Milton Stuart.

Another search pulled up addresses of two Milton Stuarts, one in Bloomfield Hills and the other in Alma, Michigan.

Preuss tried the Bloomfield Hills phone number and got the man's wife on the line. She told him her husband was an artist working a shift at the Lawrence Street Gallery, a small art cooperative on Woodward in Ferndale. Preuss got hold of him there and learned Stuart's ex-wife lived in the West Woodland house with their daughter. The wife's name was Alison Stuart, he told Preuss. And if Preuss wanted to talk with her right away, his best bet would be to try the restaurant she owned, Lord Chumley's in Madison Heights.

Milton Stuart seemed not at all curious why a police detective was looking for his wife.

Lord Chumley's was a steak house on the busy corner of John R and Twelve Mile Road in Madison Heights. It was a low Tudor building with a brick, stucco, and heavy timber façade set off from its intersection behind a row of boxwood hedges. The parking lot was packed with Happy Hour and early dinner patrons as Preuss pulled in and drove around looking for a space. Finally he pulled up in a fire lane and stuck the Ferndale Police Department card on his dash.

Inside the place was mobbed, with people standing two deep at the bar and a ragged line stretching out the door waiting for tables, mostly young professional types, the men with hair moussed into a point at the center of their heads, the women as flashy as tropical birds. All yelling as if the whole world were interested in what they had to say. The restaurant theme was Olde English, with prints of horses and what Preuss assumed was the English country-side.

Preuss elbowed his way up to the podium, where a tall, painfully thin young man stood beside a sweet-faced young woman who flashed him a toothy and practiced smile in expectation of re-ceiving his name when he walked up. He held up his badge and asked for Alison Stuart. The woman's expression changed entirely, as if a cloud had passed across the bright sunshine of her smile.

The young man standing with her, whose name tag said his name was Renn, motioned for Preuss to follow him into the main dining room.

He looked around but didn't spot the manager so he stopped a busboy with a shaved head and a load of dirty dishes in a plastic tub and asked if he had seen Alison. The busboy shook his head and continued on toward the kitchen.

"I don't see her," Renn said to Preuss. "Usually she's out on the floor at dinner time. Maybe she's in her office."

Preuss followed Renn's narrow white-shirted back through a set of swinging doors into the kitchen and past the food prep area to an office near metal racks filled with huge cans of tomato sauce. Renn knocked on the door and opened it without waiting for a re-sponse from inside, which he wouldn't have heard anyway because of the din of cooking behind them.

Alison Stuart was on the phone behind a small desk clut-tered with invoices. She held up a finger for Renn, who indicated through hand signs that Preuss wanted to see her. She pointed to-ward the hard chair on the other side of her desk. It was a tiny of-fice, crammed with cardboard boxes and a computer on a work desk behind her. On shelves on either side of her were stacked cata-logues and thick binders standing on their ends.

Alison Stuart herself had a large head with dark eyes and prominent, almost Native American features and ruddy skin, and glossy waves of black hair that shook as she listened to her caller.

She wore a dark pinstriped jacket over a white blouse and looked to be in her middle forties.

Renn nodded to Preuss and disappeared, closing the office door behind him as he left, muting the restaurant clamor.

Finally she hung up and Preuss identified himself. "What can I do for you?" she asked, smiling expectantly. He did not seem to be having his usual wet blanket effect on her.

That would change. "I'm investigating events surrounding the disappearance of a little girl in Ferndale."

As he predicted, her animated face turned grave at once. "Of course. That poor child lives down the street from me. Have you found her?"

"I guess you haven't seen the news in the past few days."

"What have I missed? Did she turn up?"

"We found her early Wednesday."

"I don't know if I want to hear this."

"I'm sorry to say she didn't make it."

The woman's high color went ashen. She put a hand to her throat. "She's *dead?*"

"Yes. Did you know her?"

"Just to say hello to. I've seen her around the neighborhood." She sat back in her chair, stunned. "Oh, her poor parents. That poor child." She shook her head, setting her cascading hair in motion. "Do you know what happened?"

"She died of an infection from a gunshot wound. I'm trying to find out where that bullet came from."

"And how can I help?"

"It's possible a gun was fired in the direction of your house on the night Madison disappeared. I think she caught one of the bullets."

"Someone was shooting at my house?"

"At this point, it's more accurate to say someone was firing in the direction of your house. We can't say for certain your house was the actual target."

"Why would someone do that?"

"That's exactly what I'm here to find out. We don't see any reason for Madison herself to have been the target. It may also have been a completely random event, but first I'm looking into the possibility someone was shooting at your house."

"Somebody shot at my house? When was this?"

"It would have been roughly 8:30 on the evening of Wednesday the fifth. Do you remember by any chance if you were home?"

"I'm quite sure I was here. I'm here almost every night. If I take a night off, it's usually Monday or Tuesday, never Wednesday. How do you know somebody shot at my house?"

He explained his activities earlier. "How late are you usually here?"

"We shut down the kitchen at ten, and I'm out by midnight, by the time I get the finances straightened out and split the tips for the staff."

"I understand you have a daughter?"

"Yes. Linda. Eighteen going on forty."

"Was she home?"

"Don't know. But I can find out for you."

She extracted a folder from one of the piles on the desk and checked through timesheets. "She works here," the woman explained as she searched. "One of the servers."

She ran a finger down a column on a spreadsheet. "It looks like she was off that night. Whether she was home or not is another story. Give me a sec and I'll find out."

She stood and squeezed past Preuss in the tight office and opened the door to call out to someone in the kitchen, "Carlos! Find Linda, would you please?"

Giving Preuss a pained smile, the woman sat back behind her desk.

"We'll need to check inside, too, for any evidence," Preuss said. "The room with the hole in the window was on the second floor front, the one with a Tot Finder decal."

"That's my daughter's bedroom."

They waited for her daughter in silence for a few moments, then she said, "Did you have dinner yet? There's a rib special tonight. When we're done here I'll set you up at a table. On the house."

Preuss realized he was starved, but shook his head. "No, thanks. As soon as we're finished, I'll need to get going."

"You sure? I can get you an order to go."

The smells from the kitchen were making his head spin.

When he didn't immediately reject the offer, she jumped up again and went out into the food prep area and shouted, "Carlos! Get me an order of ribs to go. There you are!"

Preuss turned to see a young woman rushing into the food prep area in her uniform of white shirt, black slacks, and white apron wrapped around slender hips.

"What?" the young woman said with ill-concealed annoyance. "I got an order up."

"Come in here for a minute," the woman said, and the girl stepped into the office. Preuss stood and turned toward her as much as he could in the cramped space.

"Detective Martin Preuss, Ferndale police," he said.

She eyed him warily.

"He wants to ask you some questions," Alison Stuart said.

"What about?" She had her mother's dark looks but with short spiky hennaed hair and a wide disapproving mouth.

"A week ago last Wednesday," Preuss said. "Fifth of November. Your mother told me you were off. Can you remember if you were home that night?"

"Maybe. Probably. I don't know."

That about covered all the options, Preuss thought.

"Linda," her mother said, with a sharp edge to her voice. "Were you home or weren't you?"

"A week ago Wednesday? I guess I was. For a little while."

Defensive. Teen-aged.

"Did you leave to go out at some point?" Preuss asked.

"Yeah. I was around early in the evening. Then I went clubbing with friends later on." She said it with a trace of defiance, as if her mother had forbidden it but she did it anyway.

"What time was that?"

"I don't remember." Seeing her mother aiming daggers at her, Linda said, "Maybe around nine. I don't know. It's already almost two weeks ago. How'm I supposed to remember?"

"So you might have been home around 8:30?"

"I might have been."

"Did you hear or see anything out of the ordinary?"

"Like what?"

"I don't know," Preuss said, "you tell me. Anything that doesn't usually happen? Anything you saw or heard?"

She thought for a few seconds, then shook her head.

"Maybe a sound like firecrackers," he prompted.

"Firecrackers? In November?"

"When they first hear it, sometimes people think gunfire sounds like firecrackers."

"Gunfire? Seriously? That's what you're looking for?"

"Did you hear something like that?"

"No," Linda said. "I don't remember anything like that."

"Was Keith with you?" her mother asked suddenly.

Linda raised her upper lip in a sneer, though whether for Keith or her mother wasn't clear. "No," she said. Still defensive, Preuss thought. And lying. She was a poor liar.

Something her mother no doubt already knew. "I told you I didn't want you seeing him anymore."

The girl made a guttural sound in her throat.

Alison explained to Preuss, "Keith is this *man* she's been seeing. I don't approve of him, and my daughter knows it. He was her history teacher in high school."

Preuss said nothing.

"There's nothing *wrong* with him," Linda complained. "You just don't like him because he's *older* than me."

"No," Alison said, "I don't like him because he's married with a little kid and he's got no business hanging around a teen-aged girl."

"You don't even *know* him," Linda said.

"I thought it didn't matter because you're not seeing him."

"It doesn't," Linda said. "And I'm *not*. God!"

Linda turned toward Preuss. "Is there anything else you need? I have to get my order. If that's all right with my boss," she said snarkily, aimed at her mother.

"We're finished for now," Preuss said. "If I have any more questions I'll be in touch." He gave her a business card. "If you think of anything, give me a call?"

"Sure," she said, and left the office.

Alison resumed her seat behind her desk. "Got any kids?" she asked. Preuss nodded. "Then you know how it is."

"I have boys," Preuss said. "It's a little different."

"Boys are easier to deal with, believe me. Tonight when we get home I'll have another talk with her. When she's calmer. I'll let you know if she says anything more."

"Thanks."

"How old are your boys?"

"Twenty-one and seventeen," Preuss said, and stood up so he wouldn't have to say any more about his own dysfunctional family.

The woman brought her hands down hard on the desk top. End of subject. She stood. Back to the world she could control.

"Let's get you that order of ribs," she said. "And look: let me take care of this, okay? They're on the house."

"No," Preuss said, "they're not."

As he pulled into his driveway, he felt a twinge of guilt that he and the investigation had moved on so quickly from Madison's bereaved parents. But maybe now it was best to leave them alone so they could come to terms with their grief. He assured himself that whatever he could do to help them get closure on this would be all to the good.

He brought the delicious-smelling carry-out container into the kitchen and ripped the plastic wrap away from the foil tray. The rich, succulent, glistening deep-brown slab of ribs looked and smelled as magnificent as Alison Stuart had promised.

Preuss ate two ribs, fall-off-the-bone tender, sweet and spicy, the best he had ever had, and stood staring down into the tray and realized his appetite had been slaked. This was all he could handle.

So he topped the tray with aluminum foil, placed it in the nearly empty refrigerator, and climbed the stairs to bed. Before dropping off to sleep he replayed the interview with Alison Stuart and her daughter. Then he saw in his mind's eye Toby's gorgeous face smiling up at him. And then Jason's surly glare.

And then, improbably, Shelley Larkin's wry smile.

He sat up and found her number on his cell phone. The call went into her voicemail, and he disconnected without leaving a message. He'd try later. The call list on her phone would record the effort anyway.

He lay back down and in thirty seconds his own cell rang.

Shelley Larkin calling back.

"Hey," she said. Her voice was fuzzy with sleep.

"Hey."

"You just called?"

"Did I wake you?"

"You did."

"Sorry."

"Not a problem." A deep, sleepwarm sigh. "What's up?"

"I just wanted to say hi."

"That's sweet. So I missed you at the news conference announcing the bad news."

"I thought I'd catch the flu for that one."

"Jim Cass had good things to say about you. Said you broke the case. Were your ears burning?"

"Don't want to talk about it. How's your story coming?"

"It's going to be good. I think you'll approve." Another sigh from her, mixed with the sound of rustling bedclothes.

"It's like we've both been looking for her," she said, "in our own ways."

"Let's hope your search ends better than mine."

"Me too."

Another silence. They listened to each other's soft breathing.

"I'm glad you called," she said, her voice husky and close.

"I've been thinking about you," he admitted.

"I've been thinking about you, too."

"I thought I'd try you in case you were awake."

"I wasn't."

"We've established that fact." He heard her breathy snicker and smiled despite himself.

He looked at the red numbers of the clock on the bookcase. "Can we meet?" he asked.

"Right now?"

"There are a couple of twenty-four hour places on Woodward. I'd like to see you."

"I'd love to. But I have an early interview in the morning. I have to be fresh for it. If we meet now neither one of us will get any sleep tonight and I'll be useless."

That gave him a thrill in the pit of his stomach, rich with the promise of something that had been missing in his life. For years. All he could say was, "Maybe another time."

She picked up the disappointment in his voice. "Another time for sure. Promise me?"

"I promise."

"I want to hear about your sons."

"Sure. Toby lives in a group home in Berkley. Jason's the one I was talking about who disappeared."

"I want to hear about them. I want to know everything about you."

"Likewise."

Another companionable silence stretched until he said, "I guess we should say good night."

"Thanks for the call. Talk to you again soon?"

After they hung up he lay floating in the melody of her voice until sleep overcame him.

52

Linda Stuart unlocked the door of her car, parked as usual at the far end of the lot outside the restaurant. Soundlessly Stevie Matuzik stepped out of the shadows and she jumped and shrieked.

He stood before her, trembling in the cold.

"What are you doing here?" she demanded. "You scared the shit out of me!"

"I gotta talk to you."

"Not now. I have to be someplace."

"This is important."

She sighed and they got into her car. She lit a cigarette from the pack of Merit Ultra Lights she kept in the console.

"Who was that guy?"

"What guy?"

"That guy you were talking to in your mother's office."

She shrugged. "Some cop."

"What he want?"

"Nothing to do with you, Jesse James."

"I'm serious, man. What he want to know?"

She took a quick puff of her cigarette and blew out an impatient stream of smoke. "Said he wanted to know if I heard anybody shooting a gun around my house last week."

"What'd you tell him?"

"I told him no, I didn't hear anything. Why? What's it to you?" Before he could answer she demanded, "Look, are you going to make a habit of this?"

"What?"

"Ambushing me at my car every night."

"I don't ambush you every night."

"What do you call this?"

His insides roiled with fear and anger and confusion. Finally he said, "You should be with me."

"Jesus Christ! How many times have we been through this? There isn't anything between us. There isn't any 'us.'"

"There is. There has to be."

"Why?"

"Because I love you! And I want you to love me."

In frustration she turned away and opened the car window to pitch the cigarette out. "Please get out so I can get going."

"No."

"Leave my car right now, Stevie."

"No!"

"I swear to God, that cop gave me his card, you don't get out of my car this second I'll call him and tell him it was you who fired those shots outside my home."

"No!" he cried, panicked, and as she opened her purse to look for the card he tried to grab her hands, and when she pushed him away they began to tousle and it got out of hand at once and he began to push her and then punch her and before he knew it he was raining blows on her and then she was huddled, cowering and weeping, against the driver's side door.

His heart racing, he burst out of the car and ran around to her side and threw open the door and wrestled her into the back seat, where she lay sobbing.

He jumped behind the wheel and gunned the motor and peeled out of the parking lot.

He was shaking violently in the sudden chill of what he had just done.

And was about to do.

Saturday, November 15, 2008

53

Preuss spent the early part of Saturday making calls.

Janey Cahill, to let her know the results of his field work and interview the day before. She said she would pass it along to Jim Cass, with a recommendation to get the techs out to the Stuart house.

The medical examiner's office about the progress of Madison's autopsy, which was delayed due to cutbacks on overtime.

Shelley Larkin, to say hello and make plans to meet once she was out from under her deadline on Madison's story.

After lunch he went by West Woodland, and discovered the crime scene techs were already there, scouring the Stuart house. They started with Linda Stuart's room, and had already pulled a slug from the ceiling there. It was probably going to be too damaged to be useful in matching with the bullet from Madison's body, but it helped bolster Preuss's theory of the shooting.

Alison Stuart was not there, but as he was leaving she pulled up in her Honda. He went to meet her, and when he saw the look of distress on her face he expected her to ream him out about the upset to her home.

Instead, she said, "Have you heard from Linda?"

It caught him by surprise. "No. Why?"

"She didn't come home last night. She hasn't called and I'm terribly worried."

"Is that not like her?"

"No, totally unlike her. She talks trash to me, but she's a responsible girl. She always lets me know where she is."

He followed her back inside the house. His first thought was that a rebellious teenager who dropped from sight for a night was not necessarily a problem. But after Madison he didn't want to take any chances, and the woman was beside herself with worry.

Then, too, Preuss realized, it might not be a coincidence the investigation was centering on her home at the same time as her daughter vanished.

They sat in the living room and he took the information from her. She just came from the restaurant, where she was due to work a lunch shift.

"Nobody there's heard from her," she said. "And that's not like her, either, missing a shift. She never misses a shift except when she's sick."

He took the name of the man whom her mother thought Linda had been seeing, the history teacher, and told her he would look into it immediately. He wanted to start at the restaurant, which is where she'd last been seen the night before.

"Meantime," he said, "if she shows up, or you hear from her, let me know right away."

She nodded and ran a hand through her abundant hair, pushing it back from her face.

Another missing child. Another frantic parent. Is there no end to this?

"Have you heard from Linda yet?"

Renn was standing at the podium in the entrance when he walked in. He forced an anxious breath out. "No, and we're all getting pretty worried."

"I want to ask some of the staff about when they last saw her. She was working last night?"

"Yes."

"And nobody's seen her since her shift ended?"

"I have no idea," Renn said. "Alison was just here and I thought she asked most everybody."

"I'd like to talk to them again. Can you give me a hand?"

"Sure."

Renn went to find someone to stand at the podium and then guided Preuss around the restaurant for the next forty-five minutes as they asked everyone on the floor and in the kitchen whether anybody had heard from Linda. No one had.

"Anybody who was working last night but isn't here now?"

"Let's go back to the office and check the schedule."

He led Preuss into Allison's office, where he sat at her chair and flipped through the timesheets.

"Yes," Renn said, "a couple people worked last night but they're off today."

"Could you find me their phone numbers?"

Renn wrote down the names and numbers for him. Preuss replaced him in the chair.

In the third call he spoke with the young woman who had been on the host's podium last night. Cathy Gabilondo.

"Yeah," she told him, "I saw her after work."

"After her shift, you mean, or later on someplace?"

"No, right after her shift. We walked out to our cars together."

"Did she say where she was going?"

"Home. She said she was beat. She worked a double shift."

"Did you see her get into her car and leave?"

"No. I didn't see either of them leave. I took off first."

"Either of them?"

"She was talking with Stevie."

"Who's Stevie?"

"One of the dishwashers. I don't know his last name."

"They were talking together when you left?"

"Yes. I saw him get into her car. Why, did something happen?"

"Linda hasn't been seen or heard from since last night."

"Oh shit."

"But you definitely saw her with this kid?"

Instead of answering, she said, "You're that policeman who was at the restaurant, aren't you?"

"Right."

"That's funny," she said, "because I was almost going to call the police last night."

"What happened?"

"When I was getting into my car I saw Stevie come up to her. There was something about the way she looked when she saw him. She jumped, like, when he came up next to her. Like he scared the crap out of her."

"Was there some problem between the two of them?"

"There might have been. They got in her car and it looked like they started to argue."

"Could you tell what was going on?"

"I could just tell by their gestures and the way they were talking to each other, it looked like it was getting pretty heavy. They were sitting right under a light pole so I could see it clearly."

"Why didn't you call for help?" Preuss asked.

"I guess I didn't want to get involved in whatever was happening. You never know what's going on between those two."

"Are you saying they have a relationship?"

"There's *something* going on between them, I'll tell you that. And I guess I just didn't want to do anything that would piss off Stevie."

"Why's that?"

At that, Cathy Gabilondo snorted. "The boy's a freak, you want to know the truth."

"Why do you say that?"

"Just because of the look in his eye," she said. "He's one scary little dude."

When he hung up from her, he asked Renn to find him Stevie's address. His name was Stevie Matuzik, and he lived in southeast Ferndale. From the SUV he called Cahill and told her what was happening.

"I know this kid," she said. "I've had some run-ins with him. Mostly petty shit, fights around school and so forth. Quick to anger, poor self-control, lousy self-image."

"We only see one or two hundred of those," Preuss said.

"He's actually a sad case. Smart kid, but a hair-trigger temper."

"Bad combination."

"He lives with his uncle, who's a piece of work himself."

"Where are his parents?"

"As I recall, mom took off for parts unknown a few years back, dad's on a long vacation at Jackson. Felony conviction, I'm thinking."

"I got his address from his personnel file at the restaurant." He rattled it off to her.

"Meet you at his house," she said.

54

Stevie Matuzik's home in southeast Ferndale was a bungalow, like all its neighbors, neat and tidy and tiny. A rusted Olds 98 that had once been burgundy was parked in the driveway. While sitting in front of the house, Preuss ran the plates. The car was registered to Ralph Matuzik.

Preuss rapped on the screen door and shortly the inside door opened on a tall man. He had long grey hair pulled back into a pony tail from a high forehead and a black leather vest over a black Harley Davidson tee shirt. At each side of his long, grizzled face were long sideburns and two deep trenches that may once have been dimples. Once he would have been handsome.

He gave them a wary look that barely restrained a sneer. Obviously familiar with law enforcement, Preuss thought.

Cahill said, "Ralph Matuzik?" She held up her badge, in which he had only the slightest interest, and she introduced herself and Preuss. "Mr. Matuzik, is Stevie home?"

His brown eyes disappeared into a mass of wrinkles as he squinted at them. "What's this about?"

"Is he home, sir?"

"No."

"When did you last see him?"

"Is he in some kind of trouble?"

"He may be. Do you know where he is?"

"You people never just want to talk to somebody. Unless they're in some trouble or other."

Cahill said, "We can just as easily have this conversation at the station, Mr. Matuzik. It's entirely up to you."

"Whoa. The fuck did *I* do?"

"Let's take a trip down there and we can tell you all about it," Preuss said. He made a "come on" gesture with his hand as Cahill went to open the screen door. Matuzik instinctively pulled back into the hallway.

"Hang on, there," he said, "you don't have no reason to take me in."

"Material witness to unlawful restraint of a minor, for starters," Cahill said. Preuss was already on the cell phone, calling dispatch to request a patrol car.

"Hang on just a fucking minute here," Matuzik said, holding up his hands to mollify them. "Tell me what you want and I'll tell you what you want to know."

Preuss closed his phone. "How about you start by telling us when was the last time you saw your nephew?"

"Not since yesterday. That's why I'm home now. I took the day off to look for him. He never stays out all night. I'm worried."

"You've been out looking for him, have you?" Cahill said.

"I haven't found him anywhere."

"What do you do for a living, sir?" Preuss asked.

"I'm a pressman. I work in a print shop over in Warren."

"Does Stevie have a cell phone?" Preuss asked.

"Does it look like we can afford a cell phone?"

"Stevie might have his own."

"Stevie doesn't have a cell phone."

"Point is," Cahill said, "it's important we talk to him. He'd do himself a favor by getting in touch with us." She handed him a business card. "You hear from him, you have him call us. Or you call us and tell us where he is. Understand, sir?"

"Look," Matuzik said, "can you tell me what this is all about? I'm his legal guardian. If he's done something wrong, I got a right to know."

The blue-and-white cruiser Preuss called pulled up in front of the house. The officer stepped out and came up the walk.

"A girl Stevie works with has gone missing," Cahill said, "and she was last seen with your nephew."

"A girl at the restaurant?"

Preuss nodded. "Her mother hasn't seen her since last night. Said it's not like her daughter to stay out overnight."

Matuzik pulled at his sideburns.

"He's talked about some girl at work, but I just figured he was blowing smoke up my ass. You think they're together?"

"You can help us," Preuss said, "by telling us where his hidey holes are."

"I already checked them. But I'll tell you. Come inside."

Cahill and Preuss followed Ralph into the home. It was a typical Ferndale bungalow, roomier inside than it looked from the outside but as messy as a place where two males who lived on their own would be. Cheap furniture, old food smell.

"Also," Cahill said, "any friends he hangs with."

Preuss called the informed officer up to the front door. "Mr. Matuzik here is going to give you some information." The officer nodded. Preuss noted it was Gail Crimmonds, the patrol officer who had responded to the original complaint at Walter Szymanski's house. She was a tall woman with dyed blonde hair in a Marian-the-Librarian bun and eyes that were a bright sea green.

Preuss noticed a photo on the old television set by the door. It showed Ralph and a boy standing in front of their house. Ralph had his arm around the kid, who was thin and unsmiling with a long boney nose and bad acne and blond stubble for hair.

Preuss held up the photo in its frame. "This Stevie?"

"That's him."

He was certain it was the busboy he had seen at Lord Chumley's.

Outside he checked in with Alison Stuart. Still no sign of Linda.

55

"Cmm mmm mmm," said Cahill.

"Don't talk with your mouth full," Preuss reprimanded her.

They sat around a formica table in the rear of Jimbo's, a coney island on Woodward in Ferndale. There were better places to get chili dogs in the area—the best were at a pair of coney joints downtown, American Coney Island and Lafayette Coney Island on Michigan—but they were hungry and needing to process what was happening.

The savory odor of chili sauce hung over them as they bit into hot dogs that instantly dripped chili sauce and mustard and chopped onions over their hands. As one, they reached for the flimsy paper napkins to sop up the heavy mixture.

She swallowed and took a long drink of her Diet Coke and said, "Cass is your new best friend. Praised you to the skies. Says you're good police."

Preuss swallowed his mouthful of hot dog, washed it down with iced tea, carefully wiped his lips with a handful of napkins, and stuck one finger in his mouth to comically mime puking.

"Don't knock it, man. You could have worse friends."

"I already have worse friends."

"All we have is what you got for us," she said. "Otherwise it'd be a stone whodunit. Madison would have been dropped off at the hospital dead as a doornail and we'd be clueless."

He waved it away and they ate in silence.

"So what were you up to today?" he asked.

"Spent the morning with the parents of a kid I've been working with. He was picked up for larceny from a vehicle a couple times and I wanted to talk with them about what's the best thing for him."

"What are you thinking?"

"I'm trying to get them to agree to a youth diversion program I've been setting up. Get the kid into counseling, alternative activities, like that, see if we can keep him out of the court system."

"Good luck with that."

"We'll see. It's worked pretty well other in places but I'm trying like hell to get it going here. Got a couple Juvie judges on my side."

"Do they like the way it sounds?"

She shrugged. "They're supposed to think about it and get back to me at some point today. I think they'll go for it. Who wouldn't want to keep their kid out of jail? Speaking of which, anything new with Jason?"

He shook his head and wiped a load of chili sauce off his lip. "Still locked up. My contact out in Needles is supposed to let me know when he gets out."

"What's he in for again?"

"Vagrancy," he said with a rueful smile. "Got picked up begging by the highway out there. Deputy out there said he tried to convince them they were violating his constitutional right to free speech. Apparently he was hollering about Jesus."

"And he never asked you for bail?"

"Nope. Haven't heard from him in years."

"How do you stand that? I don't know how I'd cope if one of my kids wouldn't talk to me."

"You'd manage. At least I know where he is. He's got a roof over his head and three squares a day. He wants to see America from the inside of the nation's pokies, it's his business."

They ate in silence.

"Heard from Emma lately?" she asked.

"No. Why would I?"

"No reason."

"Janey?"

"Nothing. You just have another new fan there."

"How do you know that? She pass you a note in study hall?"

"Seriously. I think she's interested in you, that's all. She asked me about you this morning. If you're with anyone. What you're like. The usual questions somebody asks."

"What you tell her?"

"Said you were a gaping asshole and she should run the other way. What you think I told her? She digs you. Ask her out for coffee, I'm sure she'd say yes in a heartbeat."

He shook his head.

"No guts, no glory."

"What's that supposed to mean?"

"I think you know."

"No," he said, "I have no idea whatsoever."

"Think about it."

They ate in silence. Then she said, "You know your problem? You haven't seen anyone in, like, how long? Since you lost Jeanette, right? What's that, five years? You haven't gotten laid since Jeanette, am I right?"

He pulled another half dozen flimsy napkins out of the silver holder and wiped his fingers clean.

"You know I'm right. There's nobody in your life besides Toby."

He thought seriously about whether he should answer that, broach the subject of Shelley Larkin, when her phone rang.

"Saved by the bell," she said. "Maybe this is my parents calling me back."

She spoke briefly on the phone, then snapped it closed and returned it to her side pocket.

She looked at him with the corner of her mouth turned up in what passed for a grin when she was both pissed and amused.

"You're not gonna believe this," she said.

56

Preuss stared in dismay at the young man sitting across the table from them. How young are the villains going to get in this town, he wondered. This one didn't even shave yet.

The kid looked about fifteen or sixteen. Next to him sat an enormously fat woman. A heavy, unpleasant fug hung in the room and seemed to emanate from her.

The kid stared at Preuss with little interest. He had a smooth baby-fat face, round like the woman's, and a short military-style haircut with a square bandage on the crown of his head and a huge bruise on his cheek that was already turning purple. Black hoody and black levis.

A real ninja, Preuss thought.

Though he perceived a quiver of fear in him, too, despite the attitude.

Cahill skimmed the police report in front of her, and passed it to Preuss to read. The kid's name was Brian Mobius. The woman was Maria Mobius, his mother. Brian was just plucked from the juvenile holding cell. Gail Crimmons found him there when she did a search of Stevie's friends.

"What's going to happen with my son?" Mrs. Mobius demanded. She had a sibilant lisp that Preuss saw came from the gap in her mouth where her two front teeth were missing. Her skin was smooth as a plump baby's and she stared at them with eyes that seemed pressed like little buttons into the fat in her pie-shaped face.

"That depends on how Brian cooperates with us," Cahill said. "If he helps us out, we might be in a position to help him. He's facing some serious charges here."

Preuss skimmed the report. "Says here you're sixteen?"

"I guess."

"You guess? You don't know how old you are?"

"He's only sixteen," his mother put in. "He's just a baby."

Brian looked away and Preuss read further. The kid had broken into a home in southwest Ferndale while the homeowner was asleep upstairs. He awoke when he heard an intruder, and found this youngster stacking his stuff into a pillowcase on the living room floor. He laid Brian out with a fireplace poker before calling the police.

"I see you came in through the kitchen window," Preuss said, hearing in his head the echoes of a Beatles song. "Just like a dozen other home invasions we've had over the past year."

"I don't know anything about those."

Preuss set the police report to the side and stared at the kid, who ignored him, suddenly finding something terribly interesting on the knuckles of his grimy hands.

Cahill said, "Brian, we understand you're a friend of Stevie Matuzik."

When he didn't say anything, she prompted, "Brian? Do you know Stevie?"

His own mother was not so patient. "Brian!" she shouted. "Talk to them! Tell them what they want to know!"

"Yeah," the kid drawled, "I know him. So?"

"When was the last time you saw him?"

"So I might have some information here I can make a deal with?"

"Ah, no," Cahill said, "that's not what's going to happen, Brian. If you have something to tell us, you might be able to help yourself when your case comes to trial. This isn't 'Let's Make a Deal.' Let's be clear about that."

"Well, what are we talking about here?" the kid asked.

Preuss held up his hands. "Okay, hold it."

He leaned forward.

"Let me tell you something, Brian. If you think you're going to knock us over with your attitude, you might as well save your breath. Neither one of us has time to sit here and listen to this bullshit from you. Excuse my French," he added for the benefit of Mrs. Mobius. "We got you cold for one house invasion. While we're chatting, the officers out there"—he jerked a thumb over his shoulder—"are collecting enough to nail you for all twelve. We'll try you as an adult and your mother'll be visiting you in Jackson before you know it. So if you have something to say to us about Stevie, say it. Otherwise don't waste our time."

The unbruised side of Brian's cheek grew pink, as though Preuss had slapped him.

"You have to help yourself here, Brian," Cahill said gently. "This is your chance to do a good turn for yourself. Thing you need to remember is, the three of us in this room? We're the ones who care about you."

"You *don't* care. You don't even know me."

"No, sweetie, we do. Detective Preuss and myself and your mom, we care about you. And it pains us when this happens to you."

The kid started to pick at the back of a hand.

"So let's start again," Preuss said. "Do you know Stevie Matuzik?"

"Yeah." Grudgingly.

"When was the last time you saw him?"

He raised a thin shoulder, then said, "Couple nights ago."

"You didn't see him last night?"

"He was working. Usually he bugs me for a ride to work, but last night he didn't."

"So you haven't seen him since when, exactly?"

"Thursday night."

"No phone calls from him? No texts?"

Brian shook his head.

"Do you know a girl named Linda Stuart?"

"Never heard of her."

"She works at the restaurant with Stevie. Friend of his?"

"If that's the chick he likes, yeah, I seen her before."

"Where?"

"When I drop him off or pick him up sometimes at the restaurant. And then that night at her house."

"What night?"

"Couple weeks ago. Stevie wanted to see her so we went over to her house."

"The house on West Woodland in Ferndale?" Preuss was instantly alert. "What happened?"

"Well, Stevie, he thinks this girl's hot for him and all, but she's like, you know, whatever."

"Yeah, let's cut to the chase here, Brian, okay?"

"So anyway we go over her house, and so we get there and she's like, she's out in a car in front of her house with this other guy. So Stevie, he freaks out, you know."

"I hear he's got a temper," Preuss said.

"Duh! Guy's a fucking powderkeg."

"Watch your language!" Mrs. Mobius said.

"Well, so anyway, so, and then, so, Stevie makes me drive him around the block and we get back to her street and she's gone, the car's gone, and Stevie, he goes like apeshit. He pulls this gun out of his pocket, and then he starts shooting."

Preuss and Cahill exchanged a glance. This was it.

"Where were you parked?" he asked.

"Down the street from her house."

"What street?"

"Dunno. Whatever that street is that runs down to Nine?"

"Livernois. How far down were you parked?"

"I don't know. Couple blocks, maybe."

Preuss thought back to where he had marked ground zero.

"Did you try to stop him?" Cahill asked.

"Did I try to stop Stevie Matuzik with a gun in his hand? Uh, no, I don't think so."

"So what happened?" Preuss asked.

"So he starts shooting at her house like he's going to fucking kill it. And he's screaming, too, at the top of his lungs about how she don't love him."

"Where'd he get the gun?"

"From his uncle."

Always the uncle, Preuss thought.

"What kind of gun was it?"

"I don't know. Some kind of handgun, that's all I know."

"Did his uncle give it to him?" Cahill asked.

"Stevie, he, um, borrowed it."

"'Borrowed it'?"

"More like snuck it out of the house when his uncle was asleep." Brian smirked.

"Does he still have it?"

"Dunno."

"So you're saying it was Stevie who shot off that gun?" Preuss said. "And he fired it at Linda's house?"

"But we were so far away, I didn't think he'd hit nothing. He was just blowing off steam."

"Blowing off steam by shooting a gun into a residential neighborhood," Cahill said. "Real genius."

Preuss considered what he had just heard. "Brian," he said, "I have to tell you something. There was a little girl out walking around that night."

"Yeah? So?"

"So in all that gunfire, this little girl got hit."

Brian looked at Cahill as though for validation that this older detective was pulling his leg. When she shook her head, he said, "You're fucking shitting me."

Even his mother was too astonished to rebuke him.

"I wish I were. You didn't see the little girl?" Preuss asked.

"No," Brian said emphatically. "No. We did not know that happened. Neither one of us even knew there was a kid out there."

"You didn't see her get hit?"

"No sir."

"Or fall?"

"No sir."

"All right, Brian," Preuss said. "This is the important question. Where can we find him?"

Brian told them where Stevie lived, in southeast Ferndale.

"Where else would he go if he was in trouble?"

Suddenly, as if the reality of his situation just penetrated, Brian started to cry, a high-pitched whine like a car struggling in first gear.

Sometimes it was hard to remember these little shits were just kids, Preuss thought, watching him.

But they were babies, teenagers whose development was behind some younger kids despite their brittle anger. That's how it was with this one. He should have been on his sofa at home, playing video games or ignoring his homework or doing something normal instead of awaiting transfer to an adult jail for multiple felonies. He should be anywhere but here. They all should.

He glanced at Cahill, who gave him a barely perceptible nod. "We've heard enough," Preuss said.

The two detectives stood to go. Before they left, Preuss said, "Brian, look at me."

The boy looked up at him with a shattered face.

"This isn't the life you want to lead, son. You've got too much going for you. Look around you. This isn't the life for a smart kid like you."

The boy's whine hit second gear.

Back at his cubicle, Preuss exploded.

"Goddamn it to hell! I'll crucify Uncle Ralph!"

57

They searched for a CCW in the name of Matuzik and got a hit on an Anita Matuzik for a .22. Same Ferndale address.

"Maybe his ex?" Preuss wondered.

Preuss prepared a request for a warrant to search Matuzik's house for the gun and for Stevie and asked the detective bureau administrative assistant to track down an ADA for a signature. As it turned out, Andrew Carnahan was in the law enforcement complex, grabbing a smoke outside. Preuss explained the situation to him, including the disappearance of Linda Stuart with Stevie and a possible connection to Madison's shooting. Carnahan signed off on the warrant right there and Preuss trotted back to the station.

He returned to his cubicle just as Officer Gail Crimmonds appeared.

"Good work finding the Mobius kid," he said.

"Wasn't hard. On the way back from the Matuzik place I checked a couple of spots the boy might be, Blair Park and an empty building on East Nine. But no sign of him."

She handed him a single sheet of paper. "Most of these are in Ferndale. The only place that isn't is his job."

"I know. Lord Chumley's in Madison Heights."

He thanked her and raced out of the station with Cahill. They sped east on Nine to Hilton, where they headed south toward the Matuzik home.

"Stevie and Linda took off together on Friday night and haven't been seen since," he said.

"Are they a couple?" Cahill asked.

"My witness didn't seem to think Linda went with him willingly."

He didn't know the kid or what he was capable of, but he knew the boy was running scared and he had a terrible feeling about what was going to happen.

At the Matuzik home, the Olds was gone from the driveway. Cahill ran around the back of the house to check for side or rear doors. While he was pounding on the front door, Preuss saw a big man watching him from the window next door.

The man came outside onto his own front stoop. He had a black and orange Harley Davidson handkerchief around his head and a long scraggly beard. He looked to be in his fifties, in a leather jacket with about a hundred patches and shorts despite the cold weather. Preuss noticed he was wearing support hose with his biker shorts and work boots.

"Hey," the man said. "Looking for Ralph?" Most of the patches on his jacket were versions of "HIM." One large patch carried a picture of a biker carrying a cross and the words, "Hogs in Ministry," in a semicircle above it.

"Seen him?"

The man nodded. "You won't find him in there." His voice was deep and resonant, like a trombone.

"Why not?"

"He took off a little while ago."

"Say where he was going?"

"Are you Detective Price?"

"Preuss."

"He asked me to tell you he was off to get his nephew." The man looked at Cahill. "Now I'm thinking he was trying to get going before you folks got here."

"I'd say that's a good bet. Did he say where he was meeting Stevie?"

"He's got a little cabin up north, out in the country. Near a place called Montrose. He's meeting the boy up there."

"Is Stevie by himself?"

"Didn't say."

"So you know where this place is, Mr. —?"

"Muller. It's Reverend Muller, actually. Pleased to meet you." He reached out a hand as large as a frying pan and Preuss shook it. "Founder of Hogs in Ministry. A biker ministry my wife and me run to bring kindred souls closer to Christ."

"You know where this cabin is, Mr. Muller?"

"I do," he said. "Ralph asked me to tell you how to get there. He just said he wanted to have some time to get to Stevie before you all did. You want, I could draw you a map."

"Mr. Muller, if you could do that, you'll be doing a great service to the City of Ferndale."

"Always ready to do my civic duty," said the man. "Long as it helps my spiritual one, of course," he said with a grin.

"I can virtually guarantee that," Preuss said.

"We need to get the state troopers in on this," Cahill said back at the station.

Preuss agreed. "If he's got Linda, it sounds like a hostage situation. It's way beyond what we can handle."

"And we don't even really know if this cabin is where they are," she pointed out.

"Can you get with Cass about making the contact with the troopers? Meantime I'm going to head up there."

"Not by yourself, I hope."

"No, don't worry about that."

She looked at him for a few seconds, then said, "Marty, please don't do this. Let the troopers deal with it."

"I intend to. But it's my fault Stevie got away without anybody stopping him. And took the girl with him. And now Matuzik is up there, too."

"How is it your fault?"

"I was too slow. I'm not going to lose another girl."

"I'll come with you," she said.

"No, you stay here. You need to coordinate between Cass and Russo and the state."

She left his cubicle to make the calls. He sat for a few moments longer, thinking about how to proceed. The one he wanted with him was Edmund Blair. He tried Blair's cell, but couldn't get through to him.

No time to leave a message. He went to see if Reg Trombley was around.

Preuss found the younger detective in his own cubicle.

"Reg," Preuss said, sticking his head in the doorway, "up for a little road trip?"

Reg's eyes lit up. "With you? I'm there."

"Better bring your Kevlar."

58

Montrose was a small farming community of fewer than two thousand people, located a little over an hour up I-75 from Ferndale. Traffic on the way up was heavy but not clogged.

Light snow swept the expressway in the darkness of the oncoming Michigan night. They wound around on 75 past Pontiac and drove into the teeth of the wind and the snow came right at them in spots. Preuss filled Reg in on what had been happening with the case, and what they had been finding about Stevie Matuzik.

"So he's up here with the Stuart girl?" Reg asked.

"I'm guessing so."

"Judging by the Kevlars, you must not think he'll come quietly."

"I hope he will. But I want to be ready if he decides to put up a fight. Apparently the kid's a hothead. Uncle seems to be on our side, but who knows what'll happen when we show up. Both a couple of wild cards with access to weapons."

"Doesn't hurt to be prepared."

"I don't know what the kid thinks is going to happen to him, or what his uncle told him, so he might resist. We probably should assume Ralph told him why we're looking for him, so he's going to be scared."

"Maybe he is anyway, and that's what brought all this on."

"Other thing is, I don't know what the situation is with Linda, whether she's a hostage or what her relationship is with him now. A witness who saw them together on Friday night said she wasn't happy to see him. My guess is, she's not a willing guest."

"How do you want to play it?"

"I'm hoping the troopers are up there and they'll have everything under control by the time we get there. If not, we're going to have to make sure everybody keeps their cool."

"Think Stevie's going to be overcome by remorse and turn himself in?"

"No, but if we can make him see the error of his ways he'll come quietly. With his uncle's help."

Reg pulled a face. "Hope you're right."

"His uncle's a tough customer but he's not stupid. He's got to know this will be best for his nephew."

When they passed over I-69, the east-west highway near Flint, they lapsed into silence. When they turned off the expressway onto M-57 toward Montrose, it was entirely dark, with no streetlights and no light from the overcast sky in the flat Michigan countryside. The snow had stopped as they rolled through the dark landscape.

Reg directed Preuss based on the map the neighbor had scrawled for them. They followed M-57 to the town of Montrose, essentially an intersection between two roads, then at the traffic light turned north on Saginaw Road to follow that out of town.

Saginaw Road became Nichols, and Preuss took that to Farrand Road, where he turned right and went east.

They followed Farrand Road for a few miles to where it wound through a remote subdivision and then, on the other side of it, dead-ended at a river bank. A paved road devolved into a dirt lane leading to the left, and Preuss guided the Explorer down the lane to the point where it headed off into the trees and became a dirt driveway that disappeared into the woods.

Preuss eased the car to a stop and turned it off. He opened the window and listened. The only sound was the soughing of the wind in the pines. Through the trees they could make out the lights of the cabin.

"I don't see the cavalry, do you?" Preuss asked.

"Nope."

"This isn't good."

He tried calling Cahill but there was no cell service.

"Damn," he said. "The troopers should be here by now."

"Maybe they couldn't find it."

"We found it easy enough and we're not even from here."

"What do you want to do?" Reg said.

Preuss considered.

"I think we should wait for them," Reg suggested.

"No. If they're not here by now, who knows how long they're going to be? I'm not going to wait any longer. Let's suit up."

He and Reg opened the doors very carefully, so the only sound in the still cold night was a faint "click" from both sides of the car. Moving as quietly as he could, Preuss popped the rear hatch and withdrew the vests. They shrugged into them in the chill damp that hung heavy in the road.

He motioned Reg close to him so he could whisper in his ear. "Why don't you hang back while I go up to the cabin by myself. I'll try to talk to them and make them see what the situation is. If they see two of us, it might upset them."

Reg gave him a thumbs-up.

The two men walked down the dirt road through the cold impenetrable forest heavy with the resin smell of pine on either side of them.

About seventy-five yards up the dirt trail winding north on the river bank they came to the small cabin.

Walking along, as the cold invaded his bones through the heavy fleece of his windbreaker, Preuss had a sudden ache of apprehension. What the hell were they doing here, in the middle of nowhere, tramping through the woods like a couple of kids playing infantry? Why weren't they waiting for the state police? And where were the troopers? What could be keeping them? What if this really had been an emergency?

Well, he thought, they were here and committed. At his side he had an armed man with known impulse control problems and they were walking straight toward a pair of crazy and perhaps desperate men—no, he corrected himself; make that one man and one boy—who were also no doubt armed, neither one of whom was likely to be a friend of law enforcement.

So, yeah. What could possibly go wrong?

The structure came into view suddenly and both men paused and hugged the side of the driveway.

Matuzik's Olds and a dark Saturn were parked close by. Fifty feet away from where they stood, the building was not so much a cabin as an overgrown shack, cluttered around the outside with the detritus of civilization, rusted mufflers and fenders and tire hubs and an engine block hanging from a tree, an old busted toilet and upside-down clawfoot bathtub, tables and broken chairs and cardboard boxes that had long since broken down in the rain and snow, spilling their contents in heaps around them. Off to the right a smaller utility shack stood with the door open.

Preuss could make out nothing inside it in the overcast night.

"Stay here," he whispered in Reg's ear, "and keep an eye on things. If it looks like I need help, come running."

Reg nodded and placed himself behind a tree at the side of the path with his weapon drawn and ready.

Preuss eased soundlessly down a path that turned from dirt to gravel. Light streamed out of two windows from the cabin on either side of the solid front door, forming two yellow trapezoids on the ground. Both windows looked into a large central room that seemed to span the entire front of the place. Nobody was visible inside.

Preuss paused before a tiny two-step porch and listened.

He could hear the rustling of the wind through the trees around him, and the sound of murmuring from inside the house, low male voices, calm and unhurried. He couldn't make out what they were saying.

There were no sounds of sirens. He and Reg were on their own.

He knew he should wait, but couldn't bring himself to linger. All he could think of was what was happening to the girl. He couldn't consider the possibility she was dead.

Stevie wouldn't do that, would he? Would he be that crazy? If so, they would all be in bigger trouble than Preuss thought.

He climbed the porch, treading carefully over the loose wood of the steps.

Standing outside the door, he turned to make sure Reg was in place, and knocked.

He stood out of the doorway, squeezing himself to the right of the door. The porch was tiny, but he didn't want to be in front of the door if it should swing open suddenly. Or blow out in an explosion of splinters.

Immediately the voices stopped.

He heard hasty shuffling behind the door, then a voice: "Who's there?"

The elder Matuzik, raw and tense.

"Ralph?"

"Who is it?"

"Martin Preuss. Ferndale PD."

Silence.

"I'd like to come in so we can talk about this."

More silence. Then the door cracked open and Ralph stepped out and pulled the door closed behind him.

"We got a little problem here," Ralph said.

"Is the girl inside?"

"Stevie's got her knocked out with some shit he gave her. He didn't tell me about this when I talked to him before."

"Is she all right?"

"I think so. Look, he's in bad shape. Says he won't come with you under any circumstances. I think I can reason with him but you got to give me some more time."

Preuss shook his head. "The state police are on their way. The only way Stevie's going to get out of this with any kind of life ahead of him is if he gives himself up and comes with us so we can sort this all out."

For several long beats Ralph thought about that.

"We have to talk some sense into the boy," Preuss said, "and you know that's true."

"Give me five more minutes," Ralph said.

"Is he armed?" Preuss asked.

Ralph nodded gravely.

"With what?"

"I keep a couple of shotguns in the cabin. He's walking around with one of them. This isn't going to be easy."

"Can you get him to give it up?"

Ralph gave him a long look and said, "Five minutes." He stepped back inside. Preuss heard hurried whispering.

Suddenly from inside Preuss heard Ralph yell, "No!"

Before Preuss could gather himself to throw the door open and bust in, Reg's voice came from the woods behind him, urgent yet muted by the trees.

"Gun!"

Preuss instinctively swung his head back to where Reg's voice had come from. He saw Reg step out from behind the tree raising his service weapon. As though in slow motion, Preuss turned his head back to the front of the little cabin and before he could make himself move he saw Stevie's skinny frame appear in the window on the left side of the house holding a rifle.

Pointed right at Preuss.

Three thoughts flew through his head in instant succession: The first was, *I'm going to die.*

Then, *I'm going to die out here in the woods.*

Then the window imploded in a shower of splinters of glass and slivers of wood simultaneous with a blast from the woods. From Reg.

A second explosion from inside the cabin deafened Preuss and the third thought came.

I'm not dead.

But his nervous system took over at that point and he dove off the porch and into the side brush. He landed hard on his shoulder and smashed his face in the gravel.

He heard another blast, this one from the cabin again, kicking up a spray of gravel nearby. In a sudden adrenaline-fueled frenzy of fear he crab-scurried into the darkness away from the cabin's front.

Ralph yelled, "NO! Stevie, STOP!" but another volley of gunfire exploded from inside, this time the crack-crack-crack of small arms fire that hissed into the brush where Preuss had been. How many weapons do they have in there?

No return fire came from Reg. Where was he? Heart pounding in his throat, trembling, Preuss threw himself against the side of the cabin and peered around the corner out toward the woods where Reg had been standing.

Preuss saw him lying on his back, arms and legs flung out to his side.

Now Preuss heard Ralph's voice screaming from inside the house as a struggle between Ralph and his nephew went crashing around the front room. Ralph cursed the boy and demanded he give up the gun, and from the sounds of struggling Preuss guessed Stevie was trying to throw his uncle off him.

Preuss heard a round of gunfire, a thud, Ralph's voice in a sharp scream, and a loud crash, as though something substantial inside had gone over. Preuss felt a shudder in the wall he was leaning against, and after a few seconds all was quiet.

From where he stood at the side of the cabin he saw Stevie appear on the porch, holding another rifle and glaring out at the spot where Preuss had been.

Jesus, Preuss thought, they must have an arsenal in there.

But what happened to Ralph and Reg? And where was Linda?

Preuss hugged the side of the building and felt his way in the darkness around to the back, where he discovered a rear entrance. He also found a sudden drop-off to the river and he almost slid down the side of a hill to the water below but caught himself by the wooden support structure of the back porch.

Who the hell built the back door of a cabin so close to the hillside by a river, he thought angrily.

He found his footing in the loose soil and worked around to the steps leading to the porch. He got himself up and with his weapon in his hand he tried the knob and found it open.

He stepped inside a small mudroom with coats hanging from hooks along one wall and boots and shoes underneath. A long filthy metal washbasin took up the other wall. Shelves lined the walls with old baskets and dusty jars from a former day when whoever stayed here did canning.

A door gave onto a narrow damp hallway that split into two bedrooms on either side and continued straight ahead toward the front room. Hugging the wall, Preuss could see into the front, which was rapidly filling with black smoke from the wood stove in the corner that had been knocked over.

Ralph lay groaning on his back beside it and on the rug small patches of flame from the wood and embers that had spilled out of the stove writhed like live things. All the furniture had been upended in the front room from the fight, like the saloon after a brawl in a western movie.

Swiftly Preuss stuck his head into the room on the right, which was small and made up as a bedroom.

Nobody there.

He tried the door to the other room. Locked, but there was a skeleton key in the lock and he turned it and opened the door to Linda Stuart sprawled face up on the bed.

Preuss rushed into the room and stood over the girl. Her eyes were open but glazed over. She looked up at him but showed no recognition. Her face was bruised and raw.

He pulled her up roughly and half-dragged, half-pushed her out of the room and into the small hallway to the mudroom. At first she was dead weight but after a few steps she started moving under her own power.

From behind them he heard Stevie's sharp screeching. The boy opened fire in their direction with the rifle but he was too shaky and too poor a marksman to do anything but blast the wall to either side of them.

Preuss shoved Linda straight ahead and out the back door, shouting, "Go! Run!"

She disappeared through the doorway and he turned and ducked behind the partition between the front room and the hall.

Another blast came from the rifle and then a "click!" Preuss was about to turn the corner and take a run at the boy when he heard the clatter of the rifle on the floor and a handgun popping. He smelled burning wood from the other room and saw tendrils of smoke drifting lazily toward him across the ceiling.

More plywood splintered from the partition. The boy kept firing as he approached the rear of the cabin. Preuss lost his footing in his own fear and as Stevie advanced Preuss scrambled back into the bedroom where Linda had been.

He leapt to the opposite wall and dropped to the ground between the bed and the wall. The room was too small to hide in.

"Drop it, Stevie!" he ordered as Stevie appeared in the doorway. "Don't make things worse for yourself!"

When Stevie moved into the room and raised the revolver he carried to take a point-blank shot, Preuss stuck his head up over the mattress and with his own Glock snapped off two shots.

Stevie's gun fell silent. The boy clutched his stomach and dropped to his knees.

Preuss took his feet shakily. Stevie looked up at him with his unformed face twisted in open hatred.

"You shot me, you motherfucker!" he shrieked.

Preuss willed himself to be calm and reached out with trembling hands to tug the boy to his feet by his shirt. "Let's get out here, the cabin's going up."

That's when he realized Stevie was still holding his gun.

Stevie's gun arm pinwheeled in a big roundhouse swing and clocked Preuss on the side of his head as he stood there trying to save the stupid asshole's life.

Preuss fell.

The cabin spun, went dark.

59

Feathers of black smoke working their way into the room.

The gathering heat from the main room.

The sudden urge to get up, go, run, get the hell out.

He slithered on his belly out to the little hallway leading to the mudroom at the back of the cabin. While combat-crawling to the safety of the cold night, which awaited him through the open doorway, he paused in his passage, momentarily overcome by a wave of dizziness and nausea from the blow to his head.

And in that moment he remembered Ralph Matuzik.

He glanced back at the front room.

It was fully aflame, filled with black smoke and tongues of fire from the burning wood that had spilled out of the stove, traveling over the wood floor to the walls and ceiling. Matuzik was immobile beside the stove.

Preuss changed the direction of his crawl and worked his way into the living room. Things were not going to last much longer. Smoke in the room left only a narrow layer of breathable air from the floor to knee level.

Bunching the collar of his jacket around his mouth with one hand, Preuss scuttled to where Matuzik lay. He reached out to grab onto the man's sweatshirt and pull him away from the burning wood. Preuss had nothing to wrap around Matuzik's shirt, no throw rugs on the floor or even towels within reach. So he whipped his jacket off and patted out the flames searing the man's front.

The door was open but blocked by flames fanned by wind sucked into the cabin. They would have to go out the back. Matuzik was too out of it to cooperate. Preuss took a deep breath and stood.

He got the man on his feet with difficulty. Matuzik gave a muffled cry of pain. Preuss could smell scorched cotton from Matuzik's sweatshirt and scorched hair from strands of his ponytail that hung loose.

Preuss pulled and pushed him out the back door as he had done with Linda.

They tripped on the steps and tumbled over the left side of the porch. But at least they were outside and didn't slide down the ravine to the river.

Still pulling Matuzik, his own head throbbing with pain, Preuss got him as far away from the house as he could. They leaned against a tree, panting and coughing and moaning. Matuzik slid to the ground as Preuss turned to stumble around to the front of the cabin.

Midway between the front steps and the perimeter of the open space around the cabin, Stevie was laying face down. Preuss run up to grab him by the collar of his shirt and pulled him further away from the blazing cabin.

As Preuss dragged him, Stevie twisted onto his back and regained sense enough to raise the gun toward Preuss's head.

Before he could get off a shot, Reg Trombley stepped forward out of nowhere and rammed the butt of his weapon into the side of Stevie's head.

The blow knocked the boy down, floppy as a rag doll.

Stevie's gun discharged into the woods and Trombley stepped across Stevie's body to stamp down on his forearm and kick the gun out of his grip across the gravel of the driveway.

Together Preuss and Trombley dragged the boy away from the house toward the tree line and let him fall.

"How are you doing?" Preuss asked Trombley.

"The vest stopped the worst of it. You?"

"Head's killing me." Trombley smiled.

Then his eyes rolled up in his head and he collapsed.

Preuss made a quick search for a bullet wound on him, but found none. Apart from his headache, Preuss himself was otherwise functional except for painful scrapes on his hands and knees.

He knelt down beside Stevie to bunch up a handful of the boy's shirt and stuffed it under his belt to stanch the belly wound as best he could.

He turned toward the cabin. Through the blown-out front windows and open doorway, he saw flames licking the walls and rolling like red-orange waves across the ceiling.

One person was still missing.

"Linda," Preuss called, "where are you?"

His voice, hoarse from the smoke and overwhelmed by the popping and cracking of timber, did not carry.

Preuss found her wrapped around a tree at the bottom of the incline that led to the river.

When she flew out of the house she must have kept going straight and slid down the side of the hill. The tree stopped her from continuing into the icy November waters, where she certainly would have died. She lay with her right leg bent under her and her face and arms ripped as if she had been in a knife fight. She was unconscious but she was breathing.

Preuss tried to get her up by himself but couldn't carry her alone. He climbed back up the ravine and collapsed in a world spinning too rapidly out of control.

When he regained consciousness a state trooper was leaning over him, staring into his face. Past the trooper's shoulder Preuss saw the house was furiously ablaze.

The trooper was not happy with the scene he walked in on, not happy at all, but he called for backup, ambulances, and the local volunteer fire department. When the fire truck arrived twenty minutes later there wasn't much the fire fighters were able to do besides douse the flames that were starting to lick at the area around the cabin. The cabin itself was all old wood so it went up entirely.

Two firemen brought Linda up. She couldn't stop crying.

60

At Hurley Medical Center in nearby Flint, Preuss was treated for smoke inhalation and a mild concussion, and released. Stevie was placed in custody and admitted for treatment of his injuries. Matuzik was not as badly burned as Preuss had feared but was admitted for observation of a head wound. Trombley was only sore from the impact of the bullet from Stevie's rifle blast, and was treated for a minor cut sustained when he fell over. Linda's broken leg was set and her cuts attended to, and she sat in the emergency department waiting for her mother.

Preuss went in to see her. She looked like hell, no longer the haughty, annoyed teenager he had spoken with—how long ago was that? Just the day before?

Her face was criss-crossed with angry red welts from her slide down the side of the hill.

"How are you holding up?" he asked. She reached out to him and grabbed him with both hands. She was still shivering, from the aftermath of fear now and not from lying frozen in the woods.

"You're safe now," he said. "It's over."

She pulled him down toward her so she could plant a kiss on the side of his face. He hugged her and straightened up.

"What's going to happen to him?" she asked.

"He's in a lot of trouble. For this and also for what happened to Madison Kaufman."

Her eyes tried to focus on him. She was still under the influence of the drugs he gave her. "What did he do to her?"

"He was the one who shot her."

She covered her mouth with a hand and began to cry again.

He stayed with her for another hour, until Alison Stuart rushed into the empty emergency center and mother and daughter fell into each other's arms and bawled.

Preuss left them to their reunion.

When Janey Cahill arrived at the medical center and saw him—he imagined he was a sight, soot-covered, dirty, bloody, bruised, and stinking of smoke—she rushed up to him and threw her arms around his aching body and held him tightly.

Then she stood back, held him at arm's length, and shook him by the shoulders. "You dumb shit! I told you not to do this!"

Then she put her arms around him again and held him close.

When they separated she led him to a chair because he was still shaky. "How's Reggie?"

"He's good. We both wore Kevlar. He took a direct hit from Stevie, but the vest stopped it. He saved my life, Janey."

He led her to the emergency department waiting room where Trombley was reclining on the sofa with his feet up. He was sleeping, so they backed away quietly.

Ralph Matuzik's cabin was now a smoldering pile of ashes in the watery early light. Nothing of the structure was saved. Half a dozen firemen were packing up their equipment.

As they worked, the volunteer fire fighters were retelling the story of the fire, which Preuss had noticed firemen often did. They would be coming back to this site for weeks, replaying it for their colleagues who had been here, and narrating it for those who had not.

Some cops were like that, but not Preuss. Retelling the stories of what he saw—the incidental cruelties, the relentless stupidity, the eruptions of violence that damaged people's lives forever for no reason whatsoever, all the crimes and transgressions that packed his days—meant reliving events he never wanted to be part of in the first place.

The need to leave this scene overwhelmed him. He told Cahill and she asked, "Can you drive?"

"I think so."

"How's your head?"

"Tolerable."

They walked to their cars through the smells of burnt, soggy wood.

"Hungry?" she asked.

"I could eat a horse."

They stopped at a diner off I-75 on the way south and had breakfast. Preuss thought about his return to Ferndale. There would be questions to answer. And acts to answer for.

"Does Russo know about all this?" he asked.

"Of course. Am I supposed to keep it a secret?"

"How'd he take it?"

"I hope you liked being a police," she said with no trace of irony. "I don't think you're going to be one much longer."

They ate in silence.

"I felt like I had to do it this way," he said. "Who knows what that twerp had in mind for her."

"Maybe," she said. "Thing is, look what you caused by doing this: you almost died, Stevie and his uncle almost died, Reg almost died, Linda almost died, and the cabin burnt to the ground. Jesus, what would Toby do if anything happened to you?"

He had no reply. She was right, of course.

"This could have ended in disaster, and the fact it didn't is just incredibly lucky."

He thought about that for a while. "I'm still convinced there wasn't time to wait for the troopers."

"Irrelevant now," she said.

"What happened to them, anyway?"

"There was a major pile-up on 75 further north and they were tied up there for hours. When they shook loose a trooper he couldn't find the cabin. I faxed them a copy of the map but evidently the copy wasn't clear enough. Comedy of errors."

"I saved that girl," he insisted.

"May that thought console you in the long years of your retirement."

Sunday, November 16, 2008

61

As Cahill predicted, Preuss was suspended as soon as he arrived at the station in the morning.

Russo didn't even bother calling him into his office. He instructed the sergeant on the front desk to let him know when Preuss showed up.

As soon as Preuss arrived at the law enforcement complex after stopping home to shower and change, Russo stormed down the hall to Preuss's cubicle and stood in the doorway, face cherry red, to tell him, "Write up your report. Then you're on administrative leave pending investigation of your actions."

Preuss would not have been surprised to see smoke emanating from his ears.

He watched the chief of detectives returning to his office without knowing how he felt about this. Hank Bellamy sitting in his cubicle across from Preuss's came over to shake Preuss's hand. He asked Preuss to tell him the story, just like the firemen, and Preuss swallowed his reluctance and obliged with an abbreviated version.

He would retell the story many times during the day. One of those times was to the police chief, who summoned Preuss to his office. The chief listened carefully, not saying anything beyond an occasional question for clarity. Then he sat nodding as he considered what Preuss had told him.

He ran a knuckle along the uneven landscape of his jaw. "Extraordinary," he said. "All because a little girl went for a walk at the exact time a kid decided to shoot a gun off because a girl dumped him."

"That's about it, unfortunately."

"We were out looking for villains and the whole time it was blind, stupid chance."

Preuss said nothing.

"Well, look," Warnock said, rousing himself from these ruminations and rocking in his desk chair, "here's the problem. Russo has a major bug up his ass, and its name is Martin Preuss."

"I gather that, sir."

"I take it you know you're on administrative leave?"

"He let me know as soon as I got in."

"That's thanks to me. He wanted to fire you outright. I talked him out of it. Told him it would be better for everybody if he suspended you with pay pending an investigation."

"Thanks."

"The Prosecutor's office will conduct the investigation."

"Yes, sir," Preuss said.

"Martin, I have to tell you, you're one lucky guy things turned out the way they did. We could have had another half dozen lives lost, including your own, because you were too impatient to do things right."

Just what Janey had said. "I understand, sir." Lucky indeed. Sometimes chance works out for the best, too.

Preuss thought of bringing up the fact that he saved the girl because the troopers were late, but thought better of it.

"As it is," the chief said, "I'm losing my best detective for who knows how long."

Preuss bobbed his head. "Thanks again."

"All right," the chief said. "It is what it is. Did you finish the report?"

"No, sir."

"Get it done and send me a copy, would you?"

"Yes, sir. I think I'm dragging it out because it may be the last thing I ever do for the Ferndale Police Department."

"Well," Warnock said, "better make it a good one, then."

"Yes, sir."

"After that, go home and get some rest. Keep out of Russo's way for a while and maybe he'll forget he doesn't like you. Spend some time with your son while things work themselves out. Think about whether you still want to be on the force."

"I will, sir."

In truth, at that moment Preuss didn't know if he wanted to stay on the force or not. He hoped the chief wouldn't ask him.

He rose to go and the chief stood with him to shake his hand. "Not how I would have done it," Warnock said, "but things turned out right in the end. I guess that's the main thing."

Preuss thanked the chief again and went off to finish his last task.

The report done and filed, with a copy to the chief, Preuss gave Paul Horvath the case file, along with his badge and weapon.

"You'll be back before you know it," Horvath assured him.

Preuss said goodbye and left the law enforcement complex already feeling disconnected. He hadn't bothered cleaning out his desk. He would take care of that another time, if it should become necessary. Right now his head was killing him and all he wanted to do was get away.

He dozed for a few hours. When he awoke late in the afternoon he went to Toby's, intending to take the boy out for dinner. Instead he discovered his son in bed with a slight temperature. Toby was glad to see him, but his greeting was subdued because he wasn't feeling well.

Preuss stayed with him for the rest of the evening, watching television with him until the young man fell asleep around eight-thirty.

Preuss kissed his son gently on the crown of his warm damp forehead, whispered into Toby's ear that he loved him, tucked the covers under his chin, said goodnight to the staff on duty, and drove back to his own house.

There he sat for hours in the silence, dark and empty as his own mind.

Monday, November 24 - Monday, December 1, 2008

62

While the investigation of him moved glacially through the Oakland County prosecutor's office, Preuss passed his first week of suspension by visiting Toby every day, playing his guitar, and getting reacquainted with his CD collection. Janey Cahill called him daily, and met him for lunch three times.

He did as the chief suggested: he thought about staying in the department or leaving it.

He came to no conclusions. He realized he was in no condition to decide.

He called Shelley Larkin twice at the beginning of the week, but each time got her voicemail. She never called him back. He tried to convince himself it was just as well.

On Friday he went to a memorial service for Madison Kaufman. The parents wanted it to be private, for family and close friends only, but they invited Cahill and Preuss because of all the two detectives had done to find their daughter.

It was a nondenominational service held at a funeral home in Ferndale. The Kaufmans turned out to have no religious affiliation. He had thought they were Jewish, but the service made no mention of any religion, or even of God.

Sharon's sister Peggy gave Madison's eulogy because Sharon wept nonstop and Stanley Kaufman, out on bail from his charges of filing a false police report and obstruction of justice, sat silent and staring, as though he were drugged. Which he may well have been. When he saw Kaufman, Preuss remembered he never spoke with him about why he had done what he did with George Schenk.

267

It was just as well. Preuss was anxious to put it all behind him. The service helped.

Overall it touched Preuss deeply. Considering all he had been through with religious people in the last two weeks, he was glad not to have to listen to any pieties about the death of a child. No one offered any comforting explanations of the intentions, benevolent or inscrutable, of any higher power toward Madison.

None would have been acceptable, considering the suffering that surrounded the end of her life.

The service confirmed his view that there was nothing beyond the visible world. It left him immeasurably saddened.

It did not help his mood that Shelley Larkin finally called on the Monday after Madison's service to wish him a happy Thanksgiving and to let him know the cover story in the new issue of the *Metro Voice* was her article, "The Life and Death of Maddie Doll."

Preuss let the answering machine take the message when he heard who it was. As much as he wanted to see her, he didn't think he could deal with the reality that whatever had been happening between them was already over.

She ended her call with, "Look, Martin. Sorry I haven't returned your calls. Long story short, I'm sort of seeing someone at the moment. But will you call me? Please? We need to talk."

He couldn't bring himself to call her back.

Later that same day Cahill called to tell him about the article, too, and he took that call when he heard her voice. She told him it was good, mostly accurate, and he was featured prominently and came off well, as did the department in general.

But the thought of the article—or more precisely, the thought of Shelley Larkin, and her message—sent him even deeper into his funk.

63

Later that day he was in his back yard raking leaves onto a blue tarp so he could pull them to the curb when he heard his cell phone ring.

He debated whether or not to answer, but decided if something had happened to Toby they would be calling his cell and he would want to know right away. So he had to answer it.

By the time he got inside the ringing had stopped, and he saw from the missed call screen it was from the Kaufmans.

What now, he wondered.

After the phone beeped with a message, he listened to what they had to say.

Sharon Kaufman's voice. Strained with fear.

"Detective Preuss," she said. "Please call me. I have a situation here. It's bad. Call me as soon as you can. Or just come over when you get this. Please! Hurry, it's Stan. He's . . . something's happening. I hope you get this message."

He called back immediately.

"Oh thank god," she said. "I called Detective Cahill but couldn't get her. Can you come over right now?"

Her voice was on the verge of skittering out of control.

"What's going on? Where are you?"

"My house. Stan's got a gun. And he's talking about shooting Roger Griswold."

A noise interrupted her and she screamed.

"Sharon," Preuss said. "Stay with me. What's happening?"

"It's Stan. He's downstairs. He's on a rampage. He's raving about killing Roger. I'm calling from my bedroom. I'm afraid!"

He heard the agony in her voice. "Did you call 911?"

"No."

"Do it now. Tell them your husband has a gun. I'll be there as fast as I can. In the meantime—Sharon, are you listening?"

He was hearing more noises from the other end of the phone, as if Stanley were crashing around the house.

"Yes."

"Can you lock your bedroom door?"

"Yes."

"Do it. And stay as far away from the door as you can."

"Yes," she said, "yes, I will."

"One more thing . . . do you know where Roger is?"

"Yes," she said. "He's downstairs. With Stanley."

"I don't understand. Why does he want to kill Roger?"

"Because I told him."

"Told him what?"

"About Madison."

"What about Madison?"

"That he isn't her real father. Roger is."

"Why would you say something like that?"

"I wanted to make him pay for what he did to Madison. I wanted to hurt him like I'm going to be hurt for the rest of my life."

"Is it true?"

"Of course it is."

Racing in the Explorer through the neighborhood streets to West Woodland, he called Cahill's cell.

"Where are you?" he asked.

"The 43rd. I'm giving testimony. We're on break."

"Did you get Sharon Kaufman's message?"

"No. I just this second turned the phone on."

"You have to get out of there and get over to the Kaufmans'. I just talked to Sharon. Stan has a gun and he's talking about shooting Roger Griswold. Bring backup."

He ended the call and ran the light across Nine Mile.

The street was calm in front of the Kaufman home. His cell rang. Cahill.

"I'm on my way," she said. "What's going on?"

"I'm in front of the Kaufmans'. Everything seems quiet." He got out of the car and walked up to the front door, examining the windows carefully and looking up and down the street. "Don't see anybody or hear anything."

"Sharon called it in. They're sending the troops."

"So where the hell are they?"

He heard what sounded like a gun shot.

"Gun," he said.

"From where?"

"Hard to tell." He held the phone away from his ear to listen for more shots, but none came. "I'm guessing inside the Kaufmans'. I'm going in."

"Watch yourself."

He took the Kaufmans' porch in one long step. He was unarmed, which was not smart but he had no choice since he had turned in his weapon with his badge.

The inside front door was hanging open.

What he saw stopped him cold.

In the living room Roger Griswold was cowering on the sofa clasping one of the little feminine throw pillows in front of his chest like an ineffective shield. The lean figure of Stanley Kaufman stood about five feet away, pointing what looked to be a .38 at him in a rock steady hand.

Preuss smelled the discharge from the gunshot he had heard, but Griswold seemed in one piece. He made a quick scan of the room: furniture and lamps overturned, all the knick-knacks swept out of the bookcases on either side of the fireplace, a hole in the plaster over Griswold's head.

When Stanley Kaufman heard Preuss behind him, he moved the gun toward Preuss as he turned his head. Preuss halted and put his hands up.

"Stan. Hang on, there, okay?"

"Stop him," Griswold pleaded. His voice was high and shaky with fear. "Make him stop, please."

"Let's all just take a breath here, okay, Stan? Let's just all be cool."

"He's going to kill me," Griswold said.

"No, he's not. Right, Stan? Let's all just calm down. Roger, I need you to be cool. Stan, how about you put down the gun and we'll talk about this?"

"There's nothing to talk about," Kaufman said in a dead calm voice. "He's right. I'm going to kill him."

"Stop him!" Roger cried.

"Roger, shut up!" Preuss ordered.

Kaufman motioned Preuss toward the sofa with a few flips of his gun, and Preuss crossed the living room. A couple of quick dips of the gun barrel told him to sit.

Hands still raised, Preuss sat on the other end of the sofa from Roger. He could hear the sirens closing in. Just come to the right house, he silently pleaded.

"Do you hear that, Stan?" Preuss said. "That's the police."

"They won't get here in time to stop what I'm going to do."

He slipped quickly across the living room and slammed and locked the front door, keeping the gun trained on the sofa the whole time.

Preuss had to wonder who was this guy, and where had he been keeping himself. This was not the Stanley Kaufman he thought he knew. This guy was cold and deliberate, with the flat eyes of a killer, not the scholarly, round-shouldered, grief-stricken man Preuss had seen throughout the investigation.

"Stan," Preuss said, "let's be reasonable. This isn't something you want to do."

"Yes," Stanley said, "it's very much what I want to do."

"Stop him!" Griswold pleaded.

"Shut up!" Preuss barked.

A sudden pounding on the door made Preuss and Griswold flinch. It didn't bother Kaufman in the least; he never took his eye off Griswold. He's either much cooler than anybody ever gave him credit for being, Preuss thought, or else he's in some kind of fugue state that's focusing his mind.

"Stay away," Kaufman yelled to whoever was at the door. "I have a gun and two hostages in here and I'm going to kill them both if you don't leave now."

Through the front window, Preuss saw the two uniformed officers who had been the first responders peer cautiously inside. They backed off the porch and withdrew to the street, where blue-and-whites had materialized around the house. One of the officers spoke rapidly into his two-way as they moved away.

"Stan," Preuss said, "listen to me. Whatever the problem is, there's another way to deal with it. You don't want to do this. He's not worth it."

"Why not?" Kaufman said. "The real question is, why have I *not* killed the man who's been fucking my wife for the past ten years? Why have I *not* killed the man who's the real father of my little girl?"

With the mention of his daughter, his cool façade wavered and his face momentarily collapsed in on itself, like a hand retracting into a fist. But it was only a temporary weakening and he steeled himself again immediately.

"Stanley, no, no," Griswold said. "You've got it all wrong. Sharon and me—it's been over for years."

A tremor of anger, like a muscle spasm, shook his head. "Don't insult my intelligence! Everybody knew but me. Everybody knew about you and my wife. And about my daughter. Who's really your daughter."

He turned the gun on Griswold again, and now his face was twisted into a mask of fury. It was a terrible sight. The barrel was three feet away from Griswold's face. Even if he were the worst shot in the world he wouldn't miss at this distance.

"She said she couldn't live with the lies anymore," Kaufman went on. "Isn't that funny? She couldn't live with the lies, so now I have to live with the truth. With the betrayal of everything I ever thought was real in my whole miserable life."

"Stan, listen, it doesn't matter," Preuss said. He needed to stop him from skittering into self-pity, where he could rationalize anything to himself because he was such a victim.

"This isn't going to make a difference in anything. Sharon stayed with *you* the whole time. You're Madison's father, in every way that matters. You know you are."

"No. No, it's all changed. It's all ruined."

"It's not. None of this is going to change the last seven years."

"It's going to change everything. It means everything that ever happened between me and my daughter was a lie."

"Stan," Preuss went on, desperate now to try anything, "you're the one who meant the world to Maddie. Not this guy. You. Would she have wanted you to do this?"

He saw Kaufman pause, as though he might be reconsidering things.

Until Griswold opened his mouth again and said, "He's right, listen to him. Please. Sharon and I, it didn't mean anything."

Kaufman looked at Griswold and a tiny smile formed on his face, a macabre grin that froze Preuss's blood.

"Lying till the end," Kaufman said. "You just never learn."

Before Preuss could move, Kaufman's gun arm went straight and hard as a bolt of iron and he shot Roger Griswold once in the center of his chest.

The bullet went through the throw pillow and made Griswold jump where he sat. He clutched the pillow more tightly to his chest, then pulled it away, incredulous, to examine what had happened. A bright red flower bloomed under his white shirt as his eyes went from abject fear to surprise and confusion.

Then he threw the pillow away and grabbed at his chest with both hands as though trying to pull the bullet out himself.

The sound of the gunshot echoed tinnily off the walls of the living room and before the reverb died away Preuss leapt from the sofa to ram his head into Kaufman's midsection.

His head exploded with pain as he made contact. Whatever violence the other man may have been carrying had spent itself and he let himself be manhandled. Clambering on top of him on the carpet, Preuss took the gun away from him with no resistance.

He left Kaufman on the floor and, pausing briefly to get his balance as a shudder of agony raced from the top of his head down his spine, he ran to Griswold.

Who, miraculously, was still breathing.

Preuss threw himself across the living room to the front door.

Ferndale was part of the Southeast Oakland SWAT team, but he saw no sign of them in the street. It had all played out too quickly for the team to arrive. They were probably still suiting up. Instead, when he opened the front door he saw a quartet of blue-and-whites diagonally in the street in front of the house and twin lines of police standing behind the cars, all on the alert after the gunshot. A fire rescue truck idled at the corner of Livernois, blocking the side street.

He waved his arms to get the EMTs inside, yelling, "Man down inside!"

Cahill was standing with Russo and the chief of police beside the chief's car at the outer perimeter of the block, all three staring at him intently. When she saw him in the doorway she sprinted toward the house, behind the paramedics trundling up the street with their equipment and folded gurney and the handful of uniformed officers who were lumbering up to the house, hands on their weapons.

Cahill came up after them. "Are you all right?"

"Seeing stars, but I'm fine. Griswold not so much."

"Is he dead?"

"Still breathing. Kaufman shot him point blank."

From inside the house, one of the officers shouted, "Drop it!"

Preuss and Cahill shared a look, then Preuss ducked inside.

He made it into the kitchen in time to see Stanley Kaufman breaking away from the grip of one of the uniforms and plunging a bread knife into his own abdomen.

The two uniforms struggled the knife away from him. After a brief and intense thrashing around, they laid Kaufman on the kitchen floor and one of the cops began to stanch the wound with a kitchen towel.

Cahill ran into the living room and returned with one of the EMTS, who made a call on his radio for reinforcements and dove into the pile of bodies.

Cahill and Preuss withdrew to the front porch.

"What the fuck is this all about?" Cahill said.

"Sharon told him Madison wasn't his kid."

"She didn't."

"She did. And Stanley was pretty focused on shooting Roger. I was trying to keep him calm, but I didn't get very far."

She put a hand on his arm and kept it there. "How are you?"

"Not my all time best." He realized he was trembling like a struck tuning fork and was starting to feel sick.

"You're turning into a real action hero."

With an arm around his shoulder, she walked him down to the street where the chief and Russo were standing. Russo gave him a hard look, which Preuss ignored.

You got nothing on me anymore, he thought.

And in that moment he understood he no longer cared if he was going to continue being a policeman or not.

"Detective," Chief Warnock said.

"Sir."

"Pretty busy for a guy on suspension."

"Yes, sir."

"Why are you here, Martin?"

Preuss took a deep breath that made his head throb. "Sharon Kaufman called me and asked me to help her," he began, then realized he didn't know where she was.

"Oh, shit. Sharon!"

He rushed back inside the house. On the second floor a door was closed. He knocked, called her name, tried the knob. Locked.

Good, he thought. Please, no more victims here.

"Sharon," he called again, knocking harder. "It's Martin Preuss. Are you all right?"

He heard her voice, small and frightened from behind the door, ask, "Where's Stan?"

"We have him in custody. You can come out."

"What about Roger?"

"Sharon, please, open up."

The door clicked and opened slowly.

"Are you hurt?" he asked.

She shook her head. He gave her a quick once-over but saw no blood on her clothes, though a nasty purple bruise was coming up on her cheek. More of her husband's work.

She looked up at him with great anticipation and hope in her eyes. When she saw the look on his face, she shook her head as though she couldn't tolerate any more bad news. Then she exploded in tears.

He held her up as they walked down stairs, Sharon weeping so hard he was afraid she would pass out. Crying for all of them, he thought. What else was there to do?

He turned her over to one of the uniformed officers outside, who gently led her away to a cruiser.

In a few minutes, the EMTs appeared in the front door of the Kaufman house and brought out two gurneys with the wounded men. They lifted the gurneys down the steps and rolled them down the street to their rigs.

From where he stood, Preuss couldn't tell if Griswold and Kaufman were alive or dead under the grey overcast November sky.

Friday, December 5, 2008

64

A large crepe paper turkey taped to the ceiling swung lazily over the table in the dining room at Toby's house, and cutouts of pilgrims and Indians marched around the walls of the living room.

Toby was in his wheelchair waiting for him, dressed, ready to go, smiling, happy as a clam.

All the supplies for his six o'clock feeding, including a can of formula, his feeding pump, and the feeding bag and extension tube that plugged into his button, were packed and hanging off the back of his chair. Preuss swept Toby's Red Wings poncho over him and pushed him out to the Explorer.

It was another cold day, in the upper twenties but clear and bright in the way early winter can be, with high clouds feathered in a crystalline sky. As they drove, Toby gazed out the window, vocalizing happily. Preuss filled him in on what he had been listening to that morning: Doc Watson, the McGonigles, Emmy Lou Harris, Pink Floyd, Jorma Kaukonen. "All your favorites," Preuss told him.

They were going to Lord Chumley's. Renn was keeping the place open while Alison Stuart stayed home to nurse Linda.

At the restaurant the young woman at the host's podium led them to their table without delay even though the restaurant was still packed with the late-lunch crowd. Preuss wheeled Toby carefully through the closely-set tables to one by the window.

It was a lunch buffet, not Preuss's favorite style of dining, in part because he hated to leave Toby alone at the table while he went to fill his plate. But the food was excellent, with stations for turkey, ham, and roast beef, and chefs in great towering hats slicing the meat with great flourishes behind the serving tables. Enough went on for Toby to keep himself occupied while Preuss got his food, and the servers came over to say hello to him, which the boy also appreciated.

Toby loved the commotion of the restaurant, and gazed around the dining room and laughed at his own private jokes while Preuss worked on his food and narrated for his son what other diners were doing.

When he finished his meal, Preuss sat for a moment, looking at the bustle around them, at the patrons sitting and laughing with their happy, apparently trouble-free lives.

How could these people be so lighthearted, he wondered. Where were the heartaches and problems in their lives? How could they sit among their happy friends and co-workers and families and smile and cackle with such delight? He looked from one table to another and saw only smiling faces, so careless of the woes that seemed always to weigh him down so heavily.

How could these people be so happy?

And how was it, he marveled, that while these happy diners went about their lives, catastrophe struck some, like the Kaufmans, so forcefully and so unpredictably? While so many others, like Stevie, had catastrophe thrust on them by the kind of parents who could visit their own misery and unhappiness on their children like a biblical curse, devastating their chances at living the happy life all these people at the restaurant seemed to enjoy?

Like everything else, it was the luck of the draw. It was pure dumb chance that allowed these diners to sail through their lives so blithely and complacently, sidestepping the misfortunes that stuck to some people like iron filings to a magnet. The same dumb chance that brought Madison Kaufman into the paths of an angry, unhappy adolescent careening around the world seeking affection and ready to lash out when he didn't get it, and then a group of zealots whose peril lay precisely in their good intentions.

The same chance that sent a drunk plowing into Jeanette's car, that caused one son to vanish and left Preuss alone with the other son, who was himself at the mercy of the accidental malformations of the neurons of his brain in his mother's womb.

Sitting across from Toby, Preuss tried to imagine what would have happened to him if he had been killed. With a pang he remembered how close he had come to serious injury in the past month. What had he been thinking? Why had he put himself in harm's way, when he had Toby—sweet, vulnerable Toby—to worry about and take care of? When he was all Toby had left from the ruins of their family?

"Toby," he said, feeling the need to apologize for things that Toby didn't even know about, "I'm sorry for what I've been doing in the past few weeks. What would we do without each other?"

At the sound of his father's voice, Toby turned his head so he was looking at Preuss in his crafty oblique look that was at once ironic and infinitely understanding. He said, "Num."

As he sat watching his son, a seizure took hold of the boy, as though deliberately to prove Preuss's meditation on the role of chance in the world. Toby's mouth twisted, his head cocked, his eyes stared off into a high corner of the room, and his arms rose and stiffened, bent at the elbows, as though prepared to fend off an adversary. His legs went straight and began to shake. He whimpered.

Preuss came out of his seat and went around to the side of the table where Toby's wheelchair was parked. He bent down to put an arm around his son's shoulder.

"Come back," Preuss said gently, "come on back, Toby. Come back. Come back."

As Preuss cooed and patted Toby's shoulder, urging him to return, the seizure gradually subsided, and as it did a smile broke across Toby's face. "Hit your funny button?" Preuss asked. Then he continued murmuring, "Come back," as the smile spread even though Toby's eyes continued their involuntary eye movements, juddering back and forth. Nystagmus, the doctors called it.

"Come back. Come back."

Preuss patted Toby's shoulder and brought his head down close to his son's to continue comforting him—"Are you back?" he asked quietly—and as the seizure subsided completely, signaled by a cough and relaxation of Toby's muscle tone, Preuss himself was suddenly overcome by something akin to his son's convulsion, an upsurge of love for the boy and simultaneously a deep spreading sorrow for everyone he had come into contact with in the past four weeks that gripped him in its own sudden attack and made him hug his son tightly, hold onto him for dear life, really, and hide in the boy's sweet-smelling hair an aching cry for them all . . . for Madison, her parents, the Griswolds, the Stuarts, Stevie and his uncle, the Schenks, and all the sad, damaged people whom Madison Kaufman's short life had touched.

Toby hummed, said his word, "Onion," and nuzzled Preuss's cheek with his nose, as though trying to comfort his father and bid him return from this seizure as Preuss had done for him.

Come back, Dad, Toby seemed to say, rubbing his nose up and down and back and forth along the grizzle of Preuss's cheek. Come on back to me.

Come back.

Come back.

CPSIA information can be obtained at www.ICGtesting.com
Printed in the USA
LVOW081620200712

290923LV00005B/71/P